"Molly Harper writes characters
you can't help but fall in love with."
—*RT Book Reviews*

PRAISE FOR
THE SOUTHERN ECLECTIC SERIES

AIN'T SHE A PEACH

"Deliciously over-the-top. . . . Straight-up fun and decidedly Southern."

—*Frolic*

"Everything you want in a Southern rom-com."

—*Fresh Fiction*

"I love Molly Harper's writing. Zany humor, eclectic characters, outrageous story lines, and pure Southern charm light up the pages."

—*Smexy Books*

"A very fun addition to Harper's laid-back series."

—*Publishers Weekly*

SWEET TEA AND SYMPATHY

"This sweet tale of the city girl finding a home in the country launches Harper's latest series and will go down as easy as honey on a deep-fried Twinkie."

—*Library Journal*

"Margot is a terrific lead for Harper's supporting cast of quirky characters. This is a promising start to Harper's Southern Eclectic series."

—*Publishers Weekly*

"This book is funny and the characters engaging. . . . Finished it in twenty-four hours and already looking forward to the next in the Southern Eclectic series."

—*Book Riot*

"Warm and cozy and full of Southern charm."

—*Dear Author*

MORE PRAISE FOR
MOLLY HARPER'S NOVELS

THE SINGLE UNDEAD MOMS CLUB

"*The Single Undead Moms Club* is frequently hilarious yet surprisingly touching."

—*Single Titles*

THE CARE AND FEEDING
OF STRAY VAMPIRES

"Filled with clever humor, snark, silliness, and endearing protagonists."

—*Booklist*

NICE GIRLS DON'T BITE
THEIR NEIGHBORS

"Terrific . . . The stellar supporting characters, laugh-out-loud moments, and outrageous plot twists will leave readers absolutely satisfied."

—*Publishers Weekly* (starred review)

NICE GIRLS DON'T HAVE FANGS

"A chuckle-inducing, southern-fried version of Stephanie Plum."

—*Booklist*

HOW TO FLIRT WITH
A NAKED WEREWOLF

"Mo's wisecracking, hilarious voice makes this novel such a pleasure to read."

—*New York Times* bestselling author Eloisa James

BOOKS BY MOLLY HARPER

THE SOUTHERN ECLECTIC SERIES
Gimme Some Sugar
A Few Pecans Short of a Pie
Ain't She a Peach
Peachy Flippin' Keen
Save a Truck, Ride a Redneck
Sweet Tea and Sympathy

THE HALF-MOON HOLLOW SERIES
Accidental Sire
Where the Wild Things Bite
Big Vamp on Campus
Fangs for the Memories
The Single Undead Moms Club
The Dangers of Dating a Rebound Vampire
I'm Dreaming of an Undead Christmas
A Witch's Handbook of Kisses and Curses
"Undead Sublet" in *The Undead in My Bed*
The Care and Feeding of Stray Vampires
Driving Mr. Dead
Nice Girls Don't Bite Their Neighbors
Nice Girls Don't Live Forever
Nice Girls Don't Date Dead Men
Nice Girls Don't Have Fangs

THE NAKED WEREWOLF SERIES
How to Run with a Naked Werewolf
The Art of Seducing a Naked Werewolf
How to Flirt with a Naked Werewolf

THE BLUEGRASS SERIES
Snow Falling on Bluegrass
Rhythm and Bluegrass
My Bluegrass Baby

ALSO
Better Homes and Hauntings
And One Last Thing . . .

Gimme Some Sugar

MOLLY HARPER

G

GALLERY BOOKS

NEW YORK   LONDON   TORONTO   SYDNEY   NEW DELHI

G

Gallery Books
An Imprint of Simon & Schuster, Inc.
1230 Avenue of the Americas
New York, NY 10020

This book is a work of fiction. Any references to historical events, real people,
or real places are used fictitiously. Other names, characters, places, and events are
products of the author's imagination, and any resemblance to actual events or
places or persons, living or dead, is entirely coincidental.

Copyright © 2019 by Molly Harper White

All rights reserved, including the right to reproduce this book or portions thereof
in any form whatsoever. For information, address Gallery Books Subsidiary Rights
Department, 1230 Avenue of the Americas, New York, NY 10020.

First Gallery Books trade paperback edition April 2019

GALLERY BOOKS and colophon are registered trademarks of Simon & Schuster, Inc.

For information about special discounts for bulk purchases, please contact Simon &
Schuster Special Sales at 1-866-506-1949 or business@simonandschuster.com.

The Simon & Schuster Speakers Bureau can bring authors to your live event.
For more information or to book an event, contact the Simon & Schuster Speakers
Bureau at 1-866-248-3049 or visit our website at www.simonspeakers.com.

Interior design by Michelle Marchese

Manufactured in the United States of America

10 9 8 7 6 5 4 3 2 1

Library of Congress Cataloging-in-Publication Data
Names: Harper, Molly, author.
Title: Gimme some sugar / by Molly Harper.
Description: First Gallery Books trade paperback edition. | New York : Gallery
    Books, 2019. | Series: Southern eclectic
Identifiers: LCCN 2018044170 (print) | LCCN 2018047008 (ebook) | ISBN
    9781501151378 (ebook) | ISBN 9781501151354 (trade pbk.. : alk. paper)
Subjects: | GSAFD: Love stories.
Classification: LCC PS3608.A774 (ebook) | LCC PS3608.A774 G56 2019 (print) |
    DDC 813/.6—dc23
LC record available at https://lccn.loc.gov/2018044170

ISBN 978-1-5011-5135-4
ISBN 978-1-5011-5137-8 (ebook)

For Kathleen, Anna, Jenn, and Therese.
You know what you did.

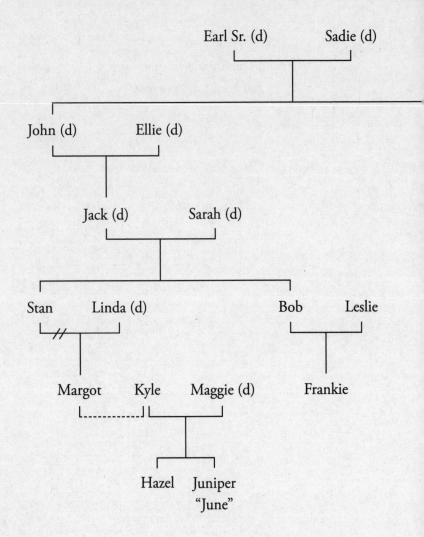

The McCready Family Tree

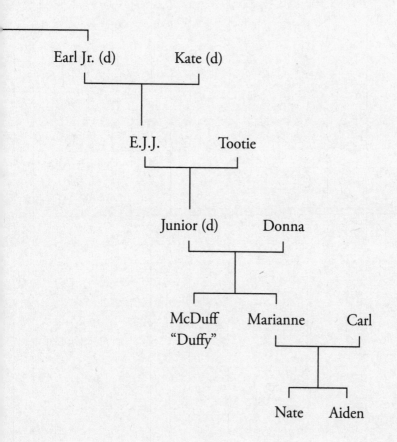

Earl Jr. (d) — Kate (d)

E.J.J. — Tootie

Junior (d) — Donna

McDuff "Duffy"   Marianne — Carl

Nate   Aiden

Gimme Some Sugar

NICE SOUTHERN GIRLS did not make money baking penis cakes.

Lucy Bowman Garten was going to hell on a road paved with devil's food and peach-toned buttercream.

Technically, she wasn't even supposed to be working in her bake shop, which would eventually be called Gimme Some Sugar, as it wasn't officially open. Hell, she'd only leased the defunct Hardison's Meat Shop two months ago, before she'd even arrived back in town. And she'd had to do that under a limited liability company so her mother-in-law wouldn't find a way to interfere with the rental agreement. Evie Garten had a surprising number of friends around town, despite the fact that she was ten pounds of mean in a five-pound sack.

While the kitchen was cleaned and ready and could easily pass a health inspector's perusal—if the mealy-mouthed, liver-spotted bastard would ever show up for his damn appointments—the displays were still fitted for the enormous hunks of pork the former meat shop used to sell, and the "café area" looked like a hoarder intervention waiting to happen. Also, as a minor point, Lucy's business license was still mired in the initial hoops set up by Sackett County's small but byzantine government. So Lucy was doing this somewhat inadvisable job for a high school friend so far under the table she was practically subterranean. She wasn't even being paid—Maddie's fiancé was going to do some plumbing work for her in return for her obscene baking skills.

The next time she got a text message that started with *So, I'm hosting a bachelorette party* . . . she was going to respond with *Do I know you?*

Lucy finished the very last swirl on the royal icing *E* and stood back to survey her work—an eighteen-inch penis lying flat across a silver-foiled cake board, with EAT ME written across its testicles in hot pink.

She would not be taking pictures of this for her shop's website.

Lucy did not understand the compulsion to eat phallic baked goods for a girl's last hurrah before marriage. She remembered how hopeful and excited she'd been before she'd married Wayne. She'd wanted to start her married life as soon as possible. She'd thought, *I can't wait to spend the rest of my days with the man I love.* She hadn't thought, *I better eat all of the buttercream-frosted appendage I can because I might not have the chance again.*

Then again, she'd been a hopeful, excited idiot before she married Wayne, so what the hell did she know?

She blew out a long sigh and said, "Well, it's grotesquely enormous and painstakingly detailed. And baking it has been the most action I've seen in years . . . so it's perfect."

Wiping her hands on her purple doughnut-themed apron, Lucy crossed to her carefully organized supplies and selected a large, unmarked sheet cake box—which, unfortunately for Lucy, had a little cellophane display window on top. She wasn't eager to show this cake off, but it was the only box large enough to accommodate it.

Once the cake was secured, she put a Braves cap over her coppery auburn curls and carried it out the front door, carefully propping it against the half-collapsed wooden flower box in front of the shop while she struggled to fit the key in the door's original and extremely tricky lock.

As usual, Main Street was bustling with midafternoon traffic: people driving home from work, ferrying their kids from school to baseball practice, the usual. She saw a couple of nearby shop owners out on the sidewalk, cleaning windows and hanging up flower baskets. February in Lake Sackett always felt like holding one's breath, the last few weeks of quiet before the tourists descended on the town's beautiful waterfront. At least, it had been that way when Lucy had been growing up—locals handed the town off to the tourists with smiles on their faces, happy to get their much-needed cash. However, it was always a relief when those same tourists cleared out in September.

After she and Wayne moved away for school, "mistakes were made" at the Sackett Dam and the Army Corps of Engineers released ten times the amount of water meant to be drained from Lake Sackett, right at the beginning of what became an extended drought. Lake levels dropped to an all-time low. Tourists didn't want to risk their boats on a diminished, sad lake where they could potentially run aground in areas that used to be safe. That meant less money coming into the businesses, which meant less capital for those businesses to make improvements, which meant dilapidated motels and shops that fewer tourists were eager to spend their time at—and on and on the cycle went. Little extras like discounts and free samples were the first thing to go, followed by friendly smiles and easy conversations. Her dad said that tourists sensed this anxious energy and booked their weekends in areas that didn't seem quite so edgy.

The town's economy had stalled to the point where Wayne claimed that visiting their families was becoming "too depressing." Wayne didn't want to see their hometown all run-down and empty, like something out of a bad horror movie. He said he wanted to remember it as it was.

Well, he was never that eager to visit Lake Sackett in the first place, but nostalgic sentimentality had been a convenient excuse. If her dad wanted to spend Christmas with them, Wayne had said, he could come to Texas and visit. Lord knew his own parents had accepted enough airline tickets on Wayne's dime.

Lucy shook her head. Thinking about her daddy, or Wayne's mama, for that matter, was not going to improve her already tense mood. So Lucy would focus on the positive. Thanks to some very concentrated effort by the recently established Lake Sackett Tourism Board, tourism to the town's hotels, rentals, restaurants, and quaint little shops was slowly coming back to the numbers enjoyed before the water dump sent the town into a tailspin. Lucy was building a business in a town on the rise, no matter who thought she was a "damn fool" to do it.

"Would you just *lock*, you sonofabitch?" she hissed, jangling her keys as she struggled to get the lock to tumble. She leaned her ball-capped forehead against the glass of the door, glad that her four-year-old wasn't around to hear her using foul language. The little sponge would probably repeat it at some terribly awkward moment, like in front of the local Baptist minister.

"Hey, let me help you with that!"

She turned . . . and screamed internally to see Duffy Mc-Cready jogging down the sidewalk of Main Street.

Duffy had been her very best friend in elementary school. She'd neglected friendships with the girls in their grade so she could play trucks in the sandbox with Duffy. She shared the Goo Goo Clusters in her lunchbox with him and only him. And in high school, well, she'd harbored a secret crush on him that reduced her to some very embarrassing diary entries, not to mention late-night-call impulses that made adult Lucy very grateful Pete Bowman had never allowed his teenage daughter a cell phone. Duffy had been one of her favorite people on the planet for years and she was so glad to reconnect with him after their years-long separation. But Holy Lord, right now, she wanted him to either go away or go blind.

Temporarily.

She wasn't evil or anything.

With the ladies-who-lunch crowd back in Texas, this was the sort of thing she would brazen her way through—smile, laugh it off, pretend it was a big joke. But this was Duffy McCready, her Lake Sackett Achilles' heel.

Duffy moved to take the keys from her while Lucy tried to angle the box out of his line of sight. This brought her closer to Duffy's tall frame as he hovered over her to work the lock. Between the warmth radiating off of his body and the smell of leather and cinnamon gum, Lucy had to brace herself against the brick to keep her knees from giving way.

Settle down, girls, she warned them. *That way lies madness*

*and tears and a crazy ex-wife who tried to push you down the stairs
in high school.*

Her knees argued that it had been a very long time since
she'd been so close to a nice-smelling man. And Duffy was a re-
liable, emotionally stable sweetheart who wouldn't mind a sniff
or two between friends. Her knees were a very bad influence.

Duffy grunted and managed to flip the key in the ancient
lock. He turned to smile at her, his face only inches from hers.
Her breath caught as she got her very first look at adult Duffy
up close, and her knees were now giving her very bad ideas. Her
childhood friend had turned into a hunk of something.

Long of limb, broad of shoulder, and possessed of *dear Lord,
don't even get me started* blue eyes, what little baby fat Duffy'd
had on his face had long since resolved into sharp cheekbones
and a strong, square jaw. She stared at his mouth, somehow soft
and inviting-looking even under that scruff of gingery beard. His
brows drew together and his mouth opened as if he was going to
say something. But his eyes cut toward the cake box, which had
shifted during Lucy's knee failure.

Duffy frowned and tilted his head. "Is that a . . . ?"

Lucy cringed, so very hard. Duffy had seen her penis.

She squeezed her eyes tight, even as she felt him move away
from her. The blood rushed to her cheeks in a hot, humiliated
wave. "Yes, yes, it is."

"Wha—Who—" Duffy's laugh burst out of him in a shocked
bark. "*Why?*"

"I don't know!"

Duffy burst out laughing. Lucy's shoulders shook with her
own giggles, despite the absolute mortification of Duffy knowing she'd spent the past few hours crafting edible genitalia from

sugar and butter. "I honestly don't know. Maddie Paxton is having her bachelorette party and she insists she can't have a cake unless it's penis-shaped. I'm just glad I wasn't asked to order the penis gummy candy."

"Women are a mystery," Duffy said, shuddering as if he was imagining those particular confections being consumed. "A beautiful, divine, horrifying mystery."

She sighed, moving toward her truck to put the cake in the passenger seat . . . far, far out of sight. "Yeah, I don't think this sort of thing counts toward the feminine mystique."

"If it makes you feel any better, it looks very realistic."

"No, that does *not* make me feel better." She shook her head and an enormous, blinding-white smile spread over his face, crinkling those big baby blues of his.

"So, welcome back to Lake Sackett," Duffy said, laughing, opening his arms in what could be construed as an invitation for a hug. She laughed and stepped toward him and he wrapped those long arms around her in an awkward embrace that didn't quite press their bodies together. A wave of disappointment swept through her, leaving her confused. Duffy was apparently one of those men—meaning pretty much all of them—who considered her a sexless nonentity now that she was a mother.

But that shouldn't affect her at all, right? Weak knees, lantern jaws, and full-body hugs had never been part of the equation for them in the first place, so why did she feel that keen sense of loss when Duffy kept his distance?

"So, what are you up to?" he said, frowning slightly as she shoved the truck door closed.

"I'm opening a bakery," she said, gesturing to the meat shop's windows.

"Really?" he said, the corners of his mouth lifting. "I thought you wanted to be a marketing guru. PR and crisis management, all that stuff? I always pictured you walking around in office buildings, barking orders while people handed you stuff to sign."

Lucy laughed, thinking of her life back in Texas, which had mostly revolved around scheduling playdates for Sam and trying to find inventive new ways to hide Wayne's phone during dinner. "Yeah, it was a real rat race."

"Well, I'm glad you got away from all that," he said. "So you're going to turn the meat shop into a bakery?"

"Sure. It's got the right wiring to support the new ovens, fridge, and cooler cases I've had installed, along with a new sink. And it's got loads of counter space for me to work with."

Lucy didn't mention the difficulty getting contractors who would work on the space on any sort of reasonable schedule, or how many she'd had walk off the job because they were distantly related to Evie or because Evie had sent Wayne's little brother, Davey, to harass them while they worked. She'd finally had to hire a crew out of Atlanta who didn't give a damn about local connections and made it clear they'd whoop Davey's ass if he kept coming around. Davey, who usually lost interest once someone his own size made it clear they would put up a fight, skulked away and the work was finally finished.

Instead, she said, "I've got all of the kitchen changes made, now I just have to finish prepping and painting the café area."

"You mean the place where people used to stand in line with deer carcasses waiting to have them processed?"

"It will be very bright paint," she told him. "People won't even recognize it."

"So are you gonna be doing wedding cakes and all that?"

"Sure, wedding cakes, birthday cakes, cupcakes, anything people will pay me to bake. It's something I started when my son, Sam, was a baby, making cakes for friends, just to relieve some stress, then doing birthday cakes for their kids as Sam got older. I got pretty good at it, took some classes and got some certifications, and now, here we are. I figured it would be a good way to make a living but have the flexibility to keep up with Sam."

"And you should be pretty popular. Ever since the Dunbars closed their bakery over Christmas, people have been getting all their bought cakes at the Food Carnival. From what I hear, they taste like freezer-burned feet."

"Which is great, because my slogan is going to be 'Doesn't taste like freezer-burned feet!'"

He barked out a laugh. "Well, you're the marketing guru," he said, nodding toward the storefront, where the former meat shop's faded weekly special signs and hanging meat hooks were still on display, like an art installation entitled *Failed Scary Commerce*. "Though the whole *Texas Chain Saw Massacre* theme, combined with the carb-based porno, might make me take that back."

Lucy spread her hands over her warm cheeks. "I will never do a bachelorette party favor for a friend. For anyone. Ever again."

"Good, I hear that's how bakers get reputations."

She laughed. She'd missed how easily Duffy could make her laugh. It was like his special talent in high school, taking everything in her life and making it seem like it wasn't so bad.

Because he's your friend, she told herself firmly. *Duffy is a* friend, *a good man who deserves a heck of a lot more than being dragged into your mess of a life right now or at any time.*

And suddenly Duffy wasn't laughing anymore. His ruddy cheeks went pale and he looked a bit sick. "Oh my Lord, I just realized, I haven't even said anything about Wayne. I just—I saw you and the penis cake and I just got so distracted."

"Oh, no," Lucy assured him. "It's okay."

"No, I was raised better than this," he said, stepping even farther away from her. "I was really sorry to hear about Wayne. That must have been awful for you. How are you holding up?"

She swallowed thickly. Right, awful. Because she'd only been a widow for six months. And she was supposedly in mourning.

Lucy had her share of regrets about Wayne. In high school, she'd thought he was one of the most interesting, ambitious people she'd ever met. He had a great sense of humor. He was charming and could be so thoughtful when it suited him. But eventually, the sense of humor became as sharp and biting as new vinegar. The charm was worn down by the grind of everyday life, and all the lead showed through the gold plating. She was left with a man who seemed like such a loving husband from the outside, a good ol' country boy who'd raised himself out of nothing to become a polished prince at Crenshaw and Associates Financial Management; but he couldn't see her as anything but a member of his "support team," a convenience, and occasionally, a source of embarrassment—certainly not as sophisticated as anyone they spent time with from his office.

Wayne had known she wasn't happy, toward the end; he just didn't understand why. He worked hard to provide for them. They lived in a beautiful home, took luxurious vacations, joined the best clubs. Sure, he had his dalliances with pretty much any female employee of Crenshaw and Associates, but that was par for the course for their circle. Hadn't the other company wives told her to expect as much? Hell, it wasn't exactly unheard of for men from Lake Sackett to stray, either. Besides, he didn't drink as much as his friends did, and he didn't spend *that* much money on his affairs. So why couldn't she at least be content with their life? And the worst part was that she couldn't make him understand, even when they'd gone two years without having sex because she wasn't about to expose herself to whatever he might have picked up from his "friends."

She didn't love him anymore. She wasn't sure she ever had, really, beyond the first wash of teenage hormones and blissfully stupid life-planning one did at eighteen. Wayne didn't see how sleeping with other women should affect his relationship with Lucy, an "evolved" opinion he'd neglected to share with her before they'd stood in front of a priest and promised to forsake all others. And while Wayne didn't see cheating as a reason to end the marriage, she wasn't about to let her actions teach Sam that those patterns were acceptable. She'd insisted on counseling, and Wayne had made a half-hearted effort. He hadn't stopped cheating, of course, but he had admitted that he should stop being so obvious about it. Then gravity had sort of ended the marriage for them, and sometimes she was at a loss as to how to feel about it.

"It's been difficult. But Sam and I are going to be okay. We're staying at my dad's place. Sam's raring to start kindergarten, but he'll settle for running the preschool like his own personal kingdom for now," she said with a snort.

Duffy's brows drew together again, noting her darker expression. "Yeah, Tootie said something about that. Is 'Mamaw Evie' still giving you a hard time about putting him in preschool instead of leaving him with her?"

Lucy rolled her dark brown eyes so hard she almost dislodged a contact lens. "No more than usual."

"It will get better," Duffy assured her. "Evie's just not used to anyone telling her no."

"Oh, she's used to it. She just refuses to hear it," she grumbled.

Duffy placed one of his enormous hands on her arm. "She's mourning. You all are. Wayne's death was a shock, and people lash out when they're grieving. They're scared, they're hurt. If anyone would know, I would."

Lucy nodded. Duffy had a unique understanding of grief. His family had owned the McCready Family Funeral Home and Bait Shop, the largest funeral home (and bait shop) in this end of Georgia, as far back as anyone could remember. While Duffy worked on the marina side of things, leading fishing tours and selling tackle, he'd seen enough funeral fistfights break out to recognize emotional wear and tear.

She'd hoped that moving with Sam back to Lake Sackett, living in her late father's home, would simplify their lives. In Dallas, she'd had "friends" that she lunched with and planned charity events with, but no one she could trust with even half of the personal details she'd mentioned in this single afternoon's conversation with Duffy. She'd hoped that things would get easier once she was in more familiar territory, with people she knew and cared about. Yes, most of her own family was gone, but she could swing a cat down Main Street and hit three people who had known her since birth. She wanted that for Sam, that permanence and familiarity, even if it did come at the cost of living near her in-laws, which was enough of a negative on her pro/con list that it had almost convinced her not to move back.

She pursed her lips and nodded. "I'm sure that's it."

"Well, if you need anything, just let me know."

Her traitorous knees could immediately name about ten things she needed, most of them requiring nudity and dim lighting. Very. Bad. Influence. Her brain scrambled for a much more appropriate and less naked answer.

"Um, actually, I need to get this cake over to Maddie. It's kind of warm out for February, and buttercream melts pretty easy. You can only imagine how much worse that thing looks when it's . . . molting."

Duffy shuddered at the image. "Yikes."

"Maybe you could come by tomorrow?"

"Ah, can't, I've got a charter tomorrow. Bunch of guys from Clarksville, want to try their hand at crappie."

"Well, text me, and we'll work out a time."

Duffy scratched the back of his neck. "I don't have your number."

"Sorry," she said, her cheeks flushing pink.

Of course Duffy had no way to contact her, beyond the gossip grapevine. They'd emailed occasionally after she'd left, and stayed Facebook friends . . . until one day she'd checked her friends list and found that he wasn't on it anymore. She'd wanted to believe it was some sort of techno-error, that he couldn't possibly have unfriended her. But she'd never had the guts to contact him and ask if he'd meant to end their digital friendship, or even to try to refriend him. And now, realizing that he didn't even have her number? It made the distance between them stand in even sharper relief.

"Give me your phone," she said, holding out her hand. He slapped a very heavy chunk of plastic in her palm. "Sweet baby

Jesus, can you call 1987 on this thing? Does it text or do I need to use Morse code?"

"Smartass," he grumbled, taking the phone back and opening his texting window. Or at least, he tried—it took him several seconds to think about it.

"I don't see a point in getting the fancy-schmancy models that can Google and scratch my back for me," he said. "It's not like I'm big on social media."

"Really?" she asked, her mouth going slightly dry. Was he really going to bring this up now? Just minutes after seeing her for the first time in years?

"Yeah, I quit Facebook years back," he said. "I just didn't see the point in it. Do I really need to know that the guy I used to sit next to in math class is 'drinking the weekend's first beer, hashtag-blessed?' And do I need to 'like' it?"

An old wound Lucy hadn't even realized was there closed just a little bit. He hadn't unfriended her; he'd walked away from the service entirely. Duffy hadn't intentionally cut her from his life. Life had just happened, as it had with so many of her old friends, and they'd lost touch. Sure, she'd thought her friendship with Duffy was different, that it would last until they were old and gray, living next door to each other and watching their great-grandkids wrestle in their backyards. If someone had told her as a teenager that they would be standing there on the sidewalk, virtual strangers, she would have laughed in their face. And maybe kicked them in the shin for good measure. But knowing that he hadn't deliberately pushed her away was welcome news.

"Probably not," she conceded. "But it's handy, when you move far from home. And when you're planning on opening a business."

"If this becomes the kind of place where people post pictures of their coffee instead of drinking it, I will boycott it," he warned her, though he was grinning. "Publicly. There may be dead fish involved."

"There's not much I can do about that," she told him. When Duffy's text function finally launched, she texted a message to her cell number. **This is Duffy.**

"You could bake ugly cupcakes that don't make for good pictures?" he suggested.

"That gets you on the Internet for other reasons," she said, pursing her lips. Duffy threw his head back and laughed.

"That's what I've been missing, that sense of humor," he told her.

"You're surrounded by women who have good senses of humor."

"Yeah, but they use them against me, which isn't as fun."

She snorted. "I've missed you, Duffy."

A truck drove by and honked, a typical greeting in Lake Sackett, but she felt oddly awkward standing on the street, where anyone could see her, laughing and typing her number into his phone. It seemed like something a widow shouldn't be doing with an old high school friend just six months after her husband's funeral. Especially a widow who was hoping to open a business that depended on community goodwill in the off-season.

"I've missed you, too, Lucy. And the rest of my family will be descending on you soon enough. Be prepared for more gossip than your ears can stand."

She grinned. "I'm looking forward to it. I was so sorry to hear about your dad passing. I'm gonna miss having someone who's willing to eat my baking mistakes, no matter how misguided. Especially now that those mistakes will be on a commercial level."

Duffy smiled, the light in his eyes going just a bit sad. "Thank you. And he would have loved to see you open this place, no matter how many mistakes you bake. He always liked you, said you were a darling."

"Well, he was right, because I am a darling," Lucy said primly.

"With a penis cake in her truck," Duffy noted.

"Come on, we'd just forgotten about the penis cake."

Duffy shook his head. "Had we?"

"Oh, I'm already pretending it never happened," she told him.

"Solid plan."

DUFFY DROVE THROUGH town at a snail's pace. He was clearly getting too old for after-charter drinks with clients. He knew a greasy breakfast from the Rise and Shine would help his sorry condition, but he wasn't sure he had the energy to get out of his truck to buy it. So he crept along Main Street and prayed for Aunt Leslie's chewy coffee to work its dark magic.

He'd meant to get up much earlier to run to the post office and pick up the shipment of lures, but he'd overslept and ended up leaving his mother to open the bait shop on her own. Donna was not going to be a happy camper when he returned. Maybe he should stop and get a greasy breakfast for her, just to avoid the inevitable ass chewing.

If Lucy's bakery were already open, that would have solved his problem. Donna was a sucker for a cinnamon roll, with the rare exception of Ike's over at the Rise and Shine. She said they tasted like "frozen, prepackaged crap," which seemed impossible given that Ike prided himself on making everything from scratch. Donna swore Bud Dunbar made the only decent cinnamon rolls in town, but Dunbar's Bakery was the last of Lake Sackett's businesses to fall victim to the water dump. Well, the bakery had also fallen victim to the fact that Bud's son, Junior, was an idiot and Bud had serious doubts about letting him run a business that involved sharp objects and hot appliances. But the water dump hadn't helped.

Cousin Margot's Founders' Festival had reversed Lake Sackett's plummet into the outhouse. His uncle Stan's girl had spent years in the big city planning parties for fancy people, and she'd channeled all of that know-how into planning the Founders' Festival the previous fall, an event so aggressively quaint that it showed up on travel blogs and magazines all over the country as a "spot to watch." And then they'd had an especially rainy winter, which was slowly building the lake back to normal levels.

Despite running late, Duffy paused and pulled to the side of the street as a funeral procession rolled into view, a nicety that his grandpa E.J.J. had drilled into his head from childhood. As his uncle Stan drove past in the hearse, he pointed at Duffy and then pointed at his watch. Duffy nodded his head and gestured back for Stan to speed it up because it was Stan's slow-ass driving dragging the funeral procession in the first place.

The key to making McCready's work was keeping the marina side fun for the boaters while remaining respectful to the people who were grieving for a lost loved one. And the poor Burtons were grieving the death of their matriarch, Mama Winnie, to a decade-long battle with breast cancer. Winnie was one of those rare women who had spent her entire life getting her way, but being so loving and supportive of her family that they never minded her total control. Grandma Tootie had aspired to be just like her, but the McCreadys were a little tougher to wrangle than the Burtons.

At one point, he'd been distantly related to the Burtons through his marriage to Lana. Her mother, Wanda, was the daughter of a distant Burton cousin. But the Burtons had always been quick to assure Duffy that they had little to do with his wife or that branch of the family, even before he married Lana . . . which should have been a red flag, he supposed.

Duffy and Lana had been "nod in the hallway" friends for years, but never thought about dating until her friend Carletta Leehigh set them up for homecoming junior year. They just sort of fell into being a couple. Lana's high school friends had teased her for years about being the only one in their group without a steady boyfriend or a pre-engagement ring. And Lana was deathly afraid of being left behind.

Like a lot of couples in Lake Sackett, they'd gotten married right out of high school. She'd come to him while they were lining up for graduation in their royal blue caps and gowns, her eyes wide in panic because her period was late. She must have gotten knocked up on prom night, she'd told him, when they'd joined the rest of their class partying on Make-Out Island. On prom night, Duffy had been six beers in when Lana sidled up to him, and he hadn't quite built up the hops tolerance he had now. Earlier that night, he'd heard that Lucy was going to follow her sweetheart, Wayne, to Texas A&M that fall instead of going to Georgia State and staying close to home. His best friend in the world was leaving him for longhorns and a shithead. Consolation sex with his not-quite-girlfriend had sounded like the best idea Duffy's beer-soaked brain had ever heard.

So when Lana had come to him with tears in her eyes, Duffy

had done the "right thing"—immediately after the graduation ceremony, he'd dropped to one knee and proposed with his class ring. After his mother, Donna, stopped screaming at him, they arranged for the quickest quickie June wedding ever performed in Lake Sackett.

Tootie said that when everything involved in the ceremony is a rental, it should be considered an omen for a short-lived marriage. Why she felt the need to cross-stitch that on a sampler and give it to them as a wedding present was another matter entirely.

And then, about three weeks after their honeymoon in exotic Knoxville, Lana told him that her period had shown up after all, that sometimes she was irregular and had these little "scares." Donna had an outbreak of the "I told you so's," insisting Duffy should have demanded a pregnancy test and an ultrasound before the wedding. Duffy started having nightmares about bear traps and having to gnaw off his own foot to escape. Between her plans to move to Texas and Duffy's new status as a married man, Lucy kept her distance and faded from his life.

And he was stuck in Lake Sackett, in more ways than one.

Duffy turned the truck onto the McCready's lot, wondering whether he should head back to town and grab that greasy breakfast after all, because he was not prepared to face a busy day tuning up boat engines. He pressed his hands over his eyes to try to relieve some of his headache. He hadn't been this hungover since the morning after he'd heard Lucy had gotten married. He and Carl had gone through four jars of Dawson family brew, which didn't sound like much, but Carl's family moonshine recipe could easily power a space shuttle launch.

His marriage had dragged on longer than it should have through mulishness (Duffy's) and infidelity (Lana's) because, well, Duffy had the unenviable combination of the McCready stubborn streak and the refusal to admit his mother was right. But Lana had gotten it into her head that sleeping with one of Duffy's well-off friends was going to lead to greener pastures, and had filed divorce papers. Duffy had recognized a reprieve when he saw it and signed them immediately.

He knew he wasn't in love with Lana anymore. He wasn't sure if he ever had been, truly, or if he had just been so blinded by loneliness and disappointment that his teenage brain had gotten its wires crossed. He did know for damn sure that he didn't want to be married to her anymore. But unfortunately, he was just attached enough to let her slip back into his life every now and again when her ego got bruised.

Every few months, Lana came to him crying, hoping for some comfort over her latest heartbreak—some dipshit ATV salesman who didn't keep his promise to take her to Daytona for the weekend or, worse, that time a dipshit Jet Ski salesman did take her to Daytona for the weekend and left her without a way to get home. And the sight of a woman he'd once thought he loved, miserable and broken . . . it was like he had no control over his pants.

In the morning, Lana would skip off with boosted self-confidence, leaving Duffy soaked in Designer Imposters perfume and resignation that the whole cycle would start over again in a few months. He knew it was unhealthy. He knew he should keep her at a distance. He just didn't want to be one of the extensive line of people who'd added to her hurt over the years. She got so caught up in attention from men, in the whirlwind of a new relationship, but she never looked before she leaped. She was sensitive. She was insecure.

She was waiting for him in the parking lot of McCready's.

Duffy opened the truck door and spotted her climbing out of her El Camino, which was parked outside the back staff entrance for the funeral home.

"Oh, shit."

E.J.J. had made it very clear that unless Lana was burying somebody, she was not welcome on the McCready's property. There had been several "confrontations" between Lana and Duffy's mama. One of them involved a boat anchor. What was she doing here, instead of following the funeral procession?

Lana leaned against her El Camino, waggling her fingers at him. He crossed to her, scanning the parking lot for Donna. If he could get Lana back in her car without incident, maybe he could get through his morning without bloodshed. He glanced toward the bait shop, where he could see his mama rummaging around in the tackle racks, facing the lot. Maybe not.

"Hey, Lana, what are you doing here?" he asked.

As she moved closer, kitten pout firmly in place, Duffy was enveloped in the familiar scent of imitation Obsession. Lana wore her usual combination of skintight jeans and a low-cut tank top in a loud tropical print. Her only concession to the late-winter weather was a jean jacket. Her short dark-blond hair was swept back from her face, which had changed over the years, mostly in the frown lines etching deep brackets around her bright red cupid's bow of a mouth.

"I brought something for you," she purred, pulling a blue plastic glasses case from her shoulder bag. "I guess I must have knocked it into my purse while I was leaving your place."

"This isn't mine," he said, lifting a gingery eyebrow as she handed him the case. "I don't wear glasses."

"Are you sure? I could swear it came from your place," she chirped, though her green, narrow-set eyes weren't quite meeting his. "Thanks for keeping me company the other night. I was just so upset about Randy. You're such a good friend to me, Duffy. Just like you always promised. I know I'll never be alone as long as you're around to make things better."

Duffy swallowed heavily. It always made him squirm inside, hearing her describe him as a "friend" so pointedly, like she was trying to friend-zone him, when she was the one who came looking for him every time she had an itch. Why did he keep doing this? Was it guilt? For leaving when he had the first chance? For not fulfilling his marriage vows of forever and endless patience?

His sister, Marianne, had always said he had a savior complex, which could stem from having so many relatives living within throwing distance, not to mention growing up with an active alcoholic and a very ill child in the extended family. Someone always needed a hand, needed a favor. Marianne also offered "being an incurable dumbass" as a potential explanation.

Lana trailed her fingers across his chest, a gesture that would have sent shivers down his spine just a few months ago. Now it made him step back, putting space between them. "They cut my hours at the store again and I've moved in with my mama. So you might be careful about calling. You know she doesn't like you since you divorced me."

"You filed the papers," he said in the flattest tone he could muster. Because she always got so upset when she thought he was mad at her, and that derailed the conversation like a couch on the tracks.

"Yeah, but she says you were a real asshole to sign them," she said, smiling sweetly. "I don't know where she gets these funny ideas. I don't say anything but nice things about you."

"Mm-hmm. I thought the cops got called the last time you moved in with your mama. Something about you setting all her shoes on fire with a can of Sterno?"

Lana's lips curled into a sneer and he knew that he'd pressed the wrong button. Lana did not like it when people reminded her of her interactions with the legal system. She snipped, "Well, I didn't have a choice. It's not like I could move back in with you with how your family feels about me."

"No, you cannot," he told her.

"I wasn't asking," she huffed, poking her bottom lip out in a pout.

He gritted his teeth. Right, like she "wasn't asking" two years before when she'd been dumped by the local weatherman and showed up on his porch with a Hefty bag full of her clothes. When Duffy refused to let her crash on his couch for "a while," Lana had told a very nice nurse he was dating at the time that he had crabs.

"Because we are not married anymore. Because *you* filed divorce papers," he said, with a little more heat in his tone than he usually used. The crabs rumor had taken months to die down.

"Well, I didn't realize it would be a federal case, wanting to spend time with a *friend*. If you don't want to see me, I'll just go."

He didn't want to disagree with her, because getting her out of the parking lot as soon as possible would prevent her from interacting with his family. But at the same time, it might be better to placate her a little bit because once he'd bolstered her up, he usually wouldn't see her for weeks. Not for the first time, Duffy realized how absolutely fucked-up it was to have to negotiate with his ex-wife like she was some sort of terrorist holding peace and quiet as her hostage.

"McDuff Marion McCready!"

Shit-fire, his mother had used his full name. This was not going to end well.

He turned to see Donna McCready standing at the steps leading to the dock, her hands propped on her hips. Her angular face, never what one would call "pleasant" these days, was thunderous.

"Son, you're already winning 'Jackass of the Week' for being late to work and leaving me to open up the shop alone," she said. "Don't compound the idiocy."

"Mother McCready, why are you always so grumpy in the mornings?" Lana asked, her tone all peaches and cream and arsenic. "You know they're making prunes in all sorts of new flavors now."

Duffy sighed in defeat. From the beginning, Lana had tried too hard to force a close relationship with his mama, who was like a cat when it came to, well, anybody. Donna only wanted to spend time with people who weren't super keen about spending time with her. And after it became clear that Donna wouldn't be penning Lana's name in the family Bible, Lana seemed to delight in poking at Donna's antisocial underbelly.

Donna growled lightly. "Don't call me 'Mother McCready.' Any family connection between us was severed by the divine wisdom of the state of Georgia!"

"Okay, let's just stop the insanity right here before I have to call Eric and he sees how bug-ass crazy our family is and runs away from the only remotely healthy relationship Frankie has ever had," Duffy barked, hurting his own head with his volume. "Lana, thank you for bringing me the glasses case. Now, Mom and I have a lot of stocking to do and we need to get to it."

"Oh, I can help!" Lana said brightly.

Donna's growl was no longer light. "March your little skinny chicken legs over to your car before I have you towed."

"Mama, calm down. You're gonna have a stroke. Get back to the shop. I'll be there in a minute. Lana, you need to leave. You're just stirring the pot right now and that's not all right," Duffy said, opening Lana's car door.

"Oh, fine." Lana sighed, rolling her eyes but smirking heavily. She straightened her shoulders and winked at him. "I'll see you later, Duffy. Mother McCready."

Donna took a threatening step toward Lana. Duffy stepped back and stopped her. "Mama, I do not have enough cash on hand to bail you out. I'll have to raid Uncle Bob's swear jar. It ain't classy to have to count out your bail money in stacks of quarters."

Lana gunned her engine and waggled her pink-frosted fingertips as she sped out of the parking lot, barely missing Duffy and Donna with the spray of gravel she threw. Donna glared at him, her whiskey-colored eyes sharp as razors over her aviators. "What sorry excuse do you have to say for yourself?"

"I know I'm late," he said. "I took those clients out for beers at the Dirty Deer, since the charter was kind of a bust, and who knew a bunch of Vols fans could drink so damn hard?"

"Oh, no, you're not late," his mother scoffed. "You're just in time to do all the restocking your damn self. I'm gonna go have a coffee with Leslie in the Snack Shack."

"I deserve that," he conceded.

"And the bait crickets got out again," she called over her shoulder as she walked down the dock.

"Wha— How?! I locked the barrel!"

"Well, I unlocked it and tipped it over!" she yelled back.

"Yeah, I deserve that, too," he muttered.

THE CRICKETS DID not go down easy. Duffy spent a good portion of his day chasing the critters around the bait shop and dumping them back into the bait cage. About a third of them escaped, which was going to cost them, so his mama had to have been pretty pissed off to do that on purpose.

Pulling into his driveway at the end of the day, Duffy stepped out of his truck and surveyed the little collection of cabins on the lake shore that his cousin Margot called a "compound." Considering the fact that the whole family worked together all day and then lived in houses within shouting distance, a body would think they'd hate the sight of each other.

But somehow, they made it work. With the exception of Frankie, McCreadys minded their own business.

The McCready family descended from a pair of brothers, John and Earl Jr. Earl built a little bait shop on what became the shore of Lake Sackett, offering tackle and lunches to fishermen and tourists. His brother, John, a carpenter by trade, was called on to give up cabinets for coffins when the Spanish flu epidemic took out a good portion of the town's population. When John needed more workspace, Earl offered him the use of the back of his shop and a family legacy was born.

Some McCreadys—his cousin Frankie, Grandpa E.J.J.,

Uncle Bob, and now Cousin Margot—buried Lake Sackett residents with all the expected pomp and frills, while others—Aunt Leslie, his mother, and himself—devoted their time to stuffing customers full of delicious deep-fried delicacies and guiding them on fishing tours through some of the best crappie beds in the county. In the best cases, one half of the family was able to help the bereaved with funeral planning and then the other half could distract the bereaved from their grief by feeding them and taking them out for some postburial cheer-up fishing. Grandpa E.J.J. loved cross-promotion.

Duffy knew his family wasn't quite normal. Most people had nightmares about mortuaries. They didn't spend Christmas in one. But he was proud that the McCready Family Funeral Home and Bait Shop was a Lake Sackett institution. Or the McCreadys belonged *in* an institution. It was a thin line.

Rolling his sore shoulders, Duffy shuffled toward his cabin, exhausted, looking forward to a cold beer and a warmed-up portion of Aunt Leslie's special macaroni and cheese. She used four kinds of cheese and none of them was Velveeta, which she called her "secret noningredient." She did use bacon, because this was Georgia and no respectable side dish should remain unbaconed. Tootie and Leslie were nice enough to deliver Tupperware dishes to him every Sunday to keep him from relying on TV dinners and carryout. His mother did not participate in this food prep relay because "he's an adult, not a dumbass teenager." Also, Donna's cooking was basically poison.

Shampooing his difficult-to-manage curls gave Duffy something to do while considering his strange encounter with his ex that morning. Something about Lana's behavior was sticking in his craw. His ex avoided Donna whenever possible. Why would she come to McCready's, where she was sure to see Donna, Frankie, or Leslie, none of whom tolerated her? Was it because she was moving in with her mom? Was she trying to wangle an invitation to stay with him? She had to know that wasn't possible. He was willing to commit to a little comfort on a long dark night, but surely she had to know they were never getting married again.

Oh, fuck a duck, what if she didn't realize they were never getting married again?

After showering and microwaving his mac 'n' cheese, Duffy settled onto the front porch swing with a beer and his laptop, an early model held together with duct tape and positive thinking. He usually checked sports stats or news while he was eating, but tonight he fired up his seldom-used email, attached a picture of the ugliest cupcake he could find on Google, and wrote, *A humble suggestion from a friend.*

He signed off with just *Duffy* and hit SEND before he could overanalyze it. And then he logged onto Facebook. Well, technically, he tried to sign into Facebook, entered an old password, and had to reset it because it had been years since his last login. He rarely updated his timeline. He didn't see the point in posting pictures of his food or deep philosophical thoughts about which pants he was going to wear that day.

Margot had informed him that his social media footprint was "shamefully small" during her revamp of McCready's online profile. But she noted that his timeline was free of political rants and inappropriate memes, which she appreciated. Tootie's account had been a mess of both, because Tootie was a bit more tech savvy and a lot less circumspect than the average senior citizen.

Duffy's updates informed him that he had more than forty

new friend requests pending, most of them from old school classmates or distant relatives on his mom's side. But other than that, his account was pretty stagnant. His real friends knew that if they wanted to contact him, they had to do it through his phone or talk to his face, like he was a person.

He scrolled by Tootie's feed because that way lay madness and dog memes. Frankie had posted a picture of her pale, smiling face snuggled up to Eric's photogenic mug. She looked so . . . weirdly and completely happy. He'd never seen her grin like that. He'd seen her smile with puckish delight, with gleeful anticipation of vengeance. And then there were those rare, scary moments when Frankie smiled because she was mentally calculating how long it would take to disintegrate your body in the crematory. But he'd never seen her beaming like her whole world was right.

Duffy was glad Frankie was settling down after so many years of "casual" dating. She had waited long enough to find someone who seemed to enjoy her crazy, even if Eric didn't seem to fully understand it. Duffy was happy for her, just like he was happy for Margot and the L.L.Bean-catalogue-perfect life she was starting with Kyle and his girls. He didn't even want to think about what happened in his sister's marriage to the guy he'd sworn blood-oath loyalty to in the sixth grade (the sister-kissing traitor). But Marianne was content, too, and that was all that counted.

A beagle mix, just out of his puppy stage and most likely one of Grandma Tootie's pack members, toddled onto Duffy's porch and sat at his feet, waggling his tail so hard that the whole back half of his body shook. "Hey, there, pup, what are you doing?"

The dog whimpered and zeroed in on Duffy's mac 'n' cheese dish with huge, glossy brown eyes.

"Oh, hell no," Duffy told him. "The minute I do that, Tootie comes over here yelling at me because I gave you something you're allergic to and I spend the rest of my night on puppy puke patrol."

The dog's butt stopped wiggling and he simply stared up at Duffy, as if he could make the mac 'n' cheese move into his belly through sheer force of will. Duffy moved the dish out of reach and pulled the dog onto the seat with him, scratching behind his ears. The dog seemed willing to accept this offering instead of cheesy, carby goodness, and leaned into the scratch.

Taking a deep breath, he typed in Lucy's name with the hand not occupied with scratching. She immediately popped up as a friend of Marianne's and Tootie's. The sight of her face seemed to make his chest tighten up. She'd been a looker ever since their elementary school days, swanning right through that awkward phase unfazed with her deep brown eyes and high cheekbones—not to mention the obstinate set to her soft pink lips that she'd inherited from her late mama.

Lucy had her arms wrapped around a boy of about four, who had Lucy's coloring but Wayne's stocky build. She gazed at her son with the sort of motherly love they wrote about in storybooks. She'd looked happy with her husband. They'd had a nice life. And he felt like an asshole for being salty over it.

She didn't need him coming at her with his unresolved feelings. She was mourning a man she loved. She needed time and space. She needed a friend. And he wasn't sure he could be her friend right now. He wanted so much more from Lucy.

He remembered the moment he fell in love with her. They'd been in seventh grade. Lucy had hit her growth spurt well before Duffy had, and stood three inches taller than his springy ginger curls. Wayne Garten and some other older boys had been poking fun at him in the cafeteria, calling Duffy a freak because his daddy cut up dead bodies all day.

Lucy had yelled, "Shut your mouth before the toilet fumes make us pass out!" And then she had walked right up to Wayne and punched him in his stupid face. Blood had spurted in a beautiful, gruesome arc from Wayne's nose as he toppled to the floor, arms windmilling comically. She planted one pink Converse on Wayne's chest and asked him if he had anything else to say to her friend Duffy. Wayne insisted that he did not.

Jimmy Greenway, the principal at the time, informed Lucy that she'd earned herself a three-page essay on alternatives to fighting. She crowed that it was worth it and she would make it four pages. Duffy knew then that no girl would ever be as awesome as Lucy Bowman, and none of them should even try.

"It's not pathetic if I close the browser now, right?" Duffy asked the dog. The dog dropped his chin on Duffy's leg and avoided eye contact. "Oh, what do you know?"

Duffy glanced up at the purr of an engine rolling toward him. Carl, the aforementioned sister-kissing traitor, was steering his massive red tow truck over the gravel drive. He rolled to a smooth stop directly in front of Duffy.

"What are you doing out here?" Duffy asked.

"I got beer that needs drinkin'," Carl said, hopping out of the truck with two six-packs of their favorite brew.

"I can help you with that," Duffy said, throwing his feet up on the porch railing.

"Marianne said you'd had a rough day," Carl said, handing him a cold can. "Frankie told her something about a plague of crickets and your mama being all pissed off?"

"I don't want to talk about it," he said.

"She also said Lana dropped by and threw her particular brand of joy around."

"It was not a red-letter day," Duffy said, cracking open his beer. "A man can't even walk across the parking lot of his workplace without getting caught in the cross fire of his mother and his ex-wife cat-fighting it out . . . and then getting ratted out by his cousin . . . who tells his sister."

"Has it occurred to you that the women in your life exercise a little too much control over you?" Carl asked.

"I try not to think about that too much," Duffy said, shaking his head.

"Yeah, one issue at a time. Every one of those women is terrifying," Carl said as he slumped onto the swing next to Duffy. He scratched behind the beagle's ears, prompting the dog to crawl into Carl's lap and attempt to lick his beer can. "I mean, I love your sister more than my own breath. But one time I ate the last peanut butter cup in the house, and she replaced the batteries in the remotes with duds she'd been saving in a drawer."

"Which remote?"

Carl took a long draw of beer and shook his head. "All of them, Duff. All of them."

Duffy nodded. "She learned that one from Frankie. I feel like I should make some sort of warning sheet for Eric. 'If you do "this stupid thing," Frankie will respond with "this particular act of pointed smartass vengeance" when you least expect it.'"

"Nah, if he's hitching into this family, he's gotta run the gauntlet. There are no shortcuts," Carl said, frowning. "So, it must have been weird seeing Lana again. After all, you told me that you haven't hung out with her in weeks. A new record, you said. Finally over her, I think you said."

Duffy tilted his beer back and drained the rest of it in one gulp.

"I knew it." Carl sighed and picked up a fresh beer.

Duffy shrugged innocently. "Knew what?"

"Dammit, Duffy! You know I don't like talking about feelings," Carl told him.

"I am really not looking forward to whatever comes after this."

"I love you like only a brother can," Carl said. "But Lana is poison. She always has been. You put up with stuff from her that you'd never allow from anybody else."

"That . . . is a fair assessment."

"Don't you want someone to share your life with? Somebody you can spend more than a few hours at a time with? Kids?"

"Are we really having this conversation?" Duffy scoffed. "This is not porch talk! This is what Marianne and Frankie talk about when they have girls' nights at Margot's. Are you gonna paint my toenails for me next?"

"I wouldn't touch your nasty-ass feet with a ten-foot pole. Answer the damn question," Carl countered.

Duffy picked at the ring of his beer can. The bitch of it was that Duff *was* lonely. With everybody in the family pairing off but him, he was starting to feel left behind. The only other singles in the family were Stan, an avowed bachelor after the disappointment of his first marriage, and Donna, who was basically a puffer fish when threatened with human interaction. So sometimes, with Lana, he felt a little bit less alone.

"Yes, I would like kids of my own one day," Duffy said. "As much as I love hanging out with the boys . . . yeah, I would like a couple of girls, I think."

"Asshole."

"Tell Aiden to stop putting his homemade superglue on people's chairs and I'll change my mind."

"That boy's either gonna be an astronaut or a supervillain," Carl said with a sigh. "But you're never gonna have one like him if you keep this crap up with Lana. Girls like Lucy Bowman—who I happen to know is back in town, thanks to my lovely wife—do not put up with playing second fiddle to crazy ex-wives and their drama. Hell, look what happened when you tried to take that cute girl from the Bass Pro Shop out to the movies."

Duffy shuddered. AnnaBeth, the fishing lure consultant, had not been amused when Lana sent an usher into the theater, searching for Duffy by flashlight, because his "wife" was having a medical emergency at the concession stand. Duffy ended up spending most of the night cleaning popcorn out of his hair, as AnnaBeth had dumped the bucket over his head. Sadly, this was not the first of Duffy's dates that had ended this way.

"You don't love Lana," Carl noted. "You just feel bad for her."

"Yep." Duffy sighed.

"Well, last time I checked, TiVo-ing a bunch of *Oprah* don't make you a life coach," Carl muttered.

"Marianne wasn't supposed to tell you about the *Oprah* thing. I feel betrayed," Duffy said.

"McDuff, one of the great things about you is the fact you're one of the nicest guys in the world. I mean, everybody in town knows that if they need something, they can call you, day or night, and you'll be right there for 'em. But maybe it's time for you to put some of that nice guy aside and think about yourself first."

"What in the hell does that mean?"

"Stop answering Lana's calls. Stop humoring her when she shows up wanting attention like a stray cat. And when she invades your dates, pretending you're still married, tell her to take her ass home."

"Fine," Duffy told him. "I will."

"And stop being such a gutless wonder and ask Lucy out on a damn date."

"I'm not a gutless wonder. I'm full of guts. And those guts know that if I tried to date Lucy and messed things up with her, that would be the end of our friendship. And I'm not willing to risk that. And hell, that's assuming she wanted to date me in the first place. I caught her loading an eighteen-inch penis cake into her van and I can't imagine I can offer her anything much in comparison."

Carl choked, spraying his beer down the front of his shirt. "What?"

"Long story."

3

LUCY SAT ON the front porch of her childhood home, on the porch swing her father had built with his own two hands, her sock feet propped up on the railing. She was wearing her black-framed glasses and an old Lake Sackett High School track and field hoodie over her pajamas as a concession to the late winter evening. She balanced a tablet in her lap, highlighting completed lines from her massive spreadsheet of to-do items in yellow. One column was marked MOVE and the other was marked BAKERY. While the MOVE column was nearly yellowed out, the BAKERY column was still distressingly incomplete.

At the top of the list was GET HERB BREWSTER TO AGREE TO AN APPOINTMENT TIME, written in shouty caps, because getting the twice-cursed local health inspector to show up for a licensing inspection was harder than trying to pin down the cable guy. She'd had everything in the kitchen ready for her inspection for weeks, but every time she got Mr. Brewster to agree to a time, he would call five minutes before, claiming that an "emergency" was keeping him from meeting her. Or he would delay their appointment until right before pickup time at Sammy's preschool.

Since she hadn't heard anything about a massive salmonella outbreak in Lake Sackett, she had to assume Herb was stonewalling her. She'd complained to his superiors at the health department, but the administrator said the director didn't like to interfere with inspectors' decisions, even if those decisions weren't getting made in the first place. Being licensed was a small but crucial part of her overall plans, and it was extremely frustrating not to be able to accomplish it because of small-town shenanigans.

Lucy sighed and wound her hair into a messy bun on top of her head. How was she ever going to get all this done? She already felt like she was being pulled in a dozen directions—taking care of Sammy, trying to make sure he was recovering from losing his daddy and having some sort of decent childhood, keeping up with the house, keeping up with their finances—and she didn't feel like she was doing any of them particularly well. Trying to open this business felt like balancing a rock on top of a house of cards.

She took her eyes off the screen for a moment to enjoy the colors of dusk bleeding across the sky. While it wasn't as carefully manicured as their landscaping back in Texas, the large front yard was neatly trimmed thanks to Lucy's steady hand with her daddy's push mower. It was perfect for Sam to run around and get muddy, something that had been sorely lacking so far in his overscheduled Gymboree-and–Baby Einstein toddlerhood. She'd already bought him a little child-size pedal tractor, which was still hidden deep within their storage unit to be unearthed for his birthday.

Unlike the McCreadys, Lucy's people hadn't lucked into lakefront property when the Army Corps of Engineers dammed the Chattahoochee River to create Lake Sackett. Then again, at least their homestead hadn't been flooded, like the Martins', who were still bitter over losing their hog farm decades before. The Bowmans had been a happy little trio on their plot of land. Before Lucy was born, her mother, Gale, worked as a waitress at the Rise and Shine. Her father, Pete, had been a mechanic at the Trinkitts' boat dealership. While neither had attended college, both of her parents were passionate readers and insisted that any day was a good day to learn something new. Even when Gale had been going through chemo, after Lucy left for college, she'd quote Lucy random facts she'd learned from magazines in the waiting room. After Gale passed, they continued playing Trivial Pursuit every Friday night and were still fairly obnoxious about yelling out the answers to *Jeopardy!*, a habit Wayne had found annoying to no end.

Welcoming Alex Trebek into her living room every night had been one of her first acts of reclaiming those little bits of "Lake Sackett Lucy" after Wayne's funeral. Calling Wayne's death a shock was a massive understatement. He'd been in such good shape, long after his college football days were over. He'd been religious about the gym and low-carb menus and eliminating fried foods from their diet—a real challenge for a woman raised in the "Yeah, we can fry that" capital of Georgia. Staying fit was "all part of the package," he'd told her. Big clients wouldn't trust a financial adviser who looked like he had no discipline. They wanted a trim, handsome family man with a picture of a pretty, smiling wife and an adorable towheaded toddler on his desk.

Unfortunately for her late husband, no amount of kale shakes could have kept that tire jack from failing and dropping a truck on Wayne's chest. It was just a fluke that he was even under the F-150 that morning. Normally he trusted professionals with car maintenance, yard work, fixing the dishwasher—he didn't even charge the battery on his golf cart. But the morning he'd died, he'd been eager to take the truck to some sort of weekend with the other executives at an exclusive golf resort outside Houston. The engine had been making a funny grinding noise and Lucy told Wayne to just drive the Mercedes so she could take the truck into the shop. But he'd wanted to play up his "good ol' boy made good" angle to impress the VPs and insisted he remembered enough from working with his stepdad to fix it himself. So he slid under the truck . . . and the rest was a 911 call.

While Lucy had *felt* clearheaded and capable the week of the funeral, she'd been left at loose ends after the burial. She'd known so little about her own life. It had taken her weeks to go through the financial paperwork, to figure out what they owned and what was leased, what could be repossessed by the bank at any moment—not because they didn't have the cash, but because she didn't know where to send the payments. Hell, she didn't even know the passwords for their online banking. Since Wayne was the financial expert and Lucy was a stay-at-home mom, it had made more sense for him to handle all the money. She'd just smiled and tried to be sensible with the credit cards as she made their life together. But it had been humbling to realize how easily she'd handed total control to her husband, to feel like a helpless child when she was trying to *raise* a child.

It had taken her months to sort through it all and arrive at a settlement with the insurance company, to zero out the accounts, to sell the house and the things they didn't need anymore, for her lawyer to reach a settlement with the manufacturer over the faulty tire jack that had led to Wayne's demise. She had a considerable nest egg now, enough to support her and Sam and pay for his tuition all the way through law school if he wanted. She'd set aside a small portion of it to start her bakery, and once she'd run through that portion, if she couldn't replenish it with earnings, she would tap out. She did not want to have one of those businesses where Gordon Ramsay showed up to yell at her about how she was running it into the ground.

Of course, no one in the Garten family knew how considerable her nest egg was, and she wanted to keep it that way.

"Here, Mama." Sam came running out of the house with her cell phone in his hand.

"Hey, I thought you were coloring a picture of a—what in the blue blazes is this?" Lucy peeled her hands away from some sticky substance on her iPhone. The phone case, custom ordered from Etsy to feature Sam's drawing of a purple dog chasing a green cupcake, was dotted with fingerprints in strawberry jelly.

"Um, Sam, dearest sweet-face, light of my life, I know this is going to sound like an odd question, but why is there jelly on my phone?"

"I'm making a sandwich," he told her, leveling her with her own brown eyes. Her eyes were one of the few features of hers that had managed to fight through Wayne's DNA and pass on to her son. His dark blond hair, the stubborn set of his chin, the long-limbed, barrel-chested build, that was all Wayne. It was like having her husband's reincarnation running around the house, something that alternately haunted her and brought her comfort.

"We just had dinner an hour ago," she reminded him. "Don't you remember the broccoli negotiations? The very foundations of our house shook with the fury of our fierce debate?"

"You're so *weird*, Mama," he said with a sigh.

"You're not wrong," she told him. "But, seriously, why are you eating again?"

"I'm still *hungry*," he groaned, rubbing his tummy.

Lucy ruffled her fingers through his (relatively clean) hair. This was something else he'd inherited from Wayne, the bottomless-pit appetite. Lucy could remember watching her late husband devour entire large pizzas on his own when he was still playing college ball. Sam seemed to be going through a growth spurt . . . which had started when he was about eighteen months old. He was stretching through his clothes faster than she could buy them. She made a note on her tablet's calendar app to call the local family practice and schedule a checkup with Dr. Laster. Sam would need one for kindergarten that fall anyway.

"Okay, I'll come in and help you make it," she said.

"No, I already did," he told her, smiling proudly.

"But the bread is up on top of the fridge. How did you reach it?" she asked.

"I didn't use bread."

"You didn't use bread . . . in a sandwich?"

He shrugged. "Didn't want it."

"So you put peanut butter and jelly in a bowl?" she asked, and when he made his *I'm trying to come up with a good explanation* face, she added, "Please tell me there was a bowl."

"I didn't use peanut butter."

"Samuel Wayne Garten, were you eating jelly out of the jar with a spoon?"

"That's the part of the sandwich I like," he said.

"Go wash your hands." She sighed, picturing the mess waiting for her on the counter. "And use a bleach wipe to de-jelly my phone."

"But it was ringing a couple of minutes ago. You said to bring you your phone when it rings," he protested, adding proudly, "And I didn't drop it in a toilet this time."

"It was ringing?" Lucy turned the phone over in her hands to check her notifications. She grimaced when she saw six missed calls on the register from Evie Garten in the last thirty minutes. Her head dropped to her chest. This was one of her mother-in-law's least fun habits. Evie didn't believe in texting or leaving voice mail. She preferred to call every five minutes until her target relented and answered out of self-defense. Lucy had set Evie's ringer to silent on her phone before driving the moving truck from Texas, otherwise the lure of turning the truck north and heading straight to Canada would have been too great.

"What's wrong, Mama? That's the face you make when strangers pinch my cheeks."

"Nothing, honey, can you just go grab me that bleach wipe? And then wash your hands?"

"Okay," he said, drawing out a sigh as if her expectations for a jelly-free phone were the most unreasonable standards ever.

Just as Sam cleared the door, Lucy's phone jolted to life, buzzing, showing Evie's number on the screen—but making no noise, because Lucy still hadn't removed the silent ringtone. For reasons.

"Nope," Lucy said, setting the phone aside and letting it ring. Evie could leave a voice mail if it was important.

Relations with Evie had been tense since Lucy moved back to Lake Sackett. Lucy had known from the start that she and her mother-in-law would not be living the Old Testament life of Naomi and Ruth. Like many older Southern women, Evie considered herself the matriarch of her family, which meant she expected approval over any and all decisions made by any family member and to take to her bed with a washcloth over her eyes whenever she was displeased. She also didn't believe in apologies—from her to other people. The most she could muster when she knew she'd made someone angry was to say, "Well, you reap what you sow." Which had never made sense to Lucy, but also never failed to make her even madder. And she seemed to think that Lucy moving back to town meant sliding firmly under her thumb.

Already annoyed that Lucy had her own plans for her future employment and that Lucy refused to move into the dilapidated vacant house next to Evie's place, Evie had been incensed to find that Lucy had enrolled Sam in the Lake Sackett Early Learners Center. The center was the only state-licensed preschool in the county, and Lucy had to fight like hell to secure a spot for Sam. But Evie had expected to be Sam's full-time care while Lucy ran her "little business." Lucy's unsweetened "no" combined with the "public embarrassment" of not being trusted to babysit was too much for Evie to bear with a smile.

But still, Lucy knew she was doing the right thing. After years of watching Lake Sackett mothers pressuring their children into believing they were all that Mama lived for, Lucy was not about to allow her preschooler to take on that burden. While Sam had been fairly resilient since the death of his daddy, he was still a little wobbly. He couldn't prop up Evie through her grief.

"Here, Mama, I brought you the wipe."

"Thanks, honey."

Sam took the phone out of her hand and methodically wiped it free of Smucker's. The phone buzzed to life again and Sam swiped his thumb over the slide to answer as Lucy yelped, "No!"

"Lucy?" Evie's voice shrieked out of the phone. "Are you there? Hello?"

Sam shrank away from the phone, his lips pulling back in distress. He never had liked the loud, booming voices so common in the Garten family. And no amount of insisting he would get used to it could erase that discomfort from Sam's face. Or stop him from running inside the house, away from the noise.

"Yes, Evie, what do you need?"

"To talk to you, of course," Evie huffed. "I haven't spoken to you in ages. I don't know what's going on with you, shutting yourself away like this. It's not healthy."

"Evie, I spoke to you two days ago."

"Yeah, and there's no excuse for it. I deserve to know what's happening with you and Sam, Evie. I thought that's why you moved back here—to be closer to us."

"I moved back here so Sam and I could live a simple, *quiet* life in a place I knew better than Dallas," Lucy countered.

"To be closer to your family."

"Even if that's the case, we're not going to see you every day, Evie. And we're probably not going to talk on the phone every day, either. That's too much."

"Says who?"

"Says me."

"Well, what if I go pick him up at that *school* tomorrow and take him home with me?" Evie suggested.

Lucy considered it, for only a moment. Evie's husband, Dewie, was Wayne's stepfather. He was a perfectly nice, hard-working man who kept to himself and tried not to interfere in Evie's dealings with her children. He liked his baseball and his beer and didn't seem to say much unless it was Evie announcing, "Well, Dewie thinks . . ." as if he weren't sitting five feet away in his easy chair.

Technically, Dewie and Evie had never married, but Dewie had spent considerably more time with the Garten kids than their father had been granted. Fred Garten had died when Wayne was eight and Wayne treasured every single memory of his father, who had taken on a near-mythical status in Wayne's head even as an adult. After the funeral, Lucy had been careful to install a frame in Sam's room with multiple photos of Wayne holding Sam, right on the wall above his bed. There may have been trouble between Wayne and Lucy, but their son would not forget his father.

Lucy took a breath through her nose and said firmly, "No, but if you want, you can meet us at the movies this weekend. They're playing the original *Jungle Book* cartoon at the Bijou. Sam's really excited about it."

"I don't want to go along with your plans, I want to do things with him on my own."

"You can meet us for lunch after the movie," Lucy offered.

"No. I want to pick him up and have him over here. He can sleep in his daddy's old room."

"He's not ready for that," Lucy insisted.

"I don't think that's fair."

"A lot about this situation isn't fair. It's not fair that Sam lost his dad. It's not fair that I uprooted him from his whole life and brought him here. But he seems to be handling it a lot better than other people."

The silence somehow grew colder on Evie's end of the line. "Well, have you thought any more about this silly preschool thing? I just don't think it's right to send him off with some stranger when I'm right here."

"No, because he loves the preschool and there's no way he's going to want to leave!" Lucy said, her voice rising. She clamped her lips shut and took a deep breath. She would not yell and upset her son before bedtime. She refused to give Evie that sort of influence in her home.

"Well, you reap what you sow. You'll see I'm right in the end."

Lucy stared at the porch ceiling and prayed for patience. "The movie starts at two on Saturday, if you want to meet us. I'm going to hang up now."

Lucy pressed the END button over Evie's shouted objections and buried her face in her hands. She was trying to give Evie a chance to see Sam, but there were limits to what she was willing to tolerate.

"Was that my grandma?" Sam asked as she walked inside the house.

Sam had built a multitiered "city" out of a mix of Duplos and Legos, whose landscape covered the entirety of her father's tiny living room. He was sprawled across the couch they'd brought from Dallas, running his trucks along the "highway" that snaked over the carpet below him.

"Yep." She knelt in front of the couch, careful not to put her knee down on a Lego.

Sam's nose wrinkled. "Did she want me to come spend the night?"

"Yeah, do you think you might want to?" Lucy asked, keeping her expression very intentionally neutral. If Sam wanted to spend the night at Evie's house, she would try to help him work up to the idea. But she certainly wasn't going to smile over it.

Sam pursed his lips. "No. I'm good."

"All right then. You still want to see *The Jungle Book* this weekend? I told Mamaw Evie about it and she might come with us."

His little face brightened and he hopped up to his knees. "Yes! She can come to the movie with us. I just don't want to spend the night. Maybe I would spend the night at Bradley's sometime, but he's my best friend, Mom. My *best* friend."

"I understand," she said, suppressing a smile. Sam had known little Bradley Curlew for all of three weeks, but their bond had been permanently forged by their mutual love of Netflix original cartoons and tiny building bricks created for the sole purpose of injuring adult feet. "Spending the night at someone's house is a pretty big deal. Even just considering it is definitely big-boy territory."

"I know. Maybe sometime soon."

"Yes, and I'm very proud of you."

"Thanks. Does that mean I can have another sandwich?" he asked.

"Absolutely not."

PEERING THROUGH THE *swish-swish* of wipers on her rain-spotted windshield, Lucy guided her truck over the familiar bumps and dips on the road to the McCready compound. There were times, when she was a kid, that she'd envied Duffy all these aunts and uncles and grandparents living nearby, in their adorable little cabins so close together. Now that she'd had a taste of living close to extended family, she was grateful for her own house on its own driveway.

Though she couldn't fault the view, she thought, sighing as the expanse of water stretched before her. The McCreadys had hundreds of yards of shoreline all to themselves, enough to build their own dock for their personal crafts. They could boat to work every morning if they wanted to. They didn't, because apparently it was impractical, but still. They had the option.

She scanned the various cabins, trying to guess which was Duffy's. Tootie and E.J.J. lived in the big white two-story "main house," central to the other homes. She knew the yellow-and-green one on the far end was Stanley's, though it looked to be in much better shape than the last time she'd seen it. Donna's cabin, the gray-and-red three-bedroom that was Duffy's childhood home, had been scrubbed clean of Marianne's misguided attempts at macramé planters and the little carved wooden doodads Junior had crafted for the porch. It was as if Duffy's family had been replaced by a stranger with a grudge against handicrafts. So in the candidates for Duffy's place, it was a toss-up between the little dollhouse cabin with a wind chime made from *Avengers* insignias or the house with the giant carved wooden bear on the porch.

"Yeah, the *Avengers* wind chime screams Frankie, so . . ." Lucy parked the truck in front of the bear-bedecked porch. "It also makes me a little sad that I know all the *Avengers* insignias. Dang it, motherhood."

As soon as she opened the truck door, sliding into the unusually warm and muggy February day, she could hear the scream of an electric saw. She turned toward the squat square cement-block building at the end of the row of houses. Despite the cosmetic improvements to some of the cabins, Junior McCready's workshop hadn't changed.

"Lucy?"

Lucy turned to see Donna McCready's lean, sharp face staring at her through the rain. Duffy's mother had always been a bit of an odd duck. She was prickly as a pissed-off cactus to most everybody, but Lucy could remember her softer side, the "Miss Donna" who threw Duffy's and Marianne's birthday parties and read books to their class on parent reading days. One of her earliest memories was of finding Miss Donna sobbing into an opened roll of paper towels at the Food Carnival, and Lucy yanking on her skirt. Donna had yelped, and bent over when eight-year-old Lucy continued tugging at the hem of her sensible JCPenney day dress.

"Miss Donna, you need to get yourself together," Lucy had told her solemnly, nodding toward a group of the meaner PTA moms standing in the dairy section, cackling like a bunch of particularly bitchy hyenas. "Don't let them see you cry, because then they'll know they got to you."

Miss Donna had sniffled and wiped her eyes, her jaw setting in a stubborn line. "All right. Thank you, honey."

Over the years, Donna had transformed from a leaky water pot to the paragon of "take no shit" before her, but had reserved nothing but sweetness and light for Lucy. She realized as an adult that Donna probably suffered from some pretty severe anxiety issues. She was nervous around people and, according to Lucy's mama, had made very few friends among the ladies of the beauty-parlor-and-prayer-circle set. Lucy found out years later Miss Donna had suffered a pretty major slight right around the time of the paper towel incident involving her removal from the PTA's Founders' Festival committee because her cooking was considered a threat to public health.

The PTA moms hadn't been wrong, but still, it wasn't a very nice thing to do.

"Aren't you a sight for sore eyes!" Donna cried with a grin. "Come on over here and give me a hug!"

"Hey, Miss Donna." Lucy giggled and threw her arms around Donna, who squeezed her with a strength that didn't seem possible in such wiry arms. "Oh, I'm glad to see you."

"Liar, you came over here to see my good-for-nothing son," Donna said, but there was no heat in it. She put her arm around Lucy, leading her toward the workshop. "But it's a good thing. You might be able to keep him from losing a thumb or something in there."

"Aw, that's a lot of pressure to put on me." Lucy chuckled.

"How's your boy doing?" Donna asked. "Frankie showed me a picture on Facebook. He's cute as a speckled pup."

"Thank you, and he's fine," Lucy assured her. "He's a bit young to understand everything that's happening, but he's fine."

"Well, kids are resilient, and I'm sure you're a far better mama than I ever was." Donna yanked the door to the workshop open. "You see the results."

Duffy's back was turned to the door, hunched over some piece of equipment. He was shirtless, sweaty, and had a tool belt hanging low on his hips, dragging the waist of his jeans down. Lucy stopped in her tracks, Donna's continued momentum pulling her forward. Lucy never would have imagined a man's back could have so many muscles. Wayne had been gym fit, but these were *work* muscles, born of hours of labor. And he was *working* them, pushing a piece of lumber through a running saw. His waist was pretty damn narrow and what she could see of his denim-clad ass—

These were very awkward thoughts to have while arm in arm with a man's mother.

"Duffy!" Donna yelled over the din of the saw.

Duffy's shoulders jerked, but his hands never faltered. He reached carefully toward the saw controls and hit the off switch. He turned, and the front view was just as nice as the back. Pectoral muscles that weren't overtly defined, but certainly present and accounted for.

"Hi, there," Lucy said, waggling her fingers.

Duffy grinned, propping his safety goggles on top of his head. "Hey!"

"She came to see you, no idea why," Donna muttered. She patted Lucy's shoulder. "Lucy, honey, I'll be stopping by your shop as soon as you're open and buying you out of anything with cinnamon. Or chocolate. Or apple. I'm gonna be buying a lot."

"That sounds good, Miss Donna."

Donna turned to Duffy and in a far gruffer tone said, "The weather's supposed to break tomorrow, be ready to work."

Donna turned on her heel and walked out of the workshop.

"I will never understand the strange hold that you have over my mother," Duffy said, pulling a shirt from the workbench and sliding it over his head.

All Lucy could think was, *Aw, ab muscles, nooooo!*

"Well, the power is a heavy burden, but I try to bear it responsibly." She cleared her throat. "So you're still doing all that carpentry stuff?"

He nodded toward the various projects in half-finished stages around the worktables—a rocking chair; a bookshelf; a set of stacking trays; a *Dr. Who*–themed birdhouse shaped like the TARDIS, which she could only imagine was for Frankie. "Yeah, not as much as I'd like, but I've gotten a lot better than I was the last time you saw my work."

"Hey, that was an amazing spice rack you made for your mom," she protested, making him laugh.

Duffy's cheeks went pink and he rubbed the back of his neck. "Well, I kept my dad's tools when he passed, and in the winters, I get to come out here and make stuff. Usually stuff to give my family for Christmas and birthday presents, because I prefer this to shopping."

"No coffins, though?" she asked, glancing around the shop.

Duffy sighed. "One—Mr. Moseley requested it specifically. He said he wanted his 'buryin' box' to be made by hands he knew."

Lucy smiled. Mr. Moseley had been the high school's gym/woodshop/driver's ed teacher and had been a fervent supporter of Duffy's "natural talent" with carpentry. "That was sweet of you."

"Eh, it was the least I could do," Duffy said, jerking his shoulders. "So what are you gonna do for cabinets, storage, and displays and such? I wouldn't think you'd wanna use the meat shop's stuff."

"I hadn't quite figured that out yet. I've been focusing on getting the kitchen equipment up and running. I just want to make the place look cozy, and you know, non–Food Carnival–y."

"You want me to see if I can put some together for you?" he asked.

"Are you kidding?" she exclaimed. "That would be amazing! But I'd hate for you to go to a lot of trouble."

"It's no trouble at all. I'd just need to look around, make some measurements."

"Are you sure it's not too much?" she asked, but before he could answer, she continued, "Oh, who the hell am I kidding, it took me weeks to get the damn kitchen updated trying to use local contractors. And you won't be intimidated if Davey shows up here giving you the evil eye."

"Not with all these power tools on my side," Duffy said.

Lucy snorted.

"Besides, I think Davey left town last week. Something about following his dream of being a demolition derby champion? He said he was going to follow the circuit in Florida."

"Yeah, that sounds like him," Lucy said, nodding and pursing her lips. "So, just let me know when you can come by and take a look at the place."

"Sure. You want to go sit on the porch? Hang out for a bit? Have a beer?"

Right, Lucy told herself, because that's the sort of thing you did with a friend—sitting on a porch and drinking beer and chatting. Not ogling their muscles . . . in front of their mother.

She grinned. "Sure, but I should probably make it a soda since I'm picking my son up from school in a few hours."

"Wow, parenting standards have changed since we were kids," he marveled.

4

*L*UCY TUGGED SELF-CONSCIOUSLY at her pale green cardigan as she walked into the Dirty Deer that weekend, Marianne McCready Dawson trailing behind her. Frankie waved at them from a booth in the corner, beckoning them closer. Lucy was seized with an illogical desire to run like hell and leave a Lucy-shaped hole in the smoke-stained wood paneling. She hadn't spent a lot of time in the Dirty Deer before she'd left town, since she hadn't been old enough to legally enter the bar. Any partying she'd done in high school was out on Make-Out Island with her classmates, and that was on the rare occasions when she'd slipped her father's careful watch.

For the first time in years, Lucy was sure she was inappropriately dressed for an occasion, even if it was just drinks at the local dive with Duffy's relatives. While they'd never enjoyed the same closeness Lucy shared with Duffy, Marianne and Lucy had been good friends in high school. So when Marianne had called to invite her for a girls' night out, because her husband, Carl, "owed her one," Lucy had accepted based on nostalgia alone.

Lucy didn't exactly have "girls' night" clothes in her pared-down wardrobe. After Wayne died, she'd donated her cute little suits and designer dresses to a women's shelter. All she had left were jeans, sensible cardigans, and the odd church dress, which didn't really fit in with the bar's "eclectic neon beer sign" decor.

Then again, Frankie was wearing a dress printed with cats firing laser guns at each other, with thick-soled sneakers and a cardigan in an eye-melting shade of electric purple. While she looked like the love child of Wednesday Addams and Rainbow Dash, Frankie McCready had always been precociously smart and determined to the point of being terrifying. Lucy was not at all surprised to hear that Frankie had taken on the mantle of family undertaker. She was the only one tough enough for the job.

"I still don't know how I feel about this," Lucy muttered to Marianne, who was making a "two" with her fingers at Sierra, the Deer's longtime waitress, and then pointing at Frankie's empty glass. "Are you sure Carl is up to watching Sam, along with your boys? I mean, Nate mentioned something about a gummy worm stash and Sam can get downright unmanageable if he gets too much corn syrup in him—"

"It'll be fine," Marianne promised. "Every year or so, Carl makes noises about maybe wanting another baby, because he thinks I look really hot pregnant and he has this fantasy about raising our own baseball team. And nights like this are a good reminder for him of why parents should not let their children outnumber them."

"He thinks you look hot pregnant?"

"My pregnancy boobs were a wonder of nature," Marianne said, shrugging.

Lucy frowned. Wayne hadn't thought much of her pregnancy, other than that it was a major inconvenience for him to have to take paternity leave. He'd been gung ho about it when he found out they were expecting a boy, but he'd still been vaguely annoyed by her snoring, the nausea, her unwillingness to accompany him to golf tournaments and charity galas when she was so big she hadn't seen her feet in months.

Then again, Marianne had married Carl Dawson, a dangerous-looking mechanic from one of the more tragic redneck families in town, who possessed a secret, gooey marshmallow center that made him one of the sweetest men on the planet. They'd been desperately in love in high school, and got married soon after Marianne graduated college. But somehow, they seemed even more in love than they'd been all those years ago. Carl looked at Marianne as if she were personally responsible for the creation of beer, pandas, and Netflix. And Marianne, for all her boob-related anti-baby bluster, had absolute faith in Carl, his affections, and his ability to parent their sons. And Lucy tried not to let the jealousy turn her stomach. Body-cramping envy was probably something that nice people didn't feel toward their friends.

"We're going to have fun," Frankie promised as they slid into a booth. "A couple of drinks, some food, we'll catch up."

"And Margot would have loved to come out, but she's got this *thing* about not showing up at a bar when she's pregnant." Frankie sighed.

"Damned unreasonable of her," Lucy said with a shake of her head. "So, how's that been, having your long-lost cousin show up after all these years? Your family's always seemed so tight-knit. I would be intimidated as hell trying to walk into that. Duffy mentioned that there have been a lot of changes."

"So, you've been talking to my brother," Marianne said, waggling her eyebrows.

"Yes, because your brother is my *friend*. And *friends* talk."

Marianne rolled her eyes, grumbling as Sierra delivered their drinks with a smile and a "We missed you, Lucy." Marianne had ordered two Georgia Peaches: a mix of moonshine, peach schnapps, and a few other ingredients sure to cause Lucy some regret in the morning.

Marianne had been trying to match Duffy up with Lucy since they were kids, going so far as to call Lucy the night before Duffy's courthouse wedding to Lana and beg Lucy to keep this "huge mistake" from happening to her brother. Lucy had respected Duffy's determination to do right by Lana, even if it made him miserable in the process. And she'd been too frightened of losing Duffy's friendship to speak out against the woman he was marrying, even if she thought Lana was a devil's helping of bad news. So she'd left the antinuptial mission to Marianne and Donna, and couldn't help but feel she'd failed her friend just a little bit.

"You know, I think my life is complicated enough without thinking about any man that way. Besides, I have a man in my life—"

Marianne lifted her hand to stop Lucy midsentence. "Oh, honey, no. Don't say your son is the man in your life. That makes me sad for you."

"Fine," Lucy shot back. "Tell me more about Margot."

"Well, getting her to accept her place in the family took some work, I'm not going to lie. Margot was a tad prickly, and some of us—not saying who, *ahem*, Frankie—may have tried a little too hard to fold her right into the family. But eventually it evened out. She relaxed a lot. We all learned about the importance of boundaries. Margot's one of us now, she just has some very polished airs about her."

"How's Stan taking the whole unwed-pregnant-daughter thing?"

"Actually, I think he's so happy that Margot is letting him be involved in her life and this pregnancy, he doesn't care if she marries Kyle or not. Kyle's a little touchy about it, but Margot's got a pretty wide streak of the McCready stubbornness in her, so I don't think that's something he can rush her on."

"Sounds like a sensible guy," Lucy noted.

"Oh, he's incredibly sensible—principal of the elementary school, a pillar of the community, which is why tongues are wagging so hard about him getting caught with his hands in the premarital cookie jar. The entire PTA is scandalized. No one even remembers how badly I screwed up the wrapping paper fund-raiser anymore."

"Well, it's good for them, gives them something to talk about besides their own lives," Lucy said. "I'm sure my name's been dropped at the Rise and Shine more than once over the last few weeks."

"Mostly among the older set," Frankie assured her. "Evie's all stirred up about you moving back to town and not immediately handing your son over for her to raise, because you're just so distraught and unable to function."

Lucy pursed her lips. "I think I'm functional."

Marianne frowned. "Well, when she tells it, you're prostrate with grief and barely able to get out of bed. You just don't have the strength of character that she does to power through your despair like she has."

"At Wayne's funeral, she told me I was a cold, greedy woman who never appreciated the roof her son put over my head while he was working himself to death," Lucy muttered into her drink.

"Well, you know Evie. She likes to play to her audience when she's spinning a yarn."

"That is true," Lucy agreed. "I try to remember what she's lost and how I would feel if it was Sam, but she only seems able to express her grief through working my last damn nerve."

"So how *are* you holding up?" Marianne asked as Sierra delivered a plate full of "possum eggs"—deep-fried, cheese-stuffed potato skins—to the table. When Lucy's eyebrow arched, she added, "I've been coming here more often lately since I started spending more time with Frankie and Margot. I don't even have to order anymore."

"Well, I am really tired of people asking how I'm holding up," Lucy told her, picking at a potato skin. "I'm tired of people walking up to me at the grocery store and giving me the 'aw, hon' face."

"What?"

Lucy tilted her head and quirked her lips into a sympathetic pout. "Aw, hon."

"I would say I'm sorry, but as your friend, you know my lying face and you would know I didn't mean it," Marianne said, pointing at her face. "I'm interested and I'm worried. And I love you, so suck it up and spill."

"Honestly, I'm probably better than I should be. I mean, rumors aside, I can get out of bed every day, and be a parent and try to get my business going. I'm very lucky that Wayne left us enough money to start over here, even if it's with less than we had in Dallas."

"I sense a 'but' coming," Marianne said.

"But you two were struggling toward the end, and you feel conflicted and guilty as hell?" Frankie supplied.

Lucy's jaw dropped. "How in the hell did you know we were struggling?"

"She's just freaky that way," Marianne intoned, taking a large bite of potato skin.

Frankie smiled, though it was a little sad around the edges. "You work on enough bodies, you notice things." She chin-pointed toward Lucy's hands. "Like you haven't worn your wedding ring in a long damn time. You don't even have that pale worn circle thing on your finger and most people have that for at least a few months after they take a longtime ring off. So you either stopped wearing your ring before Wayne died, or you did it the moment he was buried, which isn't something most people do when they're grieving for their spouse in what should have been their years of peak marital happiness."

Lucy sighed. "I don't remember you being this scary as a kid."

"She's developed a lot of terrifying life skills," Marianne said.

Lucy lowered her voice so no one at the nearby tables could hear her, because this was Lake Sackett and someone nearby was *always* listening. "Yeah, we were struggling. I don't want to go into why while we're out here in this very public place where anybody can hear. But we were. And now he's gone and I keep waiting for the other shoe to drop," Lucy said, jerking her shoulders. "From the moment the doctors told me that Wayne was gone, I've been waiting for this wave of crippling grief to bring me down. But every morning, I get up and do what needs to be done and . . . I'm happy? I can raise my son and live in a place where I don't feel so lonely and disconnected. I can see people that I've missed for years." She paused as Marianne raised her glass. "And I feel guilty for being happy, because what sort of sick person would be content and thriving in her new life without her recently deceased husband?"

"Someone who was unhappy with her recently deceased husband?" Frankie suggested.

"Still feels wrong, and doesn't exactly paint me as the most sympathetic person in the world. I wish I felt more for Wayne. I wish his death hurt more. But right now, all I'm feeling is . . . hope." Lucy blew out a long breath. "This is not the fun girls'-night-out chat I was promised."

Marianne snorted. "Well, nothing ever seems to go quite like I plan lately. But if I can give you one piece of advice? Worry about being happy and making a life for your son now. Worry about what other people think later."

"Also seems sensible," Lucy conceded, taking a long drink from her glass. "But I don't think that 'being happy' is going to include anyone besides my son for a long while, so please don't put all this pressure on me about Duffy or any other eligible Lake Sackett resident with all of his teeth."

"Why wouldn't your happy life include someone else?" Frankie asked. "Toothless or otherwise?"

"It's only been a few months since Wayne," she exclaimed, suddenly lowering her voice. "It just looks tacky . . . and suspicious if I'm taking up with someone new after my husband dies in a mysterious auto-related injury at our home. Besides, I don't know if I want to start anything like that again. I can't drag Sam into some situation that might not work out. I can't have men coming in and out of his life, confusing him, disappointing him."

"Why do you assume that any relationship you get into would go badly?"

"Because clearly, I suck at picking men. Granted, I only picked the one, but I chose him for all of the wrong reasons—his looks and his potential and the person I thought he was going to be, instead of the person he showed me he was, every day. And I just kept doubling down. Oh, you have some doubts in high school? Follow him to the college he wants to attend, just because it happens to have a decent marketing program. You love him, and think he'd *probably* be a good husband and father, but you're not sure? Accept his proposal and figure it all out later. Then have a baby with him! Build a life hundreds of miles from everything you know! Put your name on a bunch of loans! And when he cheats, don't leave, that's for quitters! It was like every time I felt any little twinge of uncertainty, my response was to dig in deeper, to prove how 'committed' I was. I mean, I honestly thought that I was going to have happy ever after with my high school sweetheart. What kind of idiot thinks that?"

"I thought that," Marianne said raising her hand. "Technically, I have that. Without the cheating, though. I'm so sorry about that part."

"Sorry, I forgot about Carl," Lucy said.

"He is the exception to all rules," Frankie assured her. "And a lot of people marry their high school sweethearts. Because they love them, because those people helped them learn what love was in the first place. It's not stupid to believe in that kind of love lasting forever. Sometimes those people grow together, they change, but the heart of them stays the same and they're happy.

And other people, they change and they grow but in different directions. They want different things. They figure out that what they thought would make them happy in life doesn't appeal all that much. It's nobody's fault, it just happens."

"That was a profound and well-thought-out statement, Frances Ann," Marianne said, raising her glass to clink against Frankie's.

"Um, thank you, and also, suck it for sounding so surprised," Frankie told her. "Anyway, you recognized the problem, which is the first step. I'm guessing you were in therapy when he died?"

"How can you tell *that* by looking at my hands?" Lucy asked.

"Eh, there's no trick to it. You're not the type of person who sits around dithering, wondering what the hell they're going to do, once they realize there's a problem," Frankie said, smirking.

Lucy rolled her eyes. She'd forgotten how challenging it could be to socialize with multiple McCreadys. "We were in therapy for the last six months before he died. I swore Wayne to secrecy over it. I did *not* want Evie knowing we were 'discussing our problems with some stranger instead of the mama who loves him.'"

Marianne shuddered. "It's times like this I am grateful Carl's mom ran away with that meat truck driver before my boys were born."

"Count your blessings," Lucy told her. "I would wake up in the morning and it was like this nagging ache in my chest, like I'd forgotten something, and then I would realize, 'Oh, yeah, your life is a lie. You don't love your husband anymore because he cheats on you regularly. You abandoned your parents. You don't have any real friends. You're far away from everything you know and you don't have any clue what to change or how to make it better.' And Wayne just couldn't figure out why I wouldn't get over 'my issues' and be happy. I thought about leaving, but the truth was, I knew I wouldn't be able to afford the lawyers Wayne could, and there was a good chance I'd lose my son. I didn't want Evie or the nannies Wayne hired to raise Sam, so I stayed. And there was a part of me that just didn't want to admit how big of a mistake I'd made."

"The impulse to avoid the 'I told you so' is strong," Frankie said. "Why do you think Duffy stayed married to Lana for so long?"

"Speak of the devil," Frankie grumbled.

"Aw, come on." Marianne sighed. Lucy followed her line of sight to a thin woman in ripped jeans and a low-cut black tank top. Her dark-blond hair was teased high and her green eyes were heavily lined. Lucy could spot the bright red lipstick bleeding into lines around her mouth from fifteen feet away. Lana was already laughing as she entered the room, like she was the life of the party, bringing the good times with her.

"My former sister-in-law, ladies and gentlemen." Marianne sighed as the woman strutted toward the bar and hollered for someone to "Get me a damn drink!"

Lucy squinted across the room at the sort of woman who would have been turned away from her club in Texas based on her shoe choice alone. "*That's* Lana?"

Marianne nodded. Lucy's chin retreated back into her neck. "But she looks . . ."

"Rode enthusiastically and put up wet?" Marianne griped. "Yeah, well, hard drinking, hard living, and avoiding sunscreen will do that to you."

Lucy watched as Duffy's former wife stumbled around the

bar from table to table, laughing and screeching and snuggling up to any man whose date didn't move fast enough to stop her. Lucy's mouth dropped open. Lana had been a dedicated flirt in high school, but she'd settled down after she'd taken up with Duffy. Lucy hadn't been thrilled that her best friend had started dating her middle school tormentor, but considering the crap Wayne had put Duffy through, she figured she didn't have a lot of room to talk.

Lucy couldn't believe she'd spent so many years being intimidated by this woman. Teenage Lana hadn't just been mean and sneaky, she'd been *unpredictable*. She'd poked and prodded in an increasingly aggravating crescendo of bullying until her targets finally snapped back, but you never knew if she'd punch you in the mouth for "disrespecting" her or go running to the nearest teacher with tears in her eyes. Lucy liked to keep that sort of volatility at a distance, so she'd avoided Lana as much as possible, especially since Lucy seemed to enrage Lana just by existing. There were times that Lucy suspected that Lana went after Duffy like a McCready-seeking missile because, well, Duffy was Lucy's. But then she considered how self-centered and weird that sounded and she dropped the idea for her own good.

High school Lucy probably would have slipped quietly out of the room to avoid Lana's notice, but this Lucy had been through the social gauntlet of a Junior League Charity Ball floral committee. By comparison, Lana was small potatoes. Sure, she still seemed mean and clearly pretty explosive, but she couldn't get Lucy's husband fired or have her son blackballed from a good preschool. The women in her Texas social circles could have done far more damage and she'd survived them. Hell, she'd even made friends with some of them.

The shove-down-the-stairs thing was still a possibility, but Lucy made direct eye contact with Lana and smiled sweetly. Lana sneered and turned her back on Lucy, focusing her attention on getting Sierra to put her drinks on Lemm Trinkitt's tab.

"How long has she been like this?" Lucy asked, as Lana swiped a trucker's shot off of his table and downed it without hesitation.

"She's always been like this," Marianne told her. "She calmed down for a while, tried to play good little housewife for a year or two. But I guess she just wanted it too badly, if that makes sense? She wanted to be a McCready. She wanted everybody to forget she was ever a Newton. I mean, McCreadys aren't exactly the Rockefellers, but I guess it's better than coming from a family that's only known for shoplifting and cheating the state out of checks. She wanted to be E.J.J.'s cherished baby-girl granddaughter. She wanted Leslie to name a special for her at the Snack Shack."

"She wanted weekends at some fancy spa in Tennessee with 'all of the McCready ladies,'" Frankie said. "And she used one of the funeral home's credit cards to book the rooms when we made polite excuses. Can you imagine Aunt Donna . . . in a spa? With other people?"

Lucy winced. "I'm picturing a sort of hybrid between ladies' mud wrestling and the rebellion in *Spartacus* if they tried to make Leslie eat three basil leaves and call it a meal."

"Honestly, I know it sounds like we didn't try, but we did," Marianne swore. "She was Duffy's wife. Even if we had our doubts about the way they started off, she was his choice and we respected that. We wanted them to make it."

"Well, maybe not Aunt Donna," Frankie interjected.

"No, my mom made it pretty clear she expected them to fail, but the rest of us, once they were married, we were pulling for them just because we didn't want to see Duffy hurt," Marianne said. "But she was just so *extra* all the time and it got old quick."

"She'd get mad if Marianne and I spent time together," Frankie murmured around a bite of cheesy potato. "She said we were intentionally trying to leave her out and hurt her feelings. My therapist would probably say she had rampaging abandonment issues out the wazoo from her father running off when she was a toddler. And her mama had a whole series of boyfriends that ran off as soon as they realized they weren't ready for an instant family."

"*You're* in therapy? But you seem so comfortable with yourself." Lucy paused to motion at Frankie's colorful clothes and hair. "And all this."

"Anxiety issues stemming from childhood illness," Frankie said casually. "Not to mention a big helping of stunted emotional growth thanks to my loving and well-meaning drone parents."

"Drone parents?"

"Helicopter parenting implies they'd let me get several hundred feet away from them," Frankie said. "Which they will not. Anyway, when Eric came along and there were some . . . outbursts, I realized I needed to talk to a professional and get my shit together so I could react to things like an adult and not a pissed-off teenager."

"It's been really good for her," Marianne said. "She hasn't staged a fake zombie apocalypse in months now."

Lucy tilted her head and stared. "Beg pardon?"

"It's a long story," Frankie said, waving her off. "And we're not here to talk about me. We were talking about our ex-cousin-in-law. Lana wanted us to be her instant adoring sitcom family, complete with 'awws' from a captive studio audience. And when we did not comply, she went crying to Duffy over it."

"What was he supposed to do about it?" Lucy asked.

"Hell if I know," Marianne said. "And Duffy didn't know, either. He just told her it would take time and that we would get to know her better eventually and everything would fall into place."

"That's our Duffy," Frankie said, sighing. "A beautiful, optimistic soul . . . trapped inside a great big idiot."

Marianne started to take exception and then shrugged and took another bite of possum egg. Around a mouthful of carbs, she said, "Then Lana tried to play us against each other. She tried to tell Tootie that Uncle Bob and Uncle Stan had plans to put her and E.J.J. in a nursing home."

"Which Tootie knew was bullshit, because part of the reason the McCready compound exists in the first place is to keep our elders at home being smartass fonts of wisdom for as long as we can," Frankie said. "Plus, Tootie's already picked out a nursing home in Florida that has a casino attached and employs attractive male nurses."

Marianne sipped her drink. "So then Lana tried to convince Aunt Leslie that Frankie had a heroin problem, otherwise she wouldn't be so skinny and pale."

"Which my mama knew was bullshit, because I'm high on life," Frankie added. "And after my chemo experience, I'm pretty selective about which needles I let near me."

"Then she tried to convince Stan that the family was about to ask him to leave the business because the stigma of his drinking problem had become too much for us," Marianne deadpanned.

"Which *Stan* knew was bullshit, because the August before we'd just thrown him a big ol' party for being fifteen years sober, and E.J.J. and Bob both told him how proud they were to run McCready's with him," Frankie said, the humor leaving her voice entirely. "Carl set off his name in fireworks, for Pete's sake."

Lucy laughed. "So she went from wannabe sitcom princess to reality show villain? And thought it was going to get her a big happy family?"

"Well, in Lana's family, people mostly screamed when they had something to say. She didn't think Duffy's relatives would discuss all these 'issues' with each other almost immediately."

"That must have been uncomfortable for Lana," Lucy said, almost feeling sorry for her.

"Oh, it was downright confrontational," Frankie said. "My mama yelled. And my mama almost never yells, but she did not appreciate somebody coming in and intentionally trying to sow trouble in her family."

"And once Aunt Leslie stops insisting we play nice, the whole family becomes a big wall of icy politeness," Marianne said.

Frankie added. "Lana took what you might call a 'withdrawal of affections' very personally and declared that our whole family was a bunch of judgmental assholes who never wanted her around in the first place."

"To be fair, she wasn't wrong," Marianne said.

Frankie noted, "Yeah, but you told her flat-out that she wasn't wrong, at Christmas, which really didn't help."

"I regret nothing," Marianne declared. "And then the cheating started, and the marriage was all downhill from there. She was being party-time Lana pretty much full-time. Slept with most of Duffy's friends, convinced herself that Paul Dabney was gonna marry her and take her to Southern Oaks to live happily ever after."

Lucy cringed. "Yeah, Duffy mentioned something about that, but I didn't want to ask a lot of questions."

"Paul decided that while it was exciting to bang his friend's wife, Lana was way less interesting after she filed divorce papers," Frankie drawled.

"Poor Duffy."

"Duffy was smart enough not to let her move into the cabin he'd built on McCready lands, but doesn't seem smart enough to cut her off entirely."

The peach schnapps and the potato skins seemed to be fighting a war in Lucy's belly. "Is he still mixed up with her?"

Marianne shook her head. "Not for a long while now. I'm not saying there haven't been moments where I was afraid he'd end up remarrying her in some terrible counterintuitive bid to lose out on life insurance, but I think he's smartened up. It must have been the universe telling him that you were on your way back to him."

"Don't start that again." Lucy sighed.

"You have feelings for him. Admit it."

"I do have feelings for your brother. Friendly feelings of friendship. A friendship I refuse to mess up with some weird postwidowing rebound that will inevitably fail because I may not be ready for any sort of relationship right now. I think I just need time to be a single adult for a while. I have enough to do with Sam and the business. I don't need to complicate things."

"Fine," Marianne conceded. "I'll drop it."

"Thank you."

"Until you're in a better mood and then I'll pick it up again."

Lucy pinched her lips together before turning to Frankie. "I have a better idea. Let's talk about your boyfriend, the cop who's built like Magic Mike."

Frankie blushed as crimson as her hair. "I would, but Marianne says I can't talk about Eric without making sex faces."

"It's true," Marianne said. "It's more than a little embarrassing. If she wasn't dating the local sheriff there would be some danger of an arrest for public indecency."

"I regret nothing, and other than that, no comment," Frankie replied. "Let's talk about the bakery instead. So about this cake Maddie Paxton ordered . . ."

Lucy sucked a bite of possum egg into her windpipe and damn near choked on it. Duffy was right, this *was* how bakers got reputations.

5

WITH THE WINDOWS shining bright and the front of the shop cleaned, Gimme Some Sugar was looking more like a charming patisserie and way less like the place hunters used to have deer turned into summer sausage. She was getting closer to opening, no thanks to Herb Brewster, the scum-sucking toad face who had just canceled yet *another* appointment with her. If she could just get her paperwork approved and her displays from Duffy, she'd be set. Someone with some business experience or a halfway cooperative local government probably could have been fully open by now. Unfortunately, there were only so many hours in the day and she did have to spend some of them feeding and caring for her son. Sure, she was feeding him frozen mini pizza bagels more often than she would like, but still, she fed him.

Lucy had put a poster in the window reading SWEET SUR-PRISES COMING SOON in the shop's signature lavender-and-white color scheme. The printing company wouldn't have her sign ready for another two weeks, and she thought it would be sort of fun to keep people guessing. But now she wondered if she was pushing too hard, too fast. She wasn't ready to open, and getting people's hopes up at this point felt a little like shooting half-cocked.

While she still lacked many of the finishing touches, the shop was finally shaped up enough that she wasn't afraid of being spotted experimenting with cake pops through the windows. The kitchen was now fully cleaned and operational. All of her pans and tools were neatly organized on the counters, waiting to be sorted into the cabinets Duffy was building. She had Sam sweeping up the café area, which was free of dangerous objects, both blunt and sharp.

Lucy wiped at a dab of cream cheese frosting she'd smeared across her pink cupcake-themed apron. She had an enormous supply of aprons, custom made by her college friend Hannah, who sold the fool things for fifty bucks a pop on Etsy. Lucy loved finding bizarre novelty fabrics and sending them to Hannah for an apron, in exchange for Hannah's favorite lemon bars. She hoped that the quirky aprons would become one of the things the shop was known for, little charming touches that made it a lot more fun to shop there than running down to the quick convenience of the Food Carnival.

"I'm a big helper, right, Mama?" Sam asked, dragging his broom across the floor. His own tiny apron, made by Hannah as a fourth birthday present, was printed with fifties-style sci-fi robots.

"You sure are, punkin," she said, pressing a lollipop stick into the last of a batch of cake pops. The rosy little bonbons of red velvet goodness were an experiment in frosting consistency that had gone surprisingly well. Lucy hadn't been sure how much the humidity would affect her recipe's ability to hold everything together, but not one of the little cake-and-cream-cheese frosting balls had fallen apart, even after she arranged the lollipop sticks in a block of floral foam.

She lifted her thick hair from her sweat-soaked neck and fanned her skin. Then again, it was only February, and she would feel like a wrung-out washcloth walking outside in June. Maybe the cake pops would be a winter special.

"Because I did a good job, does that mean I get paid?" Sam asked, all saccharine innocence.

Lucy's eyes narrowed. "How does a paycheck totaling two cookies sound?"

"Three cookies," Sam countered quickly.

"Two."

"Before dinner?" he asked with a hopeful tone. "And no oatmeal raisin. They don't count."

"One before, one after. Chocolate chips only," Lucy promised.

"Deal."

"You drive a hard bargain, sir."

Sam nodded, and then pointed out the shop window at a lanky man wearing a brand-new white button-up shirt and faded, patched jeans. The man pointed to the HELP WANTED sign she'd placed in the window and then toward the door, which Lucy had kept locked just in case . . . certain parties tried to barge in. She moved to unlock it.

Though he was a slight man, Specs Foyle moved with the heaviness of someone who'd had the wind sucked out of him by life. Lucy thought maybe his first name was Michael, but he'd worn unfortunate Coke-bottle glasses since grade school and kids that age just love mean nicknames.

"Hi, Mr. Foyle, how are you?" she asked as her son went full barnacle against her leg.

"Just fine, Lucy, just fine. And you?"

"Oh, I've been busy," she said, motioning to the half-finished shop.

The corners of his thin lips lifted. "I can see that."

Specs nodded toward Sam. "And how are you, buddy?"

Sam shook his head and buried his face in her apron. Lucy gave Specs an apologetic smile. "He's a little shy around strangers."

"Well, that's all right. Sam, you're still new in town, you've probably met more new people than you can shake a stick at, right? Gets sort of tiring after a while."

Sam nodded. Lucy's smile widened and she felt her shoulders relax ever so slightly. "Is there something I can do for you, Mr. Foyle?"

"I noticed your sign in the window," he said. "I've been outta work for a while, ever since the RV dealership closed. I worked in the service department."

"I remember," she said. "My daddy mentioned you had a dab hand with boat engines."

Specs smiled, clearly pleased to be remembered. "Your daddy was a fine man. We miss him at the Elks Lodge meetings. And your husband, I was sorry to hear about his passing."

She swallowed thickly as Sam burrowed further into her hip. She noted Specs didn't call Wayne a "fine man," which was telling. "Thank you."

"Don't suppose you'd consider me for the job," he said.

Lucy's mouth fell open and it was with more than a little embarrassment that she searched for an answer. She'd pictured hiring an older lady with a lot of home baking experience, or even an enthusiastic teenager who knew how to handle the twice-damned coffee machine. But she didn't want to be the sort of person who didn't hire someone just because of their age or the sad condition of their jeans. Specs had been known for tying on the bottle when she was a kid. Then again, today he stood before her clearly sober and steady on his feet.

"Here's my résumé," Specs said. "Miss Margot over at the funeral home helped me write it up, as a favor to her daddy. But she promised that she hadn't puffed me up too much. Everything on there is *true*. She said she just 'prioritized the information.'"

Lucy scanned over the job listings, which seemed heavy on the mechanic side, and woefully light on pastry experience.

"How much baking experience do you have?" she asked.

"Did some cooking in the navy, worked my way up to feeding a rear admiral, who was precious as all hell about his desserts," he said. "I can't do the fancy work they do on the Food Network, with the fondant and the royal icing and all, but I can read a recipe easy enough."

"He knows about the Food Network, Mama," Sam whispered, lifting his face to stare at the man speculatively. "Do you watch the *Baking Championship* show?"

Specs bent as far as his elderly knees would allow him. "Grown-up AND kids editions."

Sam tugged at Lucy's apron. "He knows about the *Baking Championship* show. He can stay."

"That's a pretty ringing endorsement," Lucy said, digging into her recipe box and pulling out what she considered to be an intermediate-level recipe—her mother's instructions for buttermilk pie. "Can you make this? Crust and all?"

He squinted at the index card through his thick lenses, a pensive expression on his wrinkled face. "Sure can. But is it a good idea for me to do a test run with a piecrust? We'll just sit here for at least an hour waiting for it to chill before I can roll it out. And I can't imagine that would be thrilling for you at the end of a long day."

Lucy grinned at him. "Excellent. You passed the first test, general knowledge. I have some dough chilling in the fridge, all ready to go. You make this pie well, and we'll talk about your own crust techniques later."

"Sneaky," Specs said, nodding with a smile of approval. "Working for you would not be boring."

"You can count on it!"

So, Lucy sat at her counter with her laptop, a cup of coffee, and Sam playing with Legos at her feet. She also happened to open the staffing website she'd subscribed to and ran a discreet background and criminal check on Michael Foyle, using the birth and address information from his résumé. When that came back relatively clean, other than a couple of drunk and disorderly charges in the 1980s, she watched him work.

Specs was meticulous in his attention to detail, from leveling the top of the measuring cup full of flour to folding the dry ingredients into the filling just a little bit at a time. He didn't take shortcuts. He didn't guess at measurements. He appreciated the science of baking, and he cleaned as he went. For that alone, he had Lucy's respect.

By the time the pie emerged from the oven, all golden-brown crackling sugar, Lucy's mouth was watering. She took a big bite of piping-hot pie and moaned. It was even better than her mother's recipe, sweet and rich with just the right amount of tangy brightness on a crust that was light and flaky as manna—if she didn't say so herself.

"Did you double the lemon zest while I wasn't looking?" she asked as Sam clamored for his own bite of pie. She fed him the tiniest bit, and then had to slide the plate and pan out of his reach across the counter.

Specs shook his head, clearly pleased with her response. "I added three tablespoons of lemon juice. Your recipe was just fine, but you have to add the juice if you want that punch to the taste buds."

"You're hired, though I'd prefer you talk to me before you start fiddling with my recipes," she said, sliding over a copy of the worksheet she'd typed up for the position's salary, schedule, and terms. "Three months probationary basis and we'll see where we stand on making it permanent and giving you a raise."

"All right, then," he said. He cleared his throat, glancing at Sam, who had given up on his mission for pie and returned to his Legos. "Though, I should tell you, I should probably stick to the kitchen and let you handle the counter work. I got a bad reputation with some of the highfalutin folks around here. I've been clean and sober for six years now. Stan McCready had one of them interventions for me, got me into AA. But I wouldn't want you to lose any business on account of me."

"If you don't want to work the counter because you don't like that side of the business, that's fine," she said. "But if you're afraid of some sanctimonious jackass turning away my cupcakes because I have a human being selling them? Well, that's a customer I can afford to lose."

His grin spread even more and he shook her hand. "Yes, ma'am."

For a brief moment, Lucy could see the future of Gimme Some Sugar, and it was beautiful and bright. She would bake special-occasion cakes and wedding cakes. She would bake brownies and cookies the size of saucers. She would sell cupcakes in so many flavors, Lake Sackett residents would gain ten pounds each just to try them all. It was going to be amazing, the end goal of the pastry classes she'd taken while Wayne worked, the achievement of all of her home baker's dreams. She was going to earn a living doing what she loved. A bubble of hope and anticipation filled her chest with a lovely warm sensation.

She should have known this euphoria would only last for a moment.

"Hey, Mama, it's my grandma!" Sam shouted, pointing to the window.

Outside her front window, Evie Garten was shading her eyes with her hands so she could peer through the glass. Lucy was briefly reminded of horror movies where the masked killer popped up out of nowhere to terrorize the heroine. But she would not flinch. She wasn't beholden to Evie anymore, in any way. Wayne wasn't around to grumble at Lucy for not appeasing his mama. Lucy could do exactly what she wanted in this situation, which was to leave Evie standing outside the shop.

And then Lucy realized she'd been foolish enough not to relock the door after she let Specs in, and now she was about to pay the price. Sam clung to her leg as Evie bustled through the entrance uninvited.

Evie Garten was a short woman, with broad shoulders she tried to disguise with distracting peplums on the dresses and suits she bought off the clearance rack at the outlet mall in

Pooler. Her round face was capped with short, graying blond curls, fluffed into a sort of pyramid formation kept in place by careful and thorough application of Aqua Net.

Lucy could see so much of her husband in Evie's pale blue-gray eyes and full mouth, which she had painted bright candy pink. But Evie's smile couldn't match the porcelain perfection Wayne had achieved by investing thousands in caps, and she lacked the polish he'd so scrupulously acquired in college. Wayne had spent every spare minute reading about wine and designer clothes and fancy vacation spots, studying people in five-star restaurants while he and Lucy split a bowl of soup and all the free bread they could get. Evie was Lake Sackett through and through, and while Lucy didn't think there was anything necessarily wrong with that, Wayne had held himself at a distance. He had been careful never to introduce his mother to his coworkers or friends when she visited them in Texas. His hesitation only made Evie cling that much tighter, and Wayne had felt a little guilty for it, but not enough to let those two streams of his life cross.

Evie's sour expression melted into delight. "Hi, Sammy!" she cooed, holding her arms out to Sam, who viewed her with a decided air of distrust from behind Lucy's leg. "Oh, you look more and more like your daddy every day. You're just the spitting image of him. Come see Mamaw, baby, and give me a hug!"

"No, thank you," Sam said. And suddenly, he ducked behind Lucy's legs and ran toward the kitchen, practically leaving a little puff of dust behind him.

"Well, that's no way to behave!" Evie gasped. "What kind of rudeness are you teaching my grandson?"

"To run from loud, threatening situations," Lucy muttered

before turning to Specs. "Would you please take the pie dishes back to the sinks and keep an eye on Sam?"

"Yes, ma'am." Specs took the plates away and followed Sam to the kitchen.

"He will sneak cookies when you're not looking," Lucy warned him. "He's basically a tiny mastermind."

"What on earth is that man even doing here?" Evie asked behind Specs's back. "Don't you know who that is?"

"Yes, Mr. Foyle is an old friend of my dad's. I just hired him as my assistant."

"Why would you ever want to do that? You don't even know if this place is going to make a go of it and you're already hiring? Not to mention"—she paused to lower her voice—"Specs Foyle is a fall-down drunk, always has been. I don't want him working here and I don't want him spending time with my grandson."

"Well, this is not your shop, so you don't get to make those decisions. And I seem to recall several members of the Garten family spending their weekends in the county jail for DUI," Lucy shot back. "So you should probably take that log out of your eye before you start counting up his splinters."

Evie turned her hardening gaze on Lucy. "Well, I hear you got a little sawdust in your own eye. I hear that you spent last night at the Dirty Deer with a bunch of *strange men*," she said, flopping her ever-present knockoff Vera Bradley bag on Lucy's counter.

Lucy sighed. "Actually, I was out with Marianne Dawson and Frankie McCready, just a girls' night, nothing more."

"And who was watching *my* grandson while you were out drinking?" Evie demanded. "I hope it wasn't Specs Foyle. I hope you have sense enough not to do that."

"Sam had a playdate with Marianne's boys. Carl watched them and they had a great time. Sam's already asking to go back."

Evie gasped. "You let that redneck Carl Dawson watch *my* grandson?"

"Yes, because Carl Dawson is a loving, attentive father who would lie down on a grenade rather than let his sons get hurt." In the interest of diplomacy and not speaking ill of the dead, Lucy didn't mention that Carl had spent more quality time with Sam the previous night than Wayne had in the last year of his life. Not because it wasn't true, but because it seemed mean-spirited.

"Well, I just don't see why you don't call me to watch him, if you're going to be running around town. It's shameful that I'm not called to take care of my grandson."

"I'm not running around town. I went out for one night with female friends. I had one drink. There's nothing wrong with doing something for myself every once in a while."

Evie slapped her hand against Lucy's counter. "There is when you're a mama. You think I didn't have dreams that I gave up for my kids? That's what motherhood *means*, sacrificing what you want, everything! That's your job!"

Lucy peered over the tops of her glasses at Evie. Wayne had always seemed to have an awful lot of stories about Evie leaving a box of Kraft mac 'n' cheese next to the stove so she could go play bingo with her friends. But bringing up something as inconsequential as reality would only distract from Lucy's point, so she said, "Well, that's really unhealthy and not the way I plan to live my life."

"Honey, I know your mama isn't around to teach you these things," Evie started, but Lucy held up one paint-covered finger.

"Let me stop you right there. You're about to cross a line that cannot be uncrossed."

"I just mean that you need to be thinking more like a Garten." Evie's tone turned wheedling.

"What does that even mean?" Lucy scoffed.

"You need to think of someone besides yourself. You need to think of Dewie and me, and Wayne's brother and sister."

"Oh, trust me, I think of you plenty," Lucy deadpanned.

"Well, that can't be true, if you're throwing my son's insurance money away on this silly idea." Evie swept her thick left arm over the café. "We had a bakery in this town for years. It closed because no one wants a bakery when we can just go to the Food Carnival."

"The bakery closed because the senior Dunbar didn't trust the junior Dunbar to run it without causing a fire that would take out the whole town. And I'm not 'throwing the money away.' It's my money to *invest* and I'm *investing* it in a business that will support me and Sam."

"But that's my point," Evie insisted. "That's not *your* money to invest. It's *Wayne's* money. Wayne would have wanted to make sure that all of us were taken care of, not just you."

"Wayne wrote a will," Lucy said. "He left you what he wanted you to have. He gave you his guns and cars and the boat and all his big toys. He gave you the things he thought would help you remember him best."

"Because he thought he would be around for years to keep taking care of us!" Evie shot back. "We've gotten used to, well, some comforts while Wayne was working. He was so good about sending us money every month."

"He did what?" Lucy gaped at Evie. She knew that Wayne

occasionally sent his family money, when they had emergencies like broken-down vehicles or that time Davey smashed all the windows out of the Dirty Deer. But she had no idea that he'd made it a monthly line item in their budget. She'd been over their bank accounts a hundred times since Wayne's death and she didn't remember seeing any checks written to his family members . . .

Shit.

The wire transfers.

Two months before, Lucy had been rooting through their checking account and discovered that Wayne had set up a wire transfer for a thousand dollars to be sent to an account at the Lake Sackett Savings and Loan every month like clockwork. She'd called the bank and inquired about the account and it turned out to be a savings account. It had made sense that Wayne was socking money away in an account, even in another town. Wayne was all about diversifying assets. Hell, Lucy thought it might have been some sort tax dodge. Wayne was good at finding those. But given that Wayne's paycheck was no longer being deposited into their checking account, Lucy had stopped the transfers. She'd decided to deal with the account when she arrived in Lake Sackett, but with all of the moving chaos, she'd completely forgotten about it.

But now she realized. He'd been making the deposits for Evie. He'd had his mom on an allowance of a thousand dollars a month. She tried not to get angry or embarrassed that she hadn't known. Wayne may have held himself at a distance from his family, but sending them money was just the sort of conscience-appeasing gesture that would keep him from losing sleep over it.

And not telling Lucy? Well, she could only imagine that Wayne hadn't thought it was any of her business. It was his income, after all. And her parents had always been a little better off than his.

So *this* was why Evie was so panicked over the idea of Lucy opening a business. She'd already lost her monthly stipend, and now Lucy was spending "family money" on herself and Sam, instead of setting up a joint checking account with her in-laws.

Evie took a crumpled Kleenex out of her pocket and dabbed at tears that . . . weren't there. "My son was a good boy whose priorities were in the right place. He wouldn't have wanted his money thrown down the toilet on some stupid idea, where you're gonna make fancy crap nobody wants. Where you're gonna hire men like—" She paused to glance at the back of the shop, where Sam was showing Specs the new lavender-and-white dish towels. "It's like you're trying to burn through Wayne's money out of spite, instead of using it to support his family like he wanted."

"Sam and I are the family he needed to support."

"I mean *all* of the Gartens!" Evie exclaimed. "We've come to depend on that money every month. You tell me how we're supposed to get by without it. How am I supposed to pay my light bill? How's Davey supposed to pay his court costs? How's Melody gonna keep gas in her car?"

"Getting a job would be my first step," Lucy said. She knew it was a low blow. Evie hadn't worked since her children were born, claiming that her children needed her too much. And her youngest, Melody, was twenty-four.

"A job isn't going to solve my problems."

"It will if the problem is 'I wonder how I'm going to pay my bills?' And if Melody and Davey have expenses they can't afford, they're grown adults and they need to figure that out for themselves. That's what most people do once they get out of high school. Look at me, I'm working at my ripe old age, despite the fact that I'm so overwhelmed with grief I can't even get out of bed," Lucy said pointedly.

"Well, that's how you're supposed to be acting," Evie hissed. "Not opening crackpot businesses and going out at all hours, leaving your child with dangerous people!"

Lucy inhaled deeply through her nose. "Look, Evie, I didn't know that Wayne was giving you money every month. And I'm sorry, but I'm not going to start that up again for you. I need what I have in the bank to support me and Sam for the long haul."

"You won't even tell me how much you have in the bank, so I don't know that for sure," Evie grumbled. "It's not too late. Jack Hitchens tells me you've only signed a six-month lease on the place. You can stop now, before you spend too much. Just cancel the lease and walk away."

Lucy smacked her hand over her face. So much for client confidentiality with her landlord. She should have known that privacy policies were no match for her mother-in-law.

"*You* need to walk away." Lucy crossed the café area and opened the front door just in time for a petite woman with frazzled strawberry-on-gray hair to toddle into the shop.

"Oh, Lucy, look at you!" Leslie McCready cried, throwing her arms around Lucy. She stepped back to survey Lucy from head to toe. "You haven't changed a bit! It's so good to see you, sweetheart!"

"Hi, Miss Leslie, how are you?" Lucy said, her residual

"mother-in-law face" making it difficult to give Leslie the smile she deserved.

"Oh, I'm just fine. I saw you through the window and just had to stop by. Duffy said you're planning on opening this place up and making it a bakery. Looks like you got your work cut out for you, but then you were never afraid of hard work, now, were you?"

Lucy snickered as Evie's face seemed to grow redder by the second. Leslie was one of the quieter members of the McCready family, but when she finally had the opportunity to speak, she could flood the Nile with words. And Evie clearly did not appreciate the interruption. Evie might lose her temper in front of Specs, but she would never act like a horse's ass in front of a pillar of the community like Leslie McCready.

"Well, hi, Evie, I didn't mean to ignore you, I was just so excited to see Lucy here," Leslie said, turning to Evie with a beaming smile on her elfin face. "You must be so proud of her. Look at what all she's done! This place is beautiful already. Everybody in my ladies Sunday school class is just so excited to see what you're going to be selling. We're probably gonna clean you out on your first day."

Evie stayed silent in response, making faces like a fish pulled out of water and slapped around a few times.

"Oh, Evie has *so much* to say about my plans," Lucy said sweetly as her mother-in-law glared. "But she was just leaving."

Evie's pale eyes narrowed at Lucy, who glared right back. Evie opened her mouth to say something, but glanced at Leslie and clamped it shut. She yanked her bag off the counter. "We're not done talking about this."

"And yet, you're still leaving." Lucy gestured toward the door.

Evie flounced out and Lucy slammed the door behind her. Lucy took off her glasses and pinched the bridge of her nose. "Next time, the door stays locked."

"Same old Evie, huh?" Leslie asked, patting Lucy's arm.

"Yep."

"Honey, don't pay her any mind. She's hurting. And she's used to getting her own way. She'll come around. And if she doesn't, you'll still be just fine, and she'll still be a pain in the butt."

"Mama, we're all done with the pie pans!" Sam exclaimed as he ran from the back of the shop. "Is Mamaw Evie gone? Is that why it's so quiet again?"

"Yes, she left, but she said she'll see you sometime soon," Lucy lied smoothly. "Sam, would you like to meet my friend Miss Leslie?"

Sam seemed to think it over for a second and then stepped closer, still hovering near his mother. "Okay."

Leslie, who had led youth programs at the local Baptist church for as long as Lucy could remember, knew enough about kids to lower her voice and not overwhelm Sam with exclamation points. "Hello there, Sam. I've heard all about you. It's nice to meet you."

Sam held out his hand for a shake. "Hello. I'm going to sweep the floor some more, to see if I can get more cookies."

"Sounds like a reasonable enough idea," Leslie said.

"Specs figured out how to get labor in exchange for cookies," Lucy said as Sam headed back to the pile of dirt he'd corralled on the floor. "That's impressive. Sam's a tough negotiator."

"I'll bet." Leslie giggled. She glanced over Lucy's shoulder at the counter. "Oh, now, what are these cute little doodads?"

"Cake pops," Lucy said. "Or at least they will be after I finish decorating them."

"Oh, I've seen those things on the Facebook," Leslie said. "My Frankie posts them all over, though Lord knows the girl never goes near a kitchen—in the interest of public health. She just likes pictures of cute food. And these? They're just adorable."

"Well, they will be. I hope."

"You mind if I try one?"

"Yeah, but they haven't been dipped in chocolate or anything."

"Well, I care a lot more about taste than I do about pretty," Leslie told her, peering over the counter until she found a plastic spoon. She carefully dipped the spoon in the frosting and spread it over a cake pop. She bit into it, far more delicately than one would expect from the creator of the deep-fried turducken in a crispy cornbread shell. Her eyebrows rose. "Nice. Dense, but moist. Real nice flavor. I never can get red velvet right. It's that whole chemical reaction with the buttermilk and the vinegar. I always end up with a sour mess. But yours is real good."

"Thank you, it took me years to get it right. The secret is mayonnaise. About a third of a cup. And it has to be 'whole egg' mayo, otherwise you don't get the right texture."

"Really!" Leslie exclaimed. "I can't believe I hadn't thought of that. I put mayo in darn near everything. How do you think this would hold up to high temperatures, like a deep fryer?" she asked, examining the remaining cake on her lollipop stick.

"Well, the frosting, not at all. You'd have nothing but a puddle of oil and melted cream cheese. But the cake? Pretty well."

Leslie grinned. "Honey, how would feel about a little collaboration?"

6

$\mathcal{D}$UFFY WALKED OUT of the post office with a box full of exotic waxworms and a head full of doubts.

The Sweethearts' Dance was coming up, a local tradition that was sort of like Sadie Hawkins Day, Lake Sackett style. Back before the lake even existed, a feud had erupted between two Sackett County families, the Dewberries and the Walkers. No one knew how it started—rumor was it had something to do with an outhouse and a property line—only that the Dewberries made their homes on the east side of the Chattahoochee River and the Walkers moved their homestead over to the west side to avoid the Dewberries. Sometime right after the Civil War, Eunice Walker fell in love with Pruitt Dewberry, and predictably both families lost their ever-loving minds. The Dewberry boy's father decided to send his son to cousins in Macon, to distract him with good hard farmwork and distance.

So Eunice rode in a johnboat down the river, right up to the Walkers' property. She stole her beloved from his bed with the help of a well-placed ladder—though obviously not well-placed from the Dewberries' perspective. She ferried Pruitt away in her little boat, as far as the river would carry them, which was about two counties over. They got married in a little chapel by a very understanding minister who thought the best way to quash a feud was with grandbabies. And it turned out that he was right. While the dozens of Walker-Dewberry descendants had mostly moved out of town by the 1960s, Eunice's brave act of defiance in the name of love had made quite an impression on the locals, and was celebrated with a Sweethearts' Dance at different locations around the county every March. No one could remember exactly when the great elopement happened, but they knew the spring rains were what helped carry the couple downriver so quickly. When the weather was still wet and cold, the dance was held indoors at places like the high school gym. When it was warm, like the unseasonably balmy February they seemed to be having, Main Street was roped off like a Valentine's-themed block party.

And in the tradition of Eunice Walker-Dewberry, girls asked the boys. Duffy had yet to be asked this year, a condition he preferred to believe was the result of local ladies' reluctance to tangle with his ex and not a commentary on his own personality. The last time he'd attended, as Julie Guffman's date, there'd been an unfortunate incident involving Lana, Julie's light blue dress, and some bright red punch.

The dance might be an opportunity to ask Lucy on an official date, but it would be breaking tradition, and honestly, a little presumptuous. And what if she assumed they were only going to go as friends? How would he make it clear that he was asking her as a romantic . . . deal? Why did the voice inside his head suddenly sound like a sixth-grade girl?

"Heel, pup!" a familiar voice shouted. "You settle down now!"

Duffy turned to see his grandmother, Tootie, getting dragged down the sidewalk by his friend the mac-'n'-cheese-loving beagle mix. The pup seemed determined to have his freedom, even if it meant taking Tootie's arm out of its socket.

Tootie somehow managed to be both a respected member of the community and the local crazy lady at the same time. She was a hundred pounds of mouthy Southern matron in a purple track suit, with a penchant for poker and collecting strays. She was at all times surrounded by a pack of adopted dogs of mixed breeds and levels of housebrokenness. That pack's number had fluctuated wildly since Margot had helped Tootie open Sackett County's first no-kill animal shelter to adopt out her canine friends.

Tootie was incredibly strict when screening potential "dog people," but so far, she'd managed to place dogs with a dozen or so families. Frankie was still trying to talk Tootie into letting her adopt a pug-giraffe mix named Mercutio, but Tootie had stamped REJECTED UNTIL YOU CAN KEEP A POTTED PLANT ALIVE on her application in bright red. (She special-ordered the stamp off the Internet just for the occasion.) So Frankie had to content herself with Herc, the retired airport security dog that had claimed Eric the minute they met.

Tootie rarely bothered with leashes, because her dogs generally followed her wherever she went. Duffy wasn't sure whether Tootie was using one now because the puppy was wearing one of those lampshade collars or because Eric had had another firm discussion with her about keeping her dogs restrained, because it looked bad for him that his girlfriend's great-aunt never got in trouble for completely ignoring leash laws. Of course, that firm discussion was accompanied by Eric's winking dimples and rock-hard biceps, so Tootie had taken it much better than the family's previous attempts to correct her.

"Hey, Tootie," he said, crouching to pet the dog. "What are you up to?"

Tootie was breathing heavily but refused to do anything as uncivilized as bend at the waist to catch her breath. "I gotta stop into the Jerky Jamboree to get Lulu's special treats. My girl only accepts exotic jerky as tribute."

"I thought the vet said that Lulu didn't need all that sodium and gristle."

"Well, the vet can explain to Lulu why a dog who is the equivalent to a seventy-seven-year-old lady doesn't deserve her favorite snack," she said, slapping the leash (a fancy canvas number with little purple and green bones printed on it) against Duffy's chest. "Here, you hold on to Prince Sparkle Cupcake while I go in. Lyle won't let me take the babies into the depot after the incident."

Duffy grimaced. The "incident" had involved four of Tootie's pack sneaking around her as she walked into the jerky depot and quickly escalating into an orgiastic fit of preserved meat gluttony. They'd done so much damage that Tootie ended up calling an ambulance for Lyle Hammond, who experienced chest pains when he saw what they did to his stock of super-rare Kobe beef jerky.

"Wait, 'Prince Sparkle Cupcake'?" he asked, glancing down at the puppy, which he now realized was sporting glittery pink polish on his nails.

"Yeah, Kyle's girls asked me to let them name the next dog we took in," Tootie said, sighing. "I tried to suggest something else, but Hazel informed me I was violating the terms of 'no takebacks.'"

"Well, it's been a while since we've had adorable and sneaky little girls running around," Duffy said. "You're out of practice."

"Yeah, I'll get back in fighting form in no time with all the new little ones coming into the family." Tootie grinned and ruffled Duffy's hair. "He just got fixed, so don't let him scratch."

Duffy frowned at the puppy while Tootie walked into the jerky store. "They got you fixed *and* they named you Prince Sparkle Cupcake? Poor bastard."

The puppy, mostly white with splotches of black and tan across his face and back, whimpered and batted his foot at Duffy's leg.

"I'm calling you Prince," he told the dog. "The rest is just too humiliating."

Prince seemed to grumble in assent and lowered his head onto his (frosted pink) front paws.

"Puppy!" he heard a little voice shriek from down the block.

Duffy glanced up to see Lucy exiting her shop with a small human, who was making a beeline for him and Prince.

"Samuel Wayne, you slow down right now!" Lucy stepped away from her door and shouted after the boy with a maternal authority he'd never imagined coming from his easygoing friend.

Watching "Samuel" was like seeing Wayne Garten running down the street in child form all over again. His dark-blond forelock flopped in the breeze while his sturdy little frame gamboled over the sidewalk. But as he moved closer, Duffy could see Lucy in the shape of the boy's mouth and the reddish cast to his hair.

Lucy smiled at him as she jogged behind her son. "Hey, Duffy."

"Um, hi," he said, waving with the hand that was holding Prince's leash, jerking at the dog's neck. If dogs could express *What the hell, man?* in a glare, Prince was throwing all sorts of visual expletives Duffy's way.

"Mister, can I pet your dog?" Sam thundered like a tiny Thor. "PLEASE?"

"Duffy, this is Sam," Lucy said, chuckling at her son's loud but polished manners. "Who communicates almost exclusively in questions, and is usually very shy, unless there is a dog in-volved . . . which is something even I didn't know about him."

Duffy grinned at the boy, surprised by the rush of affection he felt for the little guy. This was Lucy's son, a small part of one of his favorite people on the planet. And while the boy clearly had boatloads of energy and was *dying* to love on the dog, he was careful to give Prince space and keep his hands behind his back. Duffy reached out a hand and Sam extended his in return.

Instead of shaking Duffy's hand, Sam reached for Duffy's face. Despite the thin layer of fruit-snack film on the little fingers, Duffy was careful not to recoil as they twisted into his beard and pulled. To avoid the pain of a facial hair yank, he leaned closer to the little boy. "Can I pet your dog, please? How long did it take you to grow this beard? Do you have to use the no-tears shampoo on it? Does your mom make you brush it every morning like my mom makes me brush my hair?"

"Sam, that's not how we get people's attention. Keep your hands to yourself," Lucy told him sternly.

Sam sighed, as if this was an entirely unreasonable expectation from his mother, and relinquished his hold on Duffy's face. "You have a beard. I'm sorry I grabbed it without asking."

"Yes, and thank you for the apology," Duffy said, pressing his lips together so he didn't smile, because he suspected Lucy would not appreciate him undermining her discipline.

"Mama likes to read books about men with beards. They're on the covers," Sam said solemnly.

Duffy's eyes went wide, grinning at Lucy. "Really?"

"They usually don't have shirts, but they have tattoos," Sam said. "Do you have tattoos?"

"Hey, Sam," Lucy squeaked, blushing deeply, "why don't we ask Mr. Duffy something about his dog?"

"Okay," Sam said. "Can I PUH-LEASE pet your dog?"

"Yes, you can pet him," Duffy said, crouching so he was close when Sam reached the fruit-snack-covered hand toward Prince at a glacial pace. "Thanks for asking first. But be gentle, he just got back from the doctor."

"Did he get shots?" Sam asked, his lips drawn together in a serious line. "I hate getting shots. Did he bite somebody who tried to give him shots? Is that why he's wearing the lampshade on his head? Is he in a time-out?"

"No, he's just wearing the collar to keep him from hurting his stitches," Duffy said as Sam dropped to his knees to scratch Prince's ears. "My grandma will take it off in a few days."

"He's your grandma's dog? How old is *she*? What's his name?" Sam asked as the puppy used his paws as leverage to push up from Sam's knees and lick his face.

Duffy cleared his throat, trying to swallow down a laugh. His struggle made Lucy's brows rise to her hairline. "Prince."

Lucy put her hands on Sam's shoulders. "By the way, Sam,

when we meet someone, it's good manners to ask their name. So, Samuel Garten, this is my friend, Duffy McCready. We went to school together when we were your age."

"Did you ride dinosaurs to school back then?" Sam demanded. "I keep asking my mama, but she just laughs at me and won't answer."

Duffy burst out with a loud cackle, which made Sam's little brows draw together, looking even more serious. "Are you laughing at me, too, now?"

"No," Duffy said, holding up his hands in a defensive posture. "I just see why maybe your mom didn't want to answer, because you were pretty much telling her that she's real old."

"Is that why?" Sam turned to his mom. "But you *are* old, Mama."

"Thank you, sweetheart," Lucy deadpanned.

"Because if you weren't old, you couldn't have carried me around in your belly."

"Yes, so you have reminded me. Repeatedly."

"You can't beat his logic," Duffy said, shrugging.

"Quiet, you." Lucy pointed her finger at him, making Duffy laugh harder.

"So he's a big ball of lightning."

"I honestly don't know whether I'm coming or going most days," she said, sighing but smiling fondly at her son. She glanced up and her brows quirked together. "Why are you looking at me like that?"

"I feel like there's this whole other half of you now and I have no idea what changed this person in front of me and I just want to ask you about a hundred questions, which would probably be off-putting."

"Probably. We're just going to have to get to know each other all over again."

"That sounds good. So, do you still regularly eat fluffernutter sandwiches for lunch?" he asked, making her laugh.

"She does, but only on rainy days. She says it's 'comfort food,' but we don't tell Daddy about them, because he doesn't like us eating junky stuff. Were you a friend of my daddy's, too?" Sam asked, petting the squirming dog. And suddenly Duffy stopped laughing. Sam was still focused on Prince, so Duffy glanced up at Lucy. She shrugged.

"Yeah, I went to school with your daddy, too," Duffy said quietly.

"He died," Sam said, staring up at Duffy with big brown eyes.

"I heard about that. I'm sorry."

"That's why we moved to here," he said solemnly. "I like it here, but I liked my old house better. It had a pool. The lake is nice, though. My grandpa had a boat. Mama said we could go fishing. I asked my dad to take me fishing when I turn five, and then he died. So we're probably not going to go fishing. Do you go fishing with your dad?"

"I did," Duffy said. "But my dad died a few years ago."

"Really?" Sam asked. "Were you sad?"

"Very," Duffy assured him. "But that doesn't last forever. I used to be sad every day. Now, I'm only a little sad every once in a while, when it's a holiday or I'm doing something I used to do with him, like fishing or making furniture."

Lucy's own brows furrowed in an expression of grief, though Duffy couldn't tell if it was for Wayne or for Junior McCready.

"I didn't fish with my daddy. Or make furniture," Sam said, chewing his lip. "Maybe I'll be sad when I watch football."

"Maybe."

"He hasn't talked this much to anybody but me since we got to town," Lucy said as Sam returned all of his energy to petting Prince. "Normally he's burying his face in my hip anytime an unknown adult approaches. It took him days to get used to Miss Lilah at the preschool."

"Well, I have the ultimate icebreaker," Duffy said, nodding toward Prince, who was happily licking the fruit-snack residue from Sam's palms. "Yeah, you're gonna want to wash his hands."

Lucy reached into her giant purse and retrieved a packet of wet wipes, which she diligently applied to her son's hands. "So Tootie's still taking in strays, huh? How big is the pack now?"

"Down to five," Duffy told her. "Tootie opened an animal shelter a few months ago and she's been adopting her dogs out."

"Really?" Lucy's jaw dropped. "I never thought I'd see the day your grandma Tootie let her babies go home with anybody else."

Sam giggled from the sidewalk, suddenly attuned to the adults' conversation. "Your grandma's name is Tootie? That's so weird."

"It is a little bit," Duffy admitted, turning to Lucy. "And she started giving her dogs to good homes. It was a combination of trying to do the right thing and being threatened with charges by the county. She was one dog away from being officially branded a hoarder."

Sam's face lit up like a Christmas tree and a firecracker had a baby. "So she gives people dogs? Mama, can we take this dog home with us if we ask real nice?"

Having spent his formative years around Tootie, Duffy knew better than to enter into any sort of conversation in which a child asked their parent for a dog. So he shot an apologetic look toward Lucy and clamped his mouth shut. Lucy's full lips thinned, but she managed to keep her cheerful tone. "Well, a dog is a big responsibility, sweetheart. It's not something you just decide to get on the sidewalk without a plan. And you would have to help me feed him and clean up after him—"

"I would feed him!" Sam exclaimed. "I would give him all the green stuff off of my plates, all that he wanted."

"You mean the vegetables?" Lucy asked dryly.

"YES!"

"Dogs aren't really into veggies, buddy," Duffy said, even as Lucy shook her head and mouthed, *Don't help.*

"Then he could have my meat!" Sam promised. "I would give him baths and let him sleep in my bed. You wouldn't even know he was there, Mama."

"I noticed that you didn't mention who was going to be cleaning up *after* the dog," Lucy muttered. "Look, we'll talk about it. We're not going to make a decision today, no matter what. And I can't guarantee that we would get this dog, in particular, but if we can get through the next few months and you show me that you're a big responsible boy who's ready to take care of a dog, we'll talk about it."

"Aw, Mom!" he exclaimed. Prince whined almost in sync with the boy and laid his plastic-coned head against Sam's leg. He focused those big shiny puppy eyes on Lucy, who set her teeth in a firm line.

"Oh, you're good," she told the dog, while blowing out a breath. She leveled a stern look on her son and added, "That's my final word on it, Sam. And part of being a big responsible boy is listening when I say no."

And to Duffy's surprise, instead of pitching a tantrum, like Hazel, or trying a different angle to argue, like Nate, Lucy's son sighed and said, "Okay."

Lucy smiled softly and kissed Sam's hair. "Thanks, buddy."

Duffy watched her handle what could have been a knockdown, drag-out mother-child sidewalk altercation with awe. This new version of Lucy wasn't exactly the fantasy image that Duffy had held on to since high school. She was even better. She was more comfortable in her own skin and she knew the weight her word carried.

"So, bearded shirtless guys on book covers, huh?" Duffy asked as Sam busied himself with examining Prince's ears while the puppy licked Sam's face.

"I happen to enjoy the new-adult romance genre, thank you," Lucy said primly. "And I got your sketches. They look great and I like the maple finish. Are you sure I can't at least pay for materials?"

"Nope, I've got all this scrap trimming left over from when Carl and I were finishing out his and Marianne's house. It's been sitting there for years. Honestly, you're doing me a favor helping me put it to use and getting it out of the workshop." Duffy nodded toward Sam. "He seems like a very nice boy. Good manners. Firm grip. And just enough of a troll to be highly entertaining." Lucy lifted a brow, and he added, "For me."

"Lucy Bowman, oh, shug, you come on over here and let me give you a hug!" Tootie burst out of the jerky store like a purple-clad missile. Lucy grinned broadly and accepted what would no doubt be a spine-cracker. Tootie had a deceptive amount of upper-body strength hidden in her birdlike frame.

"Hey, Miss Tootie!" Lucy covered her groan with a laugh as Tootie squeezed the daylights out of her.

"I've been telling this one that he needs to bring you by the homestead, but he says you've been busy," Tootie said, glaring at Duffy.

"She has been busy," Duffy insisted. "Look at what she's done to the meat shop. It's starting to look downright respectable."

"Hmph," Tootie grumbled. "I'm sure it's very nice, Lucy, but how am I supposed to fatten you up and pump you for information if you don't come by for a cup of coffee?"

"How about Thursday afternoon?" she asked. "Sam has school in the morning."

"That'll do," Tootie said, nodding to Sam. "And be sure to bring this young man around with you. I'll introduce him to all of the dogs."

"Yes, please! I want to meet all of the dogs, Mama! Please? Hey, is your name really Tootie?" Sam asked, pulling lightly at Tootie's arm. "How did that happen?"

The older woman took Prince's leash and let him lead her down the road a bit to do some personal business. Sam followed at her heels.

"Well, my real name is Eloise. But when I was a little girl, I was learning how to tap dance and I was practicing a song called 'Tootie Tah' . . ." Tootie's voice trailed off as they moved farther away.

Duffy turned to Lucy. "I'm sorry. I should have shoved Prince behind my back or something when I saw Sam coming.

I'll tell Tootie to keep you in mind if you want, but if not, I can try to run interference."

She sighed. "It was a trap and I walked right into it. You'd think I would see them coming by now, but motherhood requires constant leveling up."

"I know it's going to sound cliché, but a boy needs a dog," he said. "It could be good for him."

Lucy scoffed. "You don't have a dog. You never did."

"I didn't need one, Tootie always had a dozen of them running around."

"That is true," she conceded.

"Trust me when I say I picked up enough leavings to have owned a hundred of them over the years."

"To be honest, it's something I've been thinking about for a while," she said, nearly whispering, even though Sam was so focused on Prince that he wouldn't have heard a dump truck full of dynamite rattling down the road. "He's been asking for a dog since he was three. I just worried that if I got him one now, it would always be 'the dog Mom got me because my dad died.'"

"Well, maybe just don't put that on its water bowl," Duffy suggested.

Lucy rolled her eyes and slapped his chest. Sam turned just in time to see this minor act of violence. His mouth dropped open and he let out an indignant squawk. "Mama, you're not supposed to hit."

"I know, but sometimes Mr. Duffy asks for it."

Sam's little hands went to his hips. "You told me that wasn't an excuse when I hit Asher at preschool."

"That is true, I did. And good for you for . . . having such a good memory."

"Frankie always had a knack for remembering that sort of thing, too," Duffy told her, and for a moment, Lucy suffered a shudder that looked like a full-body tremor.

"I love your cousin, but if my son starts coloring his hair with Sharpies, I'm coming for you," Lucy told him.

"I will tell you what I've been telling local citizens and authorities for years: I am in no way responsible for the actions of any of my relatives by blood or marriage."

"You should have that printed on little cards to hand out, to save you some time."

"I really should." He nodded. "So, uh, the Sweethearts' Dance is coming up. Are you thinking about going?"

Lucy gave a noncommittal jerk of the shoulder. "Well, sure, I have to go because I'm making about five hundred red velvet cake balls for your aunt Leslie. She took home my cake pops and experimented with different oils and frying times. She said something about setting up a mobile frying stand and selling them as treats?"

Duffy covered his grimace with a practiced smile. He'd tried to leave the invitation open-ended, but apparently he'd been so vague that it had just sounded like a general question. Carl was right. He *was* an idiot. Lucy continued on without noticing his inner turmoil. "Leslie even offered to split the profits sixty-forty under her business license. Do I want to know how your aunt Leslie has a mobile deep-frying cart?"

For a moment, Duffy thought about rephrasing his question, but like a great big coward, he latched on to the distraction of Aunt Leslie and her deep-fried wonders. "No, you do not. She's saving up for her own food truck as her 'retirement' job."

Lucy laughed. "She'll never retire. She'll be ninety years old, dropping corn dogs at the Snack Shack."

"I don't know. Tootie's almost saved enough for her and E.J.J. to take that retirement cruise to Aruba she's always talking about. And I think we're getting to that tipping point where E.J.J. standing on his feet all day, moving caskets, it's too much for him. Hell, even my mama is starting to move a little slower on the boats." Duffy raised his hand. "Please don't ever tell her I said that."

Lucy lifted her hand in the "scout's honor" sign. "So, you think the older generation is close to retiring?" she asked. "Wow, that would be a big change."

"Eh, it's not like everybody would go all at once. And Margot is learning everything Uncle Bob can teach her, she's like a sponge for anything having to do with organization. So she would have the funeral planning side covered. Nobody works like Frankie on her side of things. And I can keep the marina going. Everything else is just finding people you trust. It will still be McCready's. But things change, they always do. It's just part of it. And if Marianne's boys or, hell, Margot's girls, from the looks of it, decide they don't want to go into the family business? We'll figure something out."

"Even if it means hiring some of your McDuff cousins?"

He shuddered. "No, we don't even joke about that."

Lucy laughed. And while making her laugh was probably his favorite moment of his week so far, he was no closer to asking her to the Sweethearts' Dance—or rather, getting *her* to ask *him*. And he was just standing there staring at her like a big dope, which was starting to get awkward.

"So the dance, you're not going with anyone?" he asked, cringing a little inside at how lame he sounded, even to himself.

"Oh, no, I think it's a little early to be asking someone out on a date just yet. I'm fine just going solo, getting to see everybody without having to worry about keeping someone else entertained. It'll be my first big outing since I got back to town. How about you? Has anybody asked you?"

Duffy kept that practiced smile in place, even while he let an opportunity pass by and flip him the bird. "Well, you know me, always fielding offers."

"I guess I'll see you there, then," she said, stretching out her hands to Sam, who reluctantly left his new canine companion and joined her on their way to their truck.

Tootie and Prince came to stand alongside Duffy as they watched the pair drive away. "Duffy, you know I don't like to criticize my grandchildren, but just ask the girl out already."

"Ha! When has 'not criticizing your grandchildren' ever been your policy?" he exclaimed, only to look down at his feet as a warm, wet sensation spread over his left ankle. Prince's leg was hiked and he was contentedly peeing on Duffy's jeans and work boots. "Ah! Dammit, Prince, no!"

"Yeah, he has a tendency to do that when people raise their voices," Tootie said, her tone unconcerned.

"Have you considered training him out of it?" Duffy asked, shooing the dog away.

"Why would I want to do that?"

7

THREE HUNDRED CAKE balls in, Lucy knew that hiring Specs was the best decision she'd ever made. Not only did he follow instructions to the letter, he didn't question why destroying dozens of eight-inch round pans of red velvet cake and mixing them with frosting was a constructive idea. He worked precisely, rolling each and every ball into the exact same size and inserting the lollipop stick at the exact same angle, then rolled them in a mix of dried cake crumbs and powdered sugar to protect them in the oil.

As an added bonus, Specs kept Sam occupied by asking him questions about dogs and dinosaurs, two of Sam's favorite subjects, so Sam didn't wander around the shop causing chaos. She doubted very much she could have gotten the job done without Specs, much less have time to run Sam to E.J.J. and Tootie's house *and* go home to change into a nice dress for the occasion.

Lucy had already drawn up a baking schedule that would let her and Specs make up the cupcakes for the next day while the yeast dough for the morning pastries proofed. It would mean getting up indecently early and doing some work at home, but she figured the breakfast business would be what got people through the door, which would eventually build her clientele who would return for the bigger-ticket items like special cakes. She also planned to limit the variety of items she offered on a rotating basis, so she wouldn't end up working herself to death. Specs was a treasure, and she was already planning to give him a raise.

Tootie and her husband were electing to miss the Sweethearts' Dance for the first time in anybody's memory, because E.J.J. had a particular week involving the funeral service for Martha Mae Bronner, whose children had fought for control of the funeral services like they were playing a Japanese game show. When Tootie offered to keep Sam along with the Archer-Dawson brood for the evening, Sam had answered for his mother by shouting, "Yes! Please! I can play with the dogs! And Nate! And the dogs!"

So, if nothing else, moving back to Lake Sackett was doing a lot for Sam's shyness. Meeting new kids and spending time with responsible, trustworthy adults who were not Lucy could only be good for him.

"Well, you cleaned up nice," Specs told her as she walked back into the shop. He was loading the last of the carefully boxed cake balls into the lavender-and-white Gimme Some Sugar bags.

Lucy smoothed the skirt of one of the few party dresses she'd brought back to Lake Sackett, a red taffeta with a sweetheart neckline and a crinolined skirt that swung like a bell every time she moved. "Are you sure you don't want to go spiff up and come on over? The band's still warming up, so you've got time."

"Aw, nah, Miss Lucy, that's young people's business," he said, waving her off. "I'm just glad to help."

"Well, either way, I have something for you," she said, nodding to the tattered canvas apron Specs was wearing over his jeans and an old white T-shirt. She suspected he'd worn that apron during his military service, considering the depth of some of those stains. She set one of her reusable grocery totes on the counter and reached inside. "I asked my friend Hannah to make you some aprons of your very own, specially sewn for your tall frame."

"Um, I don't want to seem ungrateful, Miss Lucy, but I don't think I'd look right in pink cupcakes."

"There's not a pink cupcake in sight," Lucy promised, dragging two aprons out of the bag—one printed with spectacles of all different frames and colors, the other printed with famous naval battleships. "These were made just for you. And if I do say so myself, are quite manly."

"Aw, well, that's real nice of you," he said, his papery cheeks going pink under his own thick-framed glasses.

"If you want, I can get Hannah to embroider your name across the front next time," she offered.

"Don't push it," he told her, making her laugh.

"Well, you take the bag home and wear them into work. Consider it your only uniform, besides comfortable shoes." She handed him the bag and picked up the four enormous totes that she would use to carry the cake balls to the town square.

"Seems reasonable enough," he conceded, following her out the door. "You sure you don't need any help carrying those?"

"Nope," she said, locking the shop door behind her. "I'm used to lugging around fifty pounds of deadweight, also known as my sleeping child. Compared to that, this is a cakewalk. These have handles. Have a good night, Specs."

"You, too, Miss Lucy. Put some wear on those dancing shoes," he said, waving as he walked away.

Her dancing shoes were a pair of sensible red patent leather flats that she could wipe down with a rag if she dropped frosting on them. She doubted very much that she was going to wear them out. As she carried her cakey burden along Main Street, she thought wistfully of the heels she still had in storage— beautiful, stylish shoes with stilettos and kitten heels and wedges. Some of them even sparkled. But pregnancy and chasing after an energetic toddler had permanently attached sensible ballet flats to her feet for the last five years, which was a shame because her ass looked amazing when she wore stilettos. Such was the price of motherhood.

"Let me help you with that!"

She turned to see Duffy jogging down Main Street toward her.

Like most men in Lake Sackett, Duffy had a pair of "dress jeans"—dark-wash denim worn only on special occasions and sometimes to church, if the air-conditioning was broken. Duffy's were so rarely worn that the cotton damn near squeaked as he walked. Paired with a white button-up shirt and what had to be one of his dad's old gray corduroy blazers, he looked casual, if not necessarily relaxed. In fact, he looked like he was getting ready to meet with his parole officer. Not that Duffy had a parole officer, but enough of her Junior League acquaintances' husbands had gotten dinged for white-collar crime that she recognized discomfited anxiety when she saw it.

He took one of the heavy totes, lightening her load considerably.

"We have to stop meeting like this," she said, grinning.

"You should ask people for help before you try to wrestle cakes down the sidewalk."

"I can't argue with you there."

He glanced down at her dress and seemed to freeze where he stood. "Wow."

"Yeah?" she said, turning a bit so her skirt fanned out. "Thanks. I wasn't sure about it, thought maybe it was too much, but it just seems to fit the occasion, you know?"

"How can it be too much when you look so pretty?" he asked, slightly dumbfounded.

"Thank you." And Lucy's cheeks were pink and pleased again. It had been a long time since she'd seen such bald attraction in a man's eyes. Even though it was coming from Duffy, who couldn't mean it *that* way, it was nice to feel appreciated for her appearance instead of her competence or usefulness. Yeah, it made her feel about as deep as a puddle, but sometimes a girl just needed to feel like a girl.

"This is a hell of a lot of cake," Duffy noted.

"Yep, we weren't really sure how many people would be coming, or how hungry they would be," she said. "But at three bucks apiece it's not a bad deal, considering it's a full serving of cake."

"Well, I don't think you're going to have a hard time selling out," Duffy said as they rounded the corner.

Dozens of people were already gathering on Main Street, setting their camp chairs on the sidewalk, away from the crush of the town square that would become a dance floor. Main Street was done up with strings of Edison lights hanging from the streetlamps alongside red and white balloons and streamers.

March was the perfect time for such an outdoor hootenanny, as it wasn't too muggy or too buggy.

On the band shell, Clem Howard's Love Me Tender Trio was plucking through their warm-up licks. Clem was an Elvis impersonator in his midfifties whose claim to fame was that his cousin played the triangle on a B-side recording with the King himself—which in Lake Sackett was as close to greatness as most people would ever come. Clem had been trading on this celebrity for decades, cementing his place as the musical act for most community events that didn't involve a marching band, because, well, he was the best they could get. While his singing was passable, the real challenge was dancing without getting one of Clem's sweat-soaked scarves slung at you from the stage.

It was downright Rockwellian how picturesque the whole scene was, and Lucy was warmed with the sort of fulfilled nostalgia that someone hopes for when they move back to their tiny hometown. This was why she'd come back to Lake Sackett. Parties in Wayne's social circle had been so over-the-top that even a baby's first birthday shindig came across like an episode of *My Super Sweet 16*. Here there were no gift bags full of designer candles or cookies personalized with laser-etched sprinkles. Just (generally) nice people getting together to celebrate love and relationships, not with anything fancy, just a little food and music and dancing. The older couples would sit in their camp chairs with their sweethearts, chatting about how they got together. The younger couples would dance and discreetly drink the booze they'd snuck in to mix with their iced tea and lemonade.

With any luck, no one would be arrested and everybody would be home by ten.

"I'd forgotten how much I love this." Lucy sighed, setting the totes down and wringing out her pinched fingers. "I haven't been to a Sweethearts' Dance since I was in high school."

"Well, they've changed the way we do things now. All dances are the Funky Chicken. And Clem only sings Céline Dion songs," Duffy teased, making her laugh. "His version of 'My Heart Will Go On' is life-changing."

"That I would actually pay to see."

Duffy turned and lit up at the sight of a beautiful blonde in an expensive-looking black cocktail dress holding her hand over the swell of her stomach. If Lucy had to guess, she was probably five or six months along, but still gliding gracefully on a pair of black strappy heels that actually made Lucy's mouth water. Her obvious and inexplicable grace while managing her imbalanced weight on stilts appeared to make the tall bearded man hovering behind her incredibly nervous. Somehow he was in a constant state of preparing to catch her at any second.

"Duffy, hey!" the woman cried, throwing her arms around her cousin. "You clean up nice!"

"Thank you, thank you, I do try," he said, smoothing his gingery curls back in a self-conscious gesture. "Lucy, this is my cousin Margot and her soon-to-be husband, Kyle. Margot and Kyle, this is my good friend Lucy."

"I've heard so much about you," Margot said, reaching for Lucy's hand.

"You, too!" Lucy said. "Marianne and Frankie have had nothing but great things to say. I'm so glad they finally have someone to balance their, uh . . . I don't want to say 'lack of judgment,' because that sounds mean . . ."

"But Frankie did convince a kid that zombies had risen and

the world was coming to an end. I get it," Margot said. "I'm addicted to your pecan-based products. And I regret nothing. Your pies are my pregnancy craving."

"Subtle," Kyle murmured in a tone so soft Lucy was pretty sure she wasn't meant to hear.

"And you're the elementary school principal?" Lucy asked Kyle. "I'm going to be registering my son for kindergarten this fall. He said you came to visit the preschool the other day to talk to them all about moving up to the 'big kids school.' He's very excited."

"Yep, it's a very rewarding and important job," Kyle said. "Though most of the time I feel like the guy at the asylum with the big key ring."

"And then you want to marry into my family, which is so relaxing and low-key." Margot snorted.

"Hey, I resent that. Just last week, we went two whole days without anybody yelling at work. So how's it feel to actually attend a Lake Sackett community event that you didn't have to plan yourself?" Duffy asked.

"Really weird," Margot admitted. "I mean, I keep wanting to tell someone how to set up the tables for better foot traffic flow, but I honestly think that would hurt Aunt Leslie's feelings, which I would never want to do."

"And they told her that her help wasn't needed," Kyle said, smirking. "Because I think the little church ladies want to prove they can still plan something without Margot's supervision."

"They said I should take the time to enjoy myself before the baby is born," Margot said, slapping lightly at his chest. "And I happen to think they're right. Which is why I'm not correcting the table placement."

"I can tell it's a struggle for you," Lucy said.

"It really is," Margot told her.

"Lucy, honey!" Leslie cried, tugging her handsome but socially hapless husband, Bob McCready, toward their little group. Donna followed, watching the proceedings with an amused smirk. She wore black dress pants and a sparkly red cardigan, which was practically black-tie formal for Donna. She was even wearing a sweep of neutral lip color. She looked softer, somehow, but still Donna.

"Oh, you've been busy," Leslie exclaimed, taking some of the boxes from Lucy's tote bag. "Bob, Duffy, take these over to the fry stand."

"Hey, Lucy," Bob said, giving Leslie an exasperated smile as he and Duffy hauled the bags away.

"Hey, there, honey," Donna said, putting her arm around Lucy's shoulders. "I'm real proud of you for doing all this. I know Leslie's ideas can be kind of grand sometimes."

Margot stared at Donna and goggled, probably at the sweet tone of voice her aunt was using.

"Miss Donna, you look so nice. Are you here with someone?" Lucy teased.

Margot cringed, but Donna merely shrugged. "Hell no, I'm flying solo. I figured I'd help you and Leslie sell your cake things. Duffy implied that my social skills needed airing out."

"Oh, and Margot! What a pretty maternity dress!" Leslie exclaimed, cupping her hands around Margot's belly. "You're just glowing!"

Margot's smile became uncomfortably tight. "Yeah . . . everybody loves touching the belly . . ."

"You just go sit and relax and the committee will take care of everything," Leslie told her. "I'll bring you a snack in a minute."

"Thanks, Aunt Leslie," Margot said, relaxing a bit once Leslie was no longer feeling her stomach.

"Kind of funny how being pregnant makes people forget that there's a person attached to the belly, huh?" Lucy asked as Leslie departed to direct her husband and nephew in setting up the fry stand.

"Aunt Leslie is amazing in so many ways." Margot sighed. "I won't begrudge her belly rubs. But the next old man who tries to feel me up under the guise of pretending like he's trying to figure out how far along I am—as opposed to asking me? I'm going to end up on one of those 'women who snap' shows Frankie loves so much."

"Reasonable response," Lucy said. "I would tell you it gets better, but I don't want to lie to you. And it does serve as training to smack away the hands of random strangers who try to put their fingers in your baby's mouth."

Margot gasped. "Why would they do that?"

"I honestly don't know."

"Kyle, I'm buying that stroller we saw online," Margot told him.

"Sweetheart, I think that was a joke. You can't really put an electrified iron cage around a stroller."

"I don't see why not. If it works for sharks, it should protect a baby," Margot told him as he led her away. Lucy mouthed *I'm sorry* at him. He shrugged.

"*Come home to Lake Sackett,* I said. *Make new friends while connecting with old ones,* I said," Lucy muttered as she walked toward the fry stand. "Me and my big mouth."

THE CAKE BALLS were a hit. The music started and the square filled up and everywhere she looked, there were people eating deep-fried red chunks of cake and moaning in delight when they got to the surprise cream cheese frosting center. Duffy seemed to float in the periphery as she worked, talking to their old classmates, helping Leslie and Donna clean up the little paper serving cups for the cake balls. A little card on the front of the cart read, *Sweet treats provided in cooperation with GIMME SOME SUGAR, coming soon to Main Street!*

Helping Leslie with the fry station was a lesson in efficient but friendly food production. Leslie managed to scoop the cake balls out of the oil right as they reached the perfect moment of crispness, handed them off to Lucy or Donna for filling, took them back, dusted them with powdered sugar, and passed them to the next customer, all while maintaining a steady stream of conversation. She made every single person in line feel welcome and heard and eager to eat whatever Leslie was serving. Lucy was trying to absorb every detail while struggling to keep up with the orders. And never had she been so thankful for her massive collection of aprons, because Hannah's red-and-white cupid-themed creation was protecting her party dress from a fine dusting of powdered sugar and grease.

Lucy saw people she'd known since elementary school, people from her parents' church, people who could remember her from when she was "knee high." And a lot of them seemed to have the same reaction, giving her the "aw, hon" face and then staring at her like she was supposed to burst into tears at any moment. When she didn't give them the response they wanted, they seemed weirdly disappointed. Fortunately, the fast pace of serving saved her from much conversation.

She suddenly felt very visible in her red dress. Should she have worn black? It wasn't like she was a Victorian widow. But still, people were staring at her, judging her. Most of the cake balls had been filled and fried. Maybe she should head home?

"Honey, why don't you go take a break?" Donna said as the line thinned and the dancing warmed into full swing.

"Oh, but I'm supposed to be helping you two."

"Well, no one said that you had to work the whole night," Leslie said. "Go have fun!"

Leslie glanced around until she spotted her nephew. "Duffy! Sweetheart, go talk Lucy onto the dance floor. She needs a break."

Duffy seemed to grimace and Lucy tried not to take that personally. "Uh, sure. Just, uh, are your toes still kind of delicate?"

Lucy laughed. "Well, it can't be any worse than the Good Manners Dance in third grade."

He groaned and rubbed his hand over his beard, obviously recalling the little cotillion the elementary school teachers organized every spring to help the kids learn about etiquette and good behavior on fancy occasions. Lucy and Duffy had been quick to pair off as partners, but Duffy had stepped on Lucy's foot as they walked down the stage steps. Lucy fell, but Duffy's foot remained planted on her little black Mary Jane church shoe, bending her toes at an unnatural angle and breaking three of them. They'd missed the dance entirely as Lucy had to be taken to the hospital for X-rays. "Oh, don't remind me."

"I only had to wear that walking cast for a few weeks," she said as he took her hand and led her toward the twirling couples on the square. "In the summer."

He chuckled, but it sounded pained.

"And missed swim camp."

"Please stop reminiscing or I'm going to toss you into the lake," Duffy threatened as he drew her into his arms. She shivered at the sensation of his warm fingers tracing the line of her back. Standing this close, face-to-face, there was nowhere else to look, no pretending that she wasn't staring up at Duffy's mouth. It was awkward and exciting all at the same time, feeling those ripples of attraction fluttering through her belly. But agonizing, because this was Duffy, and ripples of attraction weren't exactly part of their relationship.

"I haven't danced in . . . I don't know how long," she said, sighing but holding her posture rigid. She didn't want to give in to the temptation of melting into the warm strength of his frame. She'd been so alone over the last months, carrying so much on her shoulders, it felt good to lean on someone else just for the length of "Can't Help Falling in Love." "Probably because of the toe-related PTSD."

Duffy snorted. "It's been a while for me, too. I've probably improved with age."

"Well, you couldn't get worse."

"Hey, it's been three minutes and your toes are unscathed," he said, pulling her just a bit closer.

She sniffed at his shirt. "This is going to sound weird, but you smell . . . woodsy. But not cologne woodsy. Like actual sawdust woodsy and a little sweet."

"That would be maple. I spent the afternoon sanding boards for your displays. I swear I showered, but sometimes it just kind of sinks into your skin."

"No, I like it," she said with a laugh. "You smell all woodsy because you're doing something nice for me . . . I missed you, Duffy. I really did. I'm sorry I stopped calling and writing."

"Well, I didn't exactly keep in touch," he said. "Your daddy never stopped talking about you, though. Every time I saw him, he had some new story about you or Sam."

"I called him as much as I could," she said, her throat tightening. Her daddy had never pressured her for visits because he knew how much Wayne fought against coming back home. "He didn't like flying 'all that way' to Texas to visit a 'fancy-schmancy' house that made him uncomfortable. He got to know his grandson mainly over Skype, and he was content with that."

"He never did let on how sick he was, huh?"

She shook her head. "And he swore his buddies to secrecy."

Duffy had been out of town for her daddy's funeral, she remembered. Frankie had said something about a regular charter client who asked Duffy to escort him to his first big fishing tournament in Alabama. With the tourism side of the business running slow, Donna had insisted Duffy couldn't risk alienating a client, and she had her own charters to run. At the time, it had felt like an excuse, but she had been so mired in the grief of losing her father to cancer she didn't even know he'd had, she hadn't had the emotional energy to think about it much.

"What's it like to stay in his old place?"

"Well, Wayne paid a company in Atlanta to come back and clean the house out, organize what I wanted to save. He didn't want to stay after the funeral long enough for me to do the job. So it was a blank slate, I guess. Haven't quite gotten rid of that old man smell."

"Yeah, that's not going away," he told her.

"I just wanted to give Sam a little piece of what we had, you know? I mean, I know it wasn't perfect. But it seemed safer, I guess?"

"That's not wrong. You've lost a lot, and when people are at a loss, they tend to retreat to the familiar."

"That would explain why Lana is looking at me like she wants to set my face on fire," Lucy said, nodding across the street at Lana. Just minutes before, she had been dancing with Jeremy Teague from their high school class like they were auditioning for *The Forbidden Dance*, but she still had the nerve to make snake eyes at Lucy.

"It's been a while since we've been together, but she still thinks she has a claim. I promise you she doesn't." Duffy shook his head. "Uncomfortable change of subject. Is there anything else you need help with before the opening?"

"Do you know anybody who could push my paperwork through with the county licensing office? I can't get a business license, a tax ID number. It's been six weeks since I applied. And I'm not sure that Herb Brewster is still alive. I think he died a long time ago and the people in the health department are enacting some sort of *Weekend at Bernie's* scenario."

"Still no inspection, huh?"

"No. Do you think your uncle Bob could help?"

"I'll ask him about it, but he may not be able to do much.

He takes the whole 'don't use the county commission for personal shenanigans' thing very seriously ever since Vern Lewis got tossed out. Bob got bumped up to the head spot after the incident back in October."

Lucy grimaced. "Yeah, I keep hearing about that, something about a fake zombie apocalypse?"

"Frankie got real creative to keep Lewis's kid from breaking into her morgue," Duffy said. "Do not cross my cousin when she decides she's right about something."

"Wasn't gonna," Lucy assured him.

"Vern ended up stepping down after Jared's little zombie meltdown. He was embarrassed that his son made a jackass of himself in such a public fashion, and proved what a terrible parent he is to boot. Which showed that contrary to popular opinion, the Lewis family *does* have some shame."

"Wow, maybe I should just leave the county commission out of this."

"On the other hand, Frankie is damn near living with the sheriff now. He might be able to pull some strings . . . or just steal the papers and forge some signatures," Duffy said, nodding across the dance floor to where Frankie was in the arms of a tall, muscular guy with a precise military haircut. Even in a dark blue button-up and jeans, the guy looked like a cop, and probably always would. But he looked damned delighted to be leading his girlfriend, with her bright red dress and brighter red hair, around in the crowd as she threw her head back and laughed.

"So you would expect the sheriff to commit petty crime on your behalf, but not your uncle?"

"Yep." He nodded, spinning her out and making her skirt

swirl in a perfect bell around her hips. She laughed, and people around her turned their heads. And despite herself, she didn't tamp down that smile. She reached for Duffy, who spun her back so fast she collided with his chest.

"You've gotten a little better," she conceded.

"The trick is leaning forward so your feet are out of range," he said.

She laughed again, and didn't care if people around her heard. She followed his lead around the dance floor, and one song changed into another, and all night she managed to avoid getting slapped by the sweat-soaked scarves from Clem's neck. It was the best time she'd had in years.

The crowd was beginning to thin by the time Lucy realized she hadn't returned from her "break." Her head whipped toward the fry cart, where Leslie was boxing up the supplies.

"What's the matter?" Duffy asked.

"Your mama and aunt Leslie!" she exclaimed, stepping away from him. "I can't believe I left them alone this whole time!"

Duffy followed her as she rushed across the square toward Leslie's cart. There were no cake balls left, but Leslie and Donna were packing the leftover frosting and the injector into Lucy's bags. "I'm so sorry! I just—"

"You were having fun, which I imagine is a pretty rare commodity for you these days, and you lost track of time," Leslie assured her. "It's not a problem. I'm glad you were enjoying yourself, 'cause that's what we told you to go do in the first place. Sales had pretty much slowed to a crawl, anyway. The oil's all cooled off and ready to cart away. And Bob helped me with the cleanup, because he's hoping to get lucky tonight."

Duffy and Lucy tried not to visibly recoil.

"And your share comes to a little over five hundred dollars," Leslie said, slapping a cash bag into her hand.

Minus supplies and ingredients, Lucy had just had a pretty good night. Gimme Some Sugar had a *great* night, full of product sampling and free publicity directed at her target audience. Lucy was feeling pretty damn good about herself, and she was going to call it an evening before that changed.

"Well, I think I'm going to run this stuff back to the shop," Lucy said as Leslie wrapped her in a hug that smelled of powdered sugar and canola oil.

"Aw, I'm so glad you were here tonight, shug," Leslie said. "Without you, I would have been peddling the same old corn dogs and deep-fried Twinkies."

"I appreciate a good deep-fried Twinkie as much as the next girl," Lucy said. "But I like to think we offered something a little more elevated tonight."

"People will be talking about it for weeks," Leslie said. "Now, go get some rest and enjoy your victory."

"I will," Lucy said, lifting her bags.

"Here, let me help," Duffy said, taking the bag of frosting tools from her. "Good night, everybody!"

They walked down Main Street, the light and the sound of the crowd at their backs. Lucy's feet ached like a homemade heartbreak, but the pain was well-earned. She could still remember her own father collapsing into his easy chair at the end of a long day at the shop, exhausted, but with a contented smile on his face. Her mother was always sure to give him double helpings on those nights. When she got home, she was going to treat herself to double helpings of the Ben and Jerry's she kept hidden behind the frozen fish sticks.

"I had a really good time tonight," Lucy said, smiling into the warm Georgia night.

"Me too." Duffy nudged her gently with his elbow. "I heard people talking about your bakery. I didn't get to try one, because the line was insane, but most everybody was saying if everything is as good as the cake balls, they're going to line up the day you open."

"And the people who weren't part of 'most everybody'?"

"Well, Mama always told me, life's too short to listen to stupid."

Lucy snickered as she worked aggressive magic on the stubborn bakery door. "I thought your mama always said not to fight stupid with ugly."

"Yeah, Mama has a lot of sayings about stupid. Smells good in here," he said, inhaling deeply as they walked into the bakery. Lucy flipped on the kitchen lights and he noted the paint swatches on the walls. "That's gonna look real nice, once you get all the cabinets and the tables installed. I like the whole 'not quite pastel, but still delicately pretty' thing you've got going in here. Margot would probably call it 'contemporary feminine' or something. She's into all that decor talk. She's also into your cake balls, which she ate three of, by the way, and blamed it on the baby. She'd never had red velvet cake before."

"I know it's usually a Christmas thing, but after the Sweethearts' Dance, I think there's a year-round market for it." She set the plastic container of frosting on the counter, folded up her empty tote bags, and fit them neatly into their rack.

"It's going to be amazing," he told her, peering over the counter. He spotted a six-pack storage container filled with finished red velvet cupcakes. She'd planned to take some home to

Sam, as they were his favorites. But Duffy was looking at those cupcakes like they were the very last ones on earth, and she didn't have the heart to deny him.

"Would you like to try one?" she asked super casually, holding it out to him as he rounded the counter.

"Oh no, I couldn't possibly," he said, even as he peeled the liner away from his chosen cupcake. "I mean, really, I wouldn't want to put you out."

He took an enormous bite of the cupcake and seemed to be completely frozen.

"What's wrong?"

"I don't want to scare you by making blatantly sexual sounds," he said, swallowing the bite of cake.

"You want me to leave you alone with the cupcake?" she asked.

He dropped his head until his chin touched his chest. "I might need a minute."

He closed his eyes and slowly, methodically ate the remaining cake. Watching him wrap his lips around something that she'd made like it was a religious experience was, well . . . hot as hell. His tongue swept over his thumb to lick away a stray bit of icing and her stomach clenched. He opened his eyes and grinned at her. "You're gonna be a millionaire."

She burst out laughing as he stepped closer, almost cornering her against the counter. "You have icing in your beard."

"Well, you have it right there." He gestured toward her face.

"What? Where?" she cried, raising her hands to her cheeks. If she had frosting on her face, it meant she'd had it on her face *all night* from the first test cake ball she'd eaten before the dancing started. She'd been dancing around all night with a freaking frosting mustache?

"There!" he exclaimed, popping off the top of her container and smooshing a handful of frosting against her face. She shrieked and stared at him, her mouth agape as she swiped at the white fluff on her cheek.

"I can't believe you did that!"

"You know what's worse?"

"What?"

"I'm going to do it again," he said, bringing his hand toward the other side of her face.

"No!" she yelped, catching his arm and trying to hold it away from her. He reached with his free arm and she caught that, too, and was now engaged in what looked like a game of Gladiator Hands with a crazy man covered in frosting.

"This is going to happen," he told her. "And it will mean justice is finally served after years in the making. I believe you will recall the evening of my sixteenth birthday, when you shoved my face into the cake. In front of Lisa Turnbull."

"That was an accident," she insisted. "I was pushed from behind and I bumped into you."

"You were holding the cake," he reminded her. "And I got a candle stuck up my nose."

"I really thought I was aiming more carefully," she said, smiling sweetly.

"I told you, one day, I would get back at you," he said, and smeared a handful of frosting across her jaw. "Vengeance is mine."

She squealed as he cackled, struggling not to get more frosting smeared on his face. Their eyes connected and her heart caught, warming her down to her thighs. His arms were wrapped around her and his breath was feathering across her cheek. His forehead tipped against hers. She leaned up and closed the distance between them, brushing her mouth across his. He tasted sweet, like the frosting, and yet entirely Duffy. He groaned into her mouth, running his hand up her spine and pressing her closer against him. Her dress was going to be a wreck and she just couldn't care.

She threaded her fingers through his hair, pulling him to her mouth, even as his hands slipped over her rear. He lifted her, setting her butt on the counter and stepping between her legs. She was at just the right height. Duffy took advantage of this by cupping his sticky hands around her jaw and slipping his tongue between her lips. He licked at her like she was his favorite sweet, methodically mapping every centimeter of her mouth until he knew her by heart. The pleasant warmth between her thighs grew into a white-hot star, threatening to collapse on itself if he didn't touch more, touch *there*. But before it really began, Duffy pulled away from her, inhaling like a man breaking through the surface of the water.

His face was pale, like he was horrified by what he'd just done. Lucy's heart dropped through her belly.

"Um, I need to go," he said, backing away.

Bereft, Lucy straightened her clothes, shuddering as she felt the swatches of cream cheese frosting slathered on her dress.

"Duffy, what's going on?"

"I just need to go," he said, smiling awkwardly. "Um, I'll get the displays finished this week and then come help you hang them."

"Duffy, please talk to me."

He turned toward the door and it was only the miracle of CrossFit footwork that made her speedy enough to cut him off at the pass.

"*What* is going on? Why are you running off?"

"I can't," he said. "I thought I could, but I just can't get close to you like that. I'm sorry."

She could feel her face falling. He wasn't attracted to her after all. That lovely heat she'd felt building in her belly had been completely one-sided. Duffy saw her as a friend and nothing more. She'd been so silly to think it was anything but Duffy being his sweet self.

"Well, I didn't mean to make you uncomfortable," she said. "I won't do it again. I'm sorry. I don't want to mess up our friendship."

She died just a little in those few seconds that he stared at her. Had she ruined the little bit of happiness she'd discovered here in Lake Sackett? She didn't want to uproot her life all over again, but right now, living somewhere hundreds of miles away sounded like a pretty good idea—

"I've loved you since we were kids," he blurted out, as if the words had jumped from his mouth before he could stop them.

The entire world seemed to shift. She'd never considered that Duffy could love her. Yeah, his sister had told her that he was crazy about her, but they were friends. Yeah, he was attractive, but they were friends. That was the limit of their relationship. They knew things about each other that romantic partners would never learn. He'd never even acted like he thought she was pretty until tonight. When he talked about her it was in terms of her being sweet or smart or brave. He never treated her like the other boys at school did, who stared at her chest when they thought she wasn't looking, who seemed to think being nice to her was some sort of down payment for future sex.

But he said he loved her, and had for years. Did that mean he loved her like "Hey, girl, you know I love you, you're my best platonic friend?" Or was he *in love* with her?

"I wanted to tell you, but I was an idiot and I got scared and then you were dating Wayne and I didn't want to be the jerk who messed with your life when you were happy. You seemed so happy. And then you got married and you had a baby and I didn't want to mess that up. What kind of friend messes with their best friend's happiness, but—"

She threw her arms around his neck and pulled him into another kiss. He hugged her tight as their lips danced, and she felt him retreat from her. He seemed to use all of his strength to push her gently away. "But I can't do this if you're not all in. I can't get this close to you and then lose you again. I can't get close to you if there's a chance we wouldn't work out. I don't know if I would survive it. If I'm with you and it ends, I can't go back to pretending that I'm okay with just being your friend."

"So you would rather run?" she demanded. "You act like you would be in this alone, like I never had feelings for you. Like I haven't loved you since we were kids."

"You loved me?"

"Yes, I've always been a little bit in love with you, but we were friends and I didn't want to mess it up. You never acted like you were attracted to me, at all. I mean, it was always, 'You're my best *friend*, Lucy' and 'You're such a good *friend*, Lucy' and 'I basically think of you as a dude with boobs, Lucy.'"

"I don't remember that last one," he muttered.

"I didn't want to lose our friendship, either," she said. "So I never did anything about it."

"I almost did," Duffy said. "I was going to ask you to Homecoming sophomore year, but as I was working up the nerve, Wayne asked you. It's nobody's fault but mine for waiting so long."

"And then you started dating Lana, who actively threatened to remove all of the hair from my head every time she saw me talking to you."

"I wondered why you got so distant," he said. "And then you married Wayne."

"And you married Lana."

"So we're a coward and an idiot," he said. "Quite a pair."

"I don't want to guess who is who," she said with a snort.

"Where does this leave us?"

"I think we should think about this," she said. "We don't want to rush into anything, but now that we know how we both feel, it would be stupid not to give it the full consideration."

"Are you sure it's not too soon after Wayne?" he asked.

"Once all of this is settled, you and I are going to have a long talk about my marriage," she said. "But I don't want that to figure into your thinking. I don't want what my in-laws or your family or Lana or anybody in this whole damn town thinks of this to factor in. Let's just think about what would make us happy, okay? And we'll get back to each other in a few days and talk."

"All right," he said. "I'll see you in a few days. And this is just a regular good-night kiss, between friends. Nothing else implied."

He leaned forward and kissed her gently.

"And *this* is just a regular good-night kiss, between friends.

Nothing else implied," she said, repeating the kiss, soft as a butterfly's eyelash, against his lips.

"One more," he said, kissing her deeply.

"And there's one thing you should know," she murmured against his lips. "I'm going to get you for smearing frosting all over my dress. You won't know when or how, but vengeance will be mine."

He grinned against her mouth. "I look forward to it."

TWO DAYS LATER, after another long afternoon of conditioning the rental boats' engines, Duffy walked out of the bait shop to see his grandfather sitting on the end of the dock. He was in his funeral suit, with his shoes off and his feet in the water, drinking.

Grandpa E.J.J. never drank. And he was usually in bed by nine. He'd always said "a body gets in less trouble if he's under his own covers before the news starts." So why was he sitting there in a full "Uncle Stan in the bad drinking days" funk? The last time a McCready started looking all contemplative like that, it was his father, and it was right before Junior announced that he had late-stage cancer. A few years later, he was gone.

And all Duffy could think was, *Please, no, not yet.*

He threw his tools in the back of his truck and jogged toward the end of the dock. "Grandpa?"

E.J.J. turned to see Duffy running and waved his beer bottle. "Hey there, Scooter."

"Why are you sitting out here on your lonesome? You okay?"

"Aw, sure . . . Well, my knees are still a little bit sore from trying to keep up with the full brood the other night, but yeah, other than that, I'm fine."

Duffy blew out a breath he didn't realize he was holding. "That's good. Tootie's still recovering, too, I guess?"

"Yep, but the damage was minimal. Your Lucy's little boy was best behaved out of all of them. He just sat on the couch playing with Prince most of the time."

"He seems like a really good kid," Duffy said.

"Easy to love, just like his mama," E.J.J. said, watching Duffy carefully.

"Nope," Duffy said, shaking his head. "Not going there right now. Nope."

E.J.J. cackled, lifting his feet out of the water.

"Seriously, why are you out here soaking your feet like you got the gout?" Duffy asked.

E.J.J. sighed. "Your Grandma Tootie won three hundred and twelve dollars off of her poker ladies last night."

"Isn't that a good thing? Doesn't Tootie usually win?"

"It means she's finally saved up enough to book a two-week Caribbean cruise, with the drink packages and the fancy meals and the shore excursions and the whole shebang. She booked everything online this morning. We're 'embarking' at the end of June."

"So why do you sound like you're being sent to a funeral?" Duffy asked. "Come to think of it, I've heard you much more excited about going to an actual funeral. Why do you sound like you're being sent to the urologist?"

"I've never been away from McCready's for more than a weekend," E.J.J. said, frowning. "And this cruise is *two weeks.*

What am I going to do with myself for two weeks with no work? I'll go crazy. She wants me to swim with stingrays, Duffy. What the hell am I gonna do with a stingray?"

"Avoid the stinger?"

E.J.J. elbowed his grandson in the belly. "Smartass."

"Well, it's not like you're being shipped off on an ice floe, never to be seen again. It's just a vacation. Most people take vacations. You'll come back rested and jump right back on the horse."

"I don't take vacations," E.J.J. grumbled.

"Yes, that's why Tootie has spent the last ten years saving for a luxury cruise."

"I think your grandma sees this not so much as a vacation and more like the end of my career. But I don't know if I'm ready to let go just yet. This place is my life. This is my purpose, my role in Lake Sackett. It's how I take care of my family, how I take care of my neighbors. I don't feel old, Duff. I still feel like the same man I was when your daddy was born. But more and more, I see people my age coming through the doors of the funeral chapel. When half of the obituary section is made up of people from your high school class, it makes a man step back and think."

"All the more reason for you to go out and see more of the world, enjoy yourself a little bit," Duffy told him. "You use that much of yourself taking care of other people, pretty soon you've got nothing left."

"I don't need to see much more than the state of Georgia. God set me down here for a reason." E.J.J. crossed his arms over his chest, and for just a moment, Duffy realized Frankie's stubbornness was not exclusive to great-uncle Jack's branch of the family.

"Is it because you don't think you can trust the others with running the funeral home?" Duffy asked. "I mean, if something happened to you tomorrow, would you go to your maker thinking, 'They'll burn the place down in a week'?"

"Heck no!" E.J.J. exclaimed. "Margot could sell a Frigidaire in Antarctica. Bob's doing much better now that he doesn't have to deal with people. And Frankie's almost as good with her work as Junior was."

"So why not just take the trip?"

"Maybe I'm not ready," he said. "I'm not ready to leave."

"Grandpa, you're always talking about how you can judge a man's character by whether his wife is happy. How happy do you think Tootie will be when she finally gets to take the cruise she's spent ten years saving for?"

"You know, it's a real pain in the rear when your words are thrown back in your face by your own grandchildren, just to prove a point."

"Well, then you should stop being so wise."

E.J.J. grumbled.

"Tootie's worked a long time for this, sharking her friends at poker. Put on a smile and a tacky tropical shirt and take the damn cruise like a man," Duffy told him. "And if you don't want to retire when you come back, don't. Work part-time. Work whenever you want. Swan in wearin' waders and when things get busy, tell them sorry, you've got fish to catch."

"I never have managed to take up fishing," E.J.J. said. "Which is sort of embarrassing, given the family history."

"I'll take you out on a boat myself."

"All right."

"Just make sure you take a picture with the stingrays."

"Smartass."

ACROSS TOWN, LUCY pushed her cart down the aisle at the Food Carnival, surveying its contents. She pored over the label of an enormous plastic tub of Cheez Doodles, like she didn't know they were chock-full of carbs, salt, and food colors not found in nature. She liked to think she was a good mother who provided nutritious, wholesome foods, but sometimes the lure of frozen chicken nuggets and mini pizza bagels—and Sam's enthusiasm for said nuggets and mini pizzas, as opposed to his disgust for broccoli and quinoa—was just too great a temptation. She tried to balance it out with fruits, veggies, and whole-grain bread, but she wasn't inclined to keep up the whole "kale chips and chia pudding" standard she'd tried to maintain in Texas. She'd driven herself crazy trying to make sure toddler Sam ate nothing but organic, whole foods, but the juicing and the prep work and washing all of the damn BPA-free containers had been too much.

The other moms in the Crenshaw and Associates circle had assured her that all the work was worth it, and then tried to advise her on "hacks" to make cauliflower rice more appealing to a four-year-old. But Sam was no healthier than the kids at the park who were shoving Cheez Doodles in their faces. And Lucy seemed to be a lot more tense and exhausted than the Cheez Doodle moms. Dropping her juicer and containers in a box bound for Goodwill had been one of the few enjoyable parts of her move.

She'd become a Pinterest mom in Texas. She couldn't get through a bake sale or a birthday party or a damn Valentine's Day without consulting the online idea bank for inspiration. Okay, yeah, she got some good recipes for flavored buttercream off of it. But still, she felt so trapped by the urge to live up to the examples of the other moms. She just couldn't keep up with their constantly shifting tastes and fascinations, the ever-changing list of what was in and what was "garbage." She didn't even like Sandra or Tina or Rachelle, but were wives of Wayne's coworkers and socializing with them was mandatory—even if she did suspect that Wayne had slept with one or more of them.

Everything about her life in Texas was "have to." Here in Lake Sackett, well, there was still a lot of "have to," but there was a hell of a lot more "because I wanna" in her day now.

Speaking of which.

She tossed the Cheez Doodles into her cart and pushed it down the aisle. She checked her phone and saw that she had just enough time to cruise the produce section before picking Sam up from preschool.

She turned toward the fruits and vegetables only to have her cart sideswiped by Melody Garten, Wayne's sister. Melody might have been pretty, with her mother's rounded features and striking blue eyes. But the permanently sour expression had aged her prematurely and her dark gold hair was styled into a strange pointy bouffant much like Evie's, so she looked like a cranky cockatoo.

"Lucy," Melody said with a sniff.

"Melody, how are you?" Lucy asked through gritted teeth.

"Oh, I'm just fine. I'm never troubled by the state of *my* soul," Melody chirped at her.

"Well, that sounds . . . self-assured."

Melody had never liked Lucy, but unlike the other Gartens, she didn't bother putting on a show pretending she did. The only daughter in a family that prized sons, Melody had struggled with her identity from the time she was tiny. She'd shown a lot of signs of considerable intelligence from kindergarten on, but Evie never took advantage of the gifted programs offered by Melody's teachers because Wayne was "the smart one." She showed promise as a softball pitcher, but Davey was "the athletic one" and Evie didn't think that she could keep up with another practice schedule when Davey was already involved in football and baseball and basketball. With few options available to her, Melody took on the persona of "the pious one" and it stuck. She'd been a fervent member of the Lake Sackett First Baptist Church since age twelve. She taught Sunday School, led youth groups, organized revivals, and had tried to stage a coup of the Christmas pageant committee at the ripe age of nineteen. The coup failed, due to a powerful campaign from the senior ladies' Sunday school contingent, but still it had been an admirable effort for someone so young. Melody was basically the Joan of Arc of downtrodden church volunteers.

However, Melody had made it clear from day one she didn't think Lucy had the religious fortitude necessary to be a good wife to Wayne. Melody had given her different study Bibles for every single birthday and Christmas for the last five years—in addition to the "Bride's Bible" Lucy had been gifted on her wedding day. It wasn't that Lucy didn't enjoy what she considered to be a healthy relationship with the Lord, she just wanted Melody to stay out of it and mind her own.

Melody was staring at her, hard, as if the power of her glare would be enough to intimidate Lucy into some sort of apology for . . . existing. And since Lucy wasn't in the mood for false niceties, the silence was downright excruciating.

"Okay, well, I better get going. I need to pick up Sam from school."

"You mean that 'school' where you drop him off with strangers instead of letting his mamaw take care of him in her time of grieving?" Melody sneered.

"We're all grieving, Melody. And where my son goes to school is none of your business. He's happy to go there every day, and his happiness means a lot to me right now."

"It hurts my mama, so that makes it my business," Melody shot back.

Lucy gripped the handle of her cart tight. "As much as I'd like to vacation with you on No-Logic Island, I'm gonna just stay right here on solid ground, thanks."

"I don't know what sort of ideas you got into your head when you dragged Wayne off to that fancy college, but you're not in Texas anymore. You're in Lake Sackett. And in Lake Sackett, we expect our young people to have a lot more respect for their elders."

Lucy scoffed. "What do you mean, 'we'? You're not my elder. We went to high school together."

"And *we* expect widows to have a lot more respect for their husbands' memories."

"I beg your pardon?"

"Don't you think it's a little soon for you to be prancing

around in public in a red dress?" Melody hissed. "Wayne's body is barely cold."

"I was hardly prancing. I wore a red dress to the Sweethearts' Dance, where I went without a date. Again, none of your business. Now, if you'll excuse me."

Lucy tried to push past Melody, but Melody shoved her cart forward so Lucy's was trapped against the ranch dressing display. "Everybody saw you dancing with Duffy McCready. That's not what Wayne would have wanted, you actin' like you can't wait to replace him with some stuck-up funeral director's son. You shouldn't have been out at all. You shouldn't be doing half of the things you're doing. You shouldn't be thinking about opening some silly business. Nobody wants your den of sin opening up on Main Street."

"You realize 'bakery' isn't a euphemism for anything, right?"

"No, it's just another example of you giving in to your sinful nature. It's all about sweets and indulgence and making everything all pretty and stupid and empty, just like you," Melody said. "You should be at home, focusing on being respectful and raising my nephew. You should be honoring my mama, the way my poor dead brother would have wanted you to, God rest his soul. That boy is all Mama has left of Wayne. And you don't even care. You're just thinking about yourself."

"Right now, all I'm thinking is that I don't have time to give in to my 'sinful nature' and respond to those insults with the ass-whooping you deserve. I need to leave this store and get to 'that boy' you seem so concerned about. Get out of my way or I'm gonna go Old Testament on that awful haircut."

Melody's jaw dropped. Lucy shoved her cart hard enough to knock Melody's aside and push past her.

"You just wait, you Jezebel! I'm gonna tell everybody at my church what an awful, godless heathen you are, and nobody's gonna buy a biscuit from you once word gets out. Your stupid little shop will be finished before it starts!" Melody yelled.

Lucy was so angry she didn't have the energy to be embarrassed by the other shoppers who stopped and stared. She just power-walked her cart past them, shouting back, "That's fine. I'll offer a discount to all the other godless heathens in town to balance things out!"

LUCY TRIED NOT to road rage, given her family's recent vehicular luck. And she tried not to have an angry expression on her face when she picked Sam up from preschool. And she tried not to be angry when Sam was telling her a very complicated story about his day involving finger paints, the teacher's bathroom break, and impromptu wall murals that were very funny but in no way his fault.

"Are you okay, Mama?" Sam asked from the backseat as she turned onto their road.

"Sure, baby, why do you ask?"

"Well, you've just been saying, 'Mm-hmm,' instead of asking me a bunch of questions to make sure I didn't have anything to do with Kayla and Denver painting on the walls. Most of the time, you would be asking me a lot more questions."

Lucy groaned. The whole point of her trying to make this life in Lake Sackett was so she could be a good mother to her son, and here she was half-assing her way through a conversation with him. She was spreading her focus too thin, which meant nothing was getting her full attention. And Sammy deserved as much of that attention as she could give him while safely operating a motor vehicle.

"I'm sorry, honey. I'm just a little distracted because I had a long day. But I'm glad you didn't paint on the walls, or try to tell anybody else to paint on the walls, because that's not very nice. And it probably made a lot of work for poor Miss Lilah."

"Yeah, that's what Miss Lilah said. She did *not* laugh."

"I'll bet."

"Why was your day so long?"

"Oh, Mama just had an unpleasant conversation at the grocery with somebody who seems to think she knows everything and should tell everybody what to do."

"Like June?" Sam sighed dramatically, rolling his head back against the car seat. "I like Hazel but June is so bossy when I go to play with them and Aiden and Nate."

"Well, I think June is just glad that someone younger than her came along so she can feel like the bigger kid. She'll probably stop bossing you around as soon as her little brother or sister gets here."

"Yeah, she talked a lot about that. She wants a brother real bad, because she already has a sister and she says one is *enough*," Sam said, his eyes growing wide for emphasis.

"I'll bet." Lucy snorted, remembering to file that away to tell Margot.

"So someone was mean to you at the grocery store?" Sam asked. "Were you mean back?"

"Maybe a little, but nothing Grandma Gale would have washed my mouth out with soap over," she said.

"That's so gross," Sam exclaimed with glee. He loved hearing about his grandparents' "prehistoric" punishments like soap in the mouth or copying definitions out of the dictionary. By comparison, time-outs seemed downright reasonable.

"So was she mean to you because she was mad about you dancing with Mr. Duffy?"

Lucy nearly skidded to a stop in the middle of the road. "What?"

"Mama, you said I'm supposed to ask, 'Beg pardon?' instead of shout, 'WHAT?'" Sam laughed.

"I'm sorry," Lucy said calmly as she pressed the accelerator. "I beg your pardon?"

"Well, Denver said his mom said that you were slow-dancing with Mr. Duffy at the Sweethearts' Dance. What's that mean, Mama?"

"Um, it just means that I was dancing to a slow song with Mr. Duffy."

"Because you like him?"

"Yeah, honey, he's been my friend for a long time," Lucy said as she turned into their gravel drive. While she was pretty certain that she and Duffy would be dating sometime soon, she wasn't ready to bring that up with Sam yet. Everything she'd read said not to introduce men that you date into your children's lives for months, but he'd already met Duffy. So did that count? Would it be better not to tell Sam at all until they were sure this was going somewhere?

"Well, that's nice."

"I think so."

"'Cause he's on our porch," Sam said, pointing past the windshield to where Duffy sat on the porch step, his green baseball cap in his hands.

"Huh," Lucy muttered, pulling the truck to a stop in her dad's old parking spot. "Well, I didn't expect that."

Lucy waved as she slid out of the truck. Sam unbuckled his booster seat and threw himself into his mother's waiting arms in his haste to greet their visitor. "Did you bring Prince with you?"

"Not this time, buddy," Duffy called back as Lucy lugged the heavy grocery bags out of the backseat. Duffy met her on the sidewalk and took the bags out of her hands.

"Sweetheart, can you at least say hello to Mr. Duffy before asking about the dog?"

"Hi, Mr. Duffy, where's Prince?"

"He's at home with my grandma Tootie," Duffy said. "But he said hi."

"Prince can't talk."

"Oh, sure he can. He perked up his little ears and made this sad face because I was going to visit you without him."

"Can you bring him next time?"

"Uh, we'll have to talk to your mom and see what she says."

Lucy unlocked the front door and opened it for him. "Why don't you go inside and wash up for dinner?"

"Okay!" Sam said, running inside.

"Hi," she said as Duffy set the grocery bags inside the door. "Thank you for not bringing the dog. I've been filling out the massive amount of paperwork Marianne sent over, but I just want to make sure that Sam's ready for the responsibility. I don't want to send him mixed signals."

"Tootie will also perform a background check and possibly a home visit," he said.

"She does take this seriously." Lucy shuddered.

"I thought about bringing Prince with me, but then I realized that would be a major overstep," Duffy said. "And on that note, I wanted to bring you flowers, but I thought that would be a little noticeable for Sam. So I got you this instead."

He handed her a small purple gift bag with yellow tissue poking out of the top. She reached into the tissue and found a small plastic case with a dozen small metal cones, plus what looked like a set of brightly colored plastic sculpture tools.

"You got me icing tips and fondant tools?" she said, pressing her lips together in a gratified expression.

"The lady at the craft store said it was the set that all the cake decorators want. And that even if you already had them, most cake decorators drop at least one or two in their garbage disposal at some point, so you could need replacements."

"I have lost multiple tips to my garbage disposal," she said. "Also, it's awesome to have duplicates if you're working in different-colored icings. This is a very thoughtful gift. Nicely done, sir."

Lucy glanced over his shoulder and noticed that her shutters were no longer drooping. "Did you fix my shutters?"

"I may have," he admitted. "I figured it might be harder for you to lift them and fix them on your own. And I had the tools to tighten the bolts in my truck. And I was on your porch for a long time . . . That sounds creepy. I'm sorry. I'm not stalking you."

"That was very sweet of you. Thank you."

"Well, yeah. I'm courting you, Lucy Bowman. I'm gonna woo the hell out of you."

She laughed and threw her arms around his neck. For the first time in a long time, someone had done something nice for her, for no other reason than to make her life easier. "Thank you."

"So, I am officially asking you to go out on a planned outing with me this Friday. We will wear nice clothes, and we will have dinner that you don't have to cook."

"You have no idea the real value that has for me."

"I'm getting the idea that you're not ready for Sam to know we're going to be dating?"

"No, it just seems really soon."

"You're right. We'll take things slow there. I don't want to hurt your son, Lucy. No matter what."

"Well, we may not have a choice because he's already heard that we were 'slow-dancing' at the Sweethearts' Dance from the other kids at school."

"That's just the town gossip mill. You know how it goes. He'll hear a few things, and then someone else in town will do something stupid and they'll be talking about them instead."

"I'm not scared of the gossip, I'm afraid of what Evie might do with the gossip. It's not that I don't think you're worth it. Because I do. I'm just trying to be honest with you."

Duffy slipped his fingers into hers and squeezed. "I understand how it works, trust me. I'm the one who lived through my divorce here. I want you to tell me when you're worried about something. I don't want you to be alone in this."

Duffy's hand slipped away at the sound of thundering footsteps. Sam burst out through the door and threw his arms around his mother's leg. Lucy grinned up at him. "I'm never alone."

9

DUFFY'S DECISION TO go to the Rise and Shine for dinner had been a small act of rebellious self-preservation. Tootie had invited him over for fried fish and all the fixin's at her house, but he needed a little time to himself. And if he had to hear his grandma and Aunt Leslie's "if you put sugar in cornbread, that makes it cake" argument one more time, he'd lose his damn mind.

The Rise and Shine was a traditional diner with worn red vinyl booths and a shiny black-and-white checkerboard tile floor. The jukebox in the corner played exclusively classic country-western like Hank Williams Sr. and Patsy Cline. The race car–themed pinball machines had stood sentinel by the bathrooms for decades.

He spotted several friends as he made his way to his usual booth—George Pritchett, who'd recently been widowed and begun taking all of his meals at the diner, and Dobb Cunningham, who chose to take all of his meals at the diner because he could burn water. He nodded at them and waved. Lana was sitting at the counter, giggling with the very married Gig McHale over a plate of cheese fries. She tossed her hair back as she laughed, something that she did when she was interested in a new guy.

"Hi, Duffy," she said when she saw him, her tone cool and indifferent, which was something else she did when she was interested in a new guy.

So it would appear that they were back to acquaintance mode. He shook his head, sliding into his usual booth in the back. He perused the menu, as if Ike Grandy hadn't served the same food since his family opened the diner in the 1960s, and as if Duffy hadn't been placing the same order since he was twelve—Coke, patty melt, no tomato, with tater tots. He glanced up at a familiar face one booth over.

"Marianne?" he cried.

Marianne jerked, halfway through a bite of her cheese-burger, and whipped her head toward her brother. Her mouth was full of bun as she exclaimed, "Duffy!"

"What are you doing here?" he asked. "I thought you and Margot had book club tonight. You made such a big deal about it being a bonding activity."

"Well, I went three times and hated it. It turns out that I love reading. I hate listening to other people's opinions about what I read. But I liked having a Tuesday night all to myself. I mean, I love Carl and the boys more than anything, but sometimes the noise and the constant interruptions and the smell—dear sweet baby Jesus in the manger, the smell of the socks when they're combined in the laundry room is enough to choke a horse . . . I'm getting off track. There's something to be said for just a few precious hours of alone time, is all. So I come here and read a book and have a hot meal, onion rings I don't have to share, and some blessed quiet."

Duffy stared at her for a long silent moment.

She pressed her lips together in a sheepish expression. "Please don't tell Carl."

"Of all the secrets you have told me, that is the saddest."

"Oh, please, like I don't know you and Carl are just drinking beer every Thursday when you're supposedly rebuilding that old truck," she said, her color and her gumption returning all at once.

"In our defense, we *were* rebuilding the truck. But then we got stalled a couple of weeks back when an eBay seller failed to deliver on an alternator. We were afraid you would join another book club for Thursdays if we stopped meeting up every week, because you were so damn enthusiastic about going out every Tuesday. So we've been working on Lucy's display cases. If we knew then what I know now . . ."

"Well, my point is that I knew about your little Thursday ritual and I didn't say anything, because I know that Carl needs his time away from me and the boys, just as much as I need my time."

"Then why don't you just tell Carl that you quit the book club and you're hanging out alone at the diner like some weirdo?" he asked, sitting down across the table from her.

"Because I don't want to tell him I need time away from him and hurt his feelings!" she said, shaking her head at him. "Carl may know he needs time away from me and I need time away from him, but saying it out loud would be mean."

Duffy shook his head. "I do not get married people."

"You say that because you spent so little time being married," she said, nodding toward Lana at the counter.

"Hey, keep the gloves above the belt."

"Sorry, that *was* mean," she admitted, lowering her voice and glancing at Lana. "So . . . Frankie says you and Lucy are officially courting. You fixed her shutters and everything. And that's not even a euphemism."

"Is there no privacy in this family? Have you been going through my texts? Did Frankie put some sort of spyware on my computer?"

"Well, that's a possibility, but no, we got our gossip the old-fashioned way. Lucy told Frankie, who told me."

Duffy felt oddly proud that Lucy had told people about their plans before he had. "And you don't have anything more interesting to talk about than courtship and shutter repair?"

"Something more interesting than getting you involved in a mature, emotionally healthy relationship as opposed to you falling victim to the walking Hellmouth on a weekly basis? I am confident there is nothing more dear to the female McCready hearts. Tootie made a vision board."

Duffy shuddered. "Change of subject. Did Mama tell you that Tootie finally saved up enough to send them off on their big cruise?"

"Really?" she said as Ike slid Duffy's patty melt in front of him.

"And she booked the damn thing. Thanks, Ike," Duffy said. Ike winked at Marianne and put a chocolate malt in front of her.

"So E.J.J. can't get out of it, huh?" Marianne marveled, sipping her malt. "I never thought I'd see the day. And no, Mama didn't tell me, because I'm not speaking to our mother right now."

"Again? What set her off this time?"

Marianne rolled her eyes, much in the way she used to when she was fighting with their mom as a teenager. "What always sets her off? I opened my mouth and sound came out."

"Did you give her advice again?"

"I never give her advice. I know better than that. I just mentioned that Fred Dodge asked after her and that I thought it was cute that they were still pretending not to like each other after all these years, when they were clearly sweet on each other. And it was like I tossed a match into a barrel filled with Dawson family hooch. *Fwoom!*"

"But she and Fred Dodge *are* sweet on each other, have been for years. They are the Sam and Diane of Lake Sackett. It's obvious to everybody but them."

"Yeah, well, she said something about me disrespecting Daddy's memory by suggesting she could ever be with someone besides Daddy. She said I might as well go to his grave and dance on it."

"She didn't say anything about peeing on it, right? Because that's what she says when she says I've betrayed Dad's memory."

Marianne grimaced. "No, but I have a feeling that this particular nuclear fallout will last a while. She hung up on me. And then mailed me her phone bits, just to emphasize that she was so mad at me that she smashed her cell."

"Well, that's healthy."

"I just don't know how to relate to her anymore without screaming. Somehow you always manage it."

"Oh, no, there's screaming, but I'm smart enough not to keep poking at her after the screaming starts, which is where we're different."

"I know, I can't seem to stop. It's compulsive. I'm sure Freud would say it has something to do with missing Daddy and resenting Mama for still being alive."

"No, y'all started this long before Dad died. I'm pretty sure that you started bickering when you were still in her belly."

"That's probably true," she said. "So, to review, Mama's pissed at me, Tootie and E.J.J. are off to Aruba . . . what else is happening in the family?"

"Kyle's still trying to wrestle Margot down the aisle," Duffy volunteered.

She shook her head. "Still no date set yet."

"Wow, that's got to sting for Kyle."

"I can't blame her. Tootie made more than one vision board. The 'Margot's wedding' board had glitter," Marianne said. "A lot of glitter."

"Well, that's not good."

"Maybe we can throw Frankie at the vision board as a sort of sacrificial lamb? Get Eric to propose? Surely Frankie owes Margot some sort of favor by now."

"Getting married to a guy that she's only been dating for a few months seems like a little more than a favor," Duffy said.

"Maybe this cruise is coming at just the right time to distract her," Marianne mused, sipping on her shake. "So does this mean that E.J.J. is retiring?"

"That's always been the idea."

"Kind of feels like an ending, which, with our family business, is considerable," Marianne said, frowning. "You know George is thinking about retiring? Which would put me out of a job. Frankly, I think the only reason that he's held on practicing as long as he has is because he wanted to keep me working, but the man is damn near eighty."

Duffy sat back in his booth. Even with the town's economic downturn, the McCreadys had never faced unemployment. While the marina had slowed some, death was a recession-proof business.

"Carl says I don't have to work if I don't want to, the garage is doing much better since he bought that second tow truck. But I don't know, I don't think I could be a stay-at-home mom. There's nothing wrong with it, but I love to work. I love having somewhere to go every day and having adults to talk to."

"You could always go back to law school. The town's gonna need a lawyer if George is retiring . . . and Frankie is still living here."

"It's an idea. With the tourists coming back and businesses opening up again . . . yeah, the picture's brighter around here. And the kids are able to be left alone for an hour or so without fires or pestilence breaking out. Well, Aiden is, anyway."

"You know that Leslie and Bob and any number of relatives, including me, will be willing to watch your kids if it means you can go to law school. I won't even joke about tying them up or stashing them in the closet."

For a brief moment, an excited smile broke over Marianne's face, but then she shook her head. "But law school's so expensive. I'd have to take out loans and that's not fair to the boys. They're the ones with college coming up in a few years. I had my chance and I decided not to go. I don't regret it. I've loved every minute of being married and having kids. So isn't it sort of a betrayal to go back on that now?"

"Marianne, honey, do you love the law?" Duffy asked. "All the weird legal puzzles that you get to solve digging through dusty old books?"

"Well, we mostly use Westlaw archives on a computer, but yes."

Duffy frowned at her insistent detail-picking. "So if you love it, you should go after it."

"I really hate it when you're right and get to play the wiser brother," she said, sighing. "And yet, you don't get to do it very often, so I guess I'll have to put up with it."

"Damn straight."

"Are you going to tell Carl about my secret one-person cheeseburger club?" she asked.

"No, far be it from me to mess around in other people's marriages."

"Yeah, leave that to your ex-wife," Marianne said, nodding again toward the counter, where Lana was still flirting heavily. It was humiliating for Duffy to realize it didn't even hurt or surprise him anymore. He'd seen this cycle play out so many times, he knew exactly how it would end. Gig would promise her the world. Lana would give him a little piece of her heart. And then he would fail to deliver and Lana would end up on his doorstep with Maybelline Great Lash streaking down her cheeks.

And Duffy was just so tired of it. He didn't want to be the one to prop her up. He didn't want to devote hours to cheering her up when he knew he was just going to have to do it all over again in a few weeks. It wasn't good for him or Lana and it would kill any chances he had with Lucy. It was time to let Lana go. It was time for him to develop a little dignity. But his sister didn't need to know that, because the "I told you so's" would be loud and plentiful and probably set to a gospel choir.

"Easy," he told Marianne.

"Yes, I've said so, several times. But you married her anyway."

"Not okay, Marianne. Not okay."

LUCY SWIRLED ONE last swoop of dark chocolate frosting on the devil's food cupcake. She wanted to perfect her ratios before the opening. Cupcakes were deceptively tricky. Underbake them and they were gross. Overbake them and they were dry and stuck to the inside of the throat like angry lint. Too much frosting made the treats oversweet and noxious, not enough made them underwhelming and sort of sad.

"Hey!" Duffy called, opening the front door of the shop, the glass flashing in the late-afternoon light. "I brought the shelves and cabinetwork by for you to see them."

"Hi!" she cried, rounding the counter and wiping her hands on her bacon-themed apron.

Duffy was putting those considerable arm muscles into carrying short, narrow shelves painted white through the door. She planned to install several of them around the café area and line them with glass jars filled with sprinkles and nonpareils and Jordan almonds, anything colorful and edible. Additional shelves would be installed in the kitchen to store her cake stands and more architectural pans in a pleasing display.

"Oh, they're great!" she exclaimed. "The paint job is all finished. We should probably let it cure for a day or two more before hanging them."

"One more thing!" he said, jogging back out to his truck.

Several minutes later, he wheeled in a dolly-load of varnished maple trim that almost looked like crown molding. He had a tool belt around his hips.

Duffy in a tool belt. *Holy hell.*

It took him no time at all to build a frame around the case, screwing the boards together at the corners. It looked polished and professional and when she hung the shelves and the frames, the shop would be complete.

"Thank you," Lucy said with a sigh, throwing her arms around Duffy's neck. "I really appreciate this."

He smiled down at her and she awkwardly slid her arms away from him.

"So you're almost ready, huh?"

"The opening is in two weeks, thanks to an anonymous yet effective force that pushed my paperwork through the approval process with the county." She gestured toward the wall, where her business license and tax ID were proudly displayed. "Everything except the health department, which is supposed to be coming soon. I'm hoping that 'soon' means 'next week.'"

"The Lord and small-town bureaucracy work in mysterious ways."

"And yet, somehow, I think you had something to do with it," she said.

"So no Specs today?"

"Yeah, he's been coming in to help out with the prep work, but he had to take off early for an eye appointment. Apparently he has to go through an 'annual' exam every six months," she said, frowning. "They've written in medical journals about him."

"Well, Stan wanted to tell you how tickled he is that you've given Specs a job. He's a real good man. He just needed the chance to prove himself."

"I'm happy to. He's got the talent for baking and he's been a huge help to me," she said. "I'm looking forward to Friday."

"Good! Good. Good. Good. Good. Good," he said, nodding. "That was a lot of 'goods,' wasn't it?"

She laughed, pressing her lips together. "Yes, it was. Are you nervous about our date?"

"I wouldn't say nervous, because that sort of implies that I'm dreading something. I mean, I get nervous about going to the dentist or paying taxes. And I'm definitely looking forward to our date a lot more than paying taxes."

"That's good to know."

Duffy sighed. "None of this is coming out right."

Lucy gently twisted her fingers into the neckline of Duffy's T-shirt and pulled him close. She pressed her lips to his and he seemed to melt around her, pushing her back against the glass of the unframed display case. His large hands bracketed her hips and squeezed lightly. She moaned as he nibbled along her jaw, pressing her earlobe between his teeth.

"I'm really looking forward to our date, too," she whispered in his ear. "And I'm a little nervous, but considering that kiss, I think we're going to be okay."

"Don't suppose I could have another one?"

"Just one more," she said, planting a kiss on him. "And then you have to leave, because I have to go pick up Sam from school."

Duffy poked out his bottom lip, which she kissed one last

time. She reached over the counter and presented him with a freshly frosted cupcake. "But I will give you this, to make up for rewarding this lovely cabinetry by tossing you out."

He took a bite of the cupcake, groaning.

"It's devil's food cake. It's your favorite."

"Now, this is good. I mean, mind-alteringly good," he said, licking frosting from his lips in a way that made her want to help him out. "But it's not my favorite anymore."

"What? I once saw you stuff two Hostess cupcakes into your cheeks because they were the last ones in the box and you were afraid Marianne would take them. You looked like a damn chipmunk."

"Well, people change over time, Lucy. My palate has become much more sophisticated."

Her eyes narrowed. "So what's your favorite now? German chocolate? Coconut? Ugh, please tell me it's not something involving raisins. Raisins are the worst."

His nose scrunched up as he considered. "Nope. I think it would benefit me more to let you try to guess."

He leaned forward and kissed her, the chocolate frosting making his lips all the sweeter.

"You know how hard it is for me to turn down a challenge!" she cried as he gathered his tools and backed out the door.

He grinned at her. "Yes, I do."

"I am going to make you so many cakes to try to figure this out," she growled.

He waggled his eyebrows. "Yes, I know. See you Friday."

She laughed, shaking her fist at him. "See you Friday."

10

DUFFY DUCKED DOWN in front of the tiny mirror in his proportionately small bedroom. He held up a hanger full of already knotted neckties in front of his chest, trying to figure out which one looked best with his blue-and-white checked shirt. He had a solid navy one, a green-and-red plaid number he wore every Christmas, and a dark tan one with little mallard ducks printed on it.

He frowned. None of them suited. And he wasn't sure he was supposed to wear a tie on this sort of date, but he wanted to make an effort for Lucy. Maybe he had time to run to the general store to buy another one before he picked her up?

"Knock knock!"

"Come in!" Duffy called. He turned to see Margot poke her head through the front door to his cabin. "Hey!"

"Hi, Duff." Margot stepped in and grinned at him. "Oh, you look so cute! You trimmed your beard and everything!"

Duffy swept his hand self-consciously through his shortened

beard. "Yeah, well, it's a special occasion and I didn't want to go out looking like Grizzly Adams."

"You'd be surprised how many women have a fixation for that sort of thing," she said breezily, crossing the room and taking the hanger full of ties from him. "Where are your other ties?"

"These are all of my ties."

"You only have three?"

"Margot, honey, I'd like to think we've got to the point in our relationship where you understand that I don't run across a lot of 'tie' occasions."

"Okay, fine." She sighed, taking the blue tie off the hanger and untying it.

"Hey! I worked hard on that knot!" he cried. "A few months ago."

Margot lifted her brow as she flipped his collar up. "Please."

Margot's deft hands whipped the fabric around his neck and tied a sharp square Windsor knot.

"There, that looks nice. Don't go to the general store to get another one," she told him.

He narrowed his eyes. "You don't know everything."

"It's adorable that you think that." She patted his chest. "It really is."

"So what brings you by? Besides harassing me over my accessories?"

"Frankie said that Lucy is going to be doing wedding cakes at her bakery. And if her cake balls are any indication, she'll be a much tastier alternative than, say, ordering my cake at the bulk price store in Alton."

"I would hope so."

"Well, I was hoping that you would ask her if she would

be willing to do a tasting sometime? And give her my cell number?"

"Why don't you just call her? I can give you her number."

"Two reasons: One, so she can say no if she doesn't want to do it. And two, if she does want to do it, you're the guy who delivered her the good news and gets to talk to her about all of her exciting plans. Women love that. It's instant awkward-first-date conversation balm."

"You're a truly devious person," he told her.

"Not as devious as Frankie, but far less likely to end up in jail."

"There are times when I wonder if that's the whole reason she's dating Eric," Duffy said.

Margot waggled her dark-blond brows. "That's not the only reason, trust me."

"I don't want to think about that. Just let me have my illusions," he said.

She laughed, giving him a hug. Margot wasn't much of a hugger, so he took full advantage of the familial affection, squeezing her tight. She sniffled as she leaned away from him, still encircled in his arms.

"I hope you have a really good time tonight, Duff. Lucy's a sweetheart. And you deserve someone nice like her." Her eyes shimmered with unshed tears. "I just get so sad, thinking about you all alone in this little cabin, with no one to talk to. You don't even have one of the dogs!"

Duffy cringed as the tears broke free and rolled down Margot's cheeks. "What is happening here? I've never seen you cry before. I'm not sure what to do."

"I don't know, either!" Margot squeaked, hugging Duffy

again but carefully keeping her tear-streaked face away from his good shirt. He awkwardly patted her back as she pulled out a fancy handkerchief she just happened to have in her suit pocket and dabbed at her cheeks. She was prepared for anything, his cousin. Except for, apparently, the emotional strain of helping him get ready for a date night.

"Hey, Sweet Tea, you about ready for me to run you to Kyle's?"

He never thought he would say this, but he was very grateful his uncle Stan lived so close. Stan's jaw may have dropped at the sight of his polished, poised daughter weeping delicately into Duffy's shoulder, but he immediately crossed the room and pried Margot loose from Duffy's neck and transferred the tearful burden to his own shoulder. "It's okay, baby. Just cry it out."

"I don't know what's wrong," Duffy said. "One minute she was fine, and the next she was boo-hooing."

"I just got so sad, thinking of Duffy living in this tiny place, all alone. It's just so sad! So very, very sad!"

"Easy," Duffy told her.

"The hormones are just sending a bunch of messages to your brain all at once. It happens all the time with pregnant women. Your mama was a leaky watering pot the whole time she was expecting you," Stan told her. "Hell, Donna cried for two days over dropping a bag of rice on the floor."

"Really?" Duffy said, shuddering.

"Well, your mama was way less intimidating in those days," Stan said. "How about I take Margot home and you go pick up some flowers for your gal?"

Duffy cringed. "Flowers?"

"I left some in a little vase in your fridge." Margot sniffed.

"Lucy seems to like purple and that goes well with blue, so I got you some delphiniums and hydrangea."

"You're a life-sav— Wait, did you sneak flowers out of the funeral arrangements to make my date a bouquet?" Duffy asked.

"No comment," Margot said.

Stan shook his head. "Honey, that's not right."

"It was just the ones that the Burtons didn't take home," Margot told her father as he walked her out of the cabin. "We were going to compost them anyway. Good night, Duffy!"

"Good night!" Duffy called.

"Don't go to the general store to buy another tie!" she yelled from outside.

"She does know everything," he grumbled.

DUFFY TRIED NOT to run up the stairs to Lucy's house, because that would seem scary. He knocked and could hear the cheerful music of some kids' show through the door. She opened it, wearing a dark blue knit dress that knew the curves of her in ways that he wished his hands could. Her hair flowed around her shoulders in waves. And she was wearing lip stuff that made her mouth all shiny and peachy.

"Wow," he murmured. "I thought the red dress was nice, but . . . wow."

"Thanks," she said, smiling, but suddenly her face fell. "I'm sorry. Marianne just called. Nate and Aiden have been throwing up since they stepped off the school bus this afternoon. The whole school has a vicious stomach bug going around. And these things never stay contained within one school. That means my child has probably been exposed to some sort of virus that will turn him inside out *Alien* style within the next few hours. He's already getting pale and his temperature is up to ninety-nine point five, which means my stop on the vomit express is swiftly approaching."

"Okay," he said, shrugging out of his jacket and stepping into the house.

"Which means I can't go out tonight," she said, her brows furrowing. "Because there are laws against child abandonment."

"Okay," he said, handing her the bouquet. "These are for you. You should probably put them in some water."

"Thanks, they're really pretty," she said, her tone even more confused as he walked over to the old beige couch, where Sam was draped listlessly across one of the corners. His eyes were closed as he dozed against the arm of the sofa. He had a ragged blue baby quilt tucked under his chin and his skin was indeed pale and cheesy-looking.

"You need Popsicles or Jell-O or anything?" he asked. "Marianne keeps the boys in a constant orange-red-purple Popsicle rotation when one of them's sick. She says it's the only way to get fluids into them. I can run to the store if you need me to."

She stopped and smiled, her eyes a little glassy. "Yes, I have a freezer full of Popsicles. I also happen to have a batch of lemon meringue bars boxed up in the kitchen, since I thought we weren't exchanging flowers. And I'm pretty sure those are your favorite. But considering they've been here in the red zone, you may want to burn them or throw them into the lake to avoid contamination."

"Well, I'm sure I would have loved every virus-covered bite, but lemon meringue bars aren't my favorite."

"What!" she whispered. "You bought an entire tray of them at the senior bake sale!"

"Well, yeah, because you were selling the lemon meringue bars. And I wanted you to sell out before anybody else, as a point of pride. I took them home to my family and we ate them for days. They were delicious, but they weren't my favorite."

"I will figure this out," she told him.

"And I will look forward to it," he told her, sitting on the couch.

"Why are you settling in?" Lucy asked, the flowers still in her hand.

"Because, as long as it's all right with you, I plan on staying and helping you take care of Sam. Marianne always looks like the walking dead when she's done taking care of the boys in a stomach flu war, and not in the fun zombie kind of way. And that's with Carl helping her. I don't want you doing this alone."

"You can't mean that," she told him, her brown eyes bottomless and wide. "There is no more horrifying part of parenting than the stomach flu. We're talking endless cups of flat Sprite, constant washing of soiled sheets and pajamas, and if we're lucky, we'll only have to watch the same Pixar movie twelve times."

"Will it be easier if I'm here, or harder?" he asked.

"How easily do you throw up?" she asked. "Because if you have a sympathetic vomiting thing going, I am not taking care of two patients."

"I'll be fine, I promise. Remember, I have two adorable but disgusting nephews."

She laughed and plucked at her skirt. "Do you mind if I go change? Because this is more of an overalls-and-hairnet situation. Maybe even safety goggles."

"I have some in my truck," he said. "I'll yell if he wakes up."

"Okay, thank you," she said, bolting toward the hallway Duffy knew led to the bedrooms. The house hadn't changed much since Pete Bowman lived there. The same worn but clean furniture, the same lamp shaped like a leaping bass, the old brick fireplace that rarely got used in the Georgia heat but looked nice at Christmas. Lucy had cleaned the place down to the bone, and he could see the touches she'd added to make it more "her." A bright blue rag rug covered the threadbare carpet. Framed pictures of Lucy, Sam, and Wayne were hung artfully on the walls in configurations that Marianne would have described as "Pinterest-y."

It was sobering to be reminded of Wayne, in this moment, sitting in a living room with his son, thinking of Wayne's wife as his date. But Lucy said she was ready, and he had to trust her word. What sort of man would claim to love a woman but not believe she knew her own mind?

And he loved Lucy—not just the puppy love he'd known in school, when she'd been one of the only non-blood-related girls he could talk to without making an absolute doofus out of himself. As he'd come to know this new adult Lucy over the last few weeks, he'd come to love everything about her that was new yet familiar. He loved that she'd managed to grow and become fiercer and funnier, and still remain the sweet person who made very small pot holders for everybody she knew in a failed attempt to learn how to knit.

The question was, how did she feel, and how would he fit into her life if she let him? Maybe he shouldn't have been so insistent on staying. Maybe her refusals weren't just polite. What if he was being intrusive and weird? But it sort of felt like he was committed at this point.

He heard Sam stirring to his left, unearthing himself from the blue quilt. His face had taken on a sort of pea soup cast and there seemed to be sweat dotting his upper lip.

"Hey, Sam, your mom is down the hall. You want me to get her?"

"I don't feel so good, Mr. Duff." Sam moaned while crawling to his knees and inching toward Duffy.

"I know, buddy."

"I think I'm gonna—" He leaned over and promptly threw up in Duffy's lap. Duffy's eyes went wide, but he bit his lip to keep from shouting or doing anything that would frighten Sam, who had already burst into tears.

"Uh, Lucy. We've got a situation in here," he whisper-yelled, patting Sam's back awkwardly and trying so hard not to shudder at the sight of his pant legs.

Lucy emerged from the hallway dressed in an old Braves T-shirt and yoga pants. Her hair was out of its fancy style and wound into a loose bun on top of her head.

"And so it begins," Lucy intoned, sounding very much like Gandalf at the beginning of the War of the Ring.

LUCY HAD NOT been exaggerating about the bottomless cups of Sprite. Just after Sam had sicked up, Lucy had moved her son to the bathroom with expert swiftness, calling, "You can throw your jeans in the laundry!" as she started the shower. It sounded like she'd set up a sort of human car wash situation and had Sam washed, dried, and in a fresh set of jammies within a few minutes.

Fortunately, Duffy had spare clothes out in the truck, in case of fish guts, and wasn't forced to wear another pair of Lucy's yoga pants. And he'd managed to find the upholstery cleaner under the sink and defunk the couch before anything set.

The next few hours became a blur of Popsicles and temperature checks and Technicolor gastric issues. (The damn Popsicles.) Just when he thought maybe they had it handled, Sam's fever would spike or he would go from comfortable to crying and miserable within seconds. While Duffy wasn't sick himself, he did feel like he'd been hit with the business end of a backhoe.

Sometime around midnight, when he'd originally thought he and Lucy might be wrapping up their evening, Duffy dozed off on the couch and his head dipped back so hard that he jerked awake. The credits to one of the *Shrek* movies were scrolling down the screen.

Lucy was sprawled against the opposite side of the couch, her hair coming loose from its bun in chunks and her mouth slightly open. Sam was standing beside her, tugging on the sleeve of her T-shirt.

Duffy sat up, rubbing his hands over his eyes. "Hey, your mama's finally getting some sleep, so why don't we just let her stay that way, okay?"

"I don't feel good," Sam grumbled.

"I know, buddy."

"But I don't think I'm gonna throw up again."

"Well, that's a relief. Because I only have the one extra pair of pants."

"Can I have some Gatorade?" Sam asked.

"Sure thing."

Duffy stood and reached for the pitcher on the kitchen counter, which contained a perfectly blended mix of water and sports drink that only moms could calculate for maximum hydration without sugar overload.

"I'm sorry I threw up on you, Mr. Duff," Sam said as Duffy sat on the couch and handed him his dinosaur cup with the lid and special brontosaurus-head straw.

"That's okay."

"Twice," Sam added, clambering across the couch to lean against Duffy's arm.

"That's okay, too."

Sam's breath, frankly, was awful. But Duff pushed his sweaty hair back from his forehead, which was feeling considerably cooler than it had a few hours before. But he reached for the ear thermometer and gently tucked it into Sam's ear canal. It read 100.2, which was a considerable improvement from the spikes they'd seen earlier that night.

"I like that one better than the other thermometer," Sam said. "I always talked while it was in my mouth and Mama would make this face." Sam bent his features into a caricature of an irritated, stressed adult.

Duffy nodded. "That seems about right."

The boy settled into his side and lodged his head against Duffy's ribs.

"Can we watch *Up* again?" Sam asked.

Duffy sighed. The first ten minutes of that movie were an emotional beating, but Sam loved the bits with the talking dogs. "Sure."

He ran his hand over Sam's hair while they watched the damn balloon movie for the umpteenth time. He found he wasn't scared off by the idea of spending his evenings this way. Dealing with a stomach flu wasn't exactly a picnic, but he'd seen far more disgusting sights at the marina. Hell, he'd watched grown men, green with seasickness, throw up more off the side of his boat. And then there was that incident when Frankie went a little too far with the haunted house special effects for the elementary school. But this wasn't so bad. Sam was a bright kid, and funny and inquisitive. And he didn't seem to dislike Duffy, which was always a good way to start.

But holy hell, he didn't know if he could watch old Carl lose Ellie one more time without throwing up himself.

He was very grateful that Sam drifted off to sleep before the hill scene. He leaned his head back against the couch and let the sweet relief of changing the DVD to *Cars* wash over him.

On the opposite side of their couch-shaped life raft, Lucy gasped and her head shot up. For a moment, he saw panic in her eyes at not knowing where she was and what was happening, where Sam was. She scanned her surroundings until she spotted her son curled against Duffy's side, and her expression instantly relaxed.

"It's okay," Duffy whispered. "He's fine. I checked his temp a couple of minutes ago, it's one hundred point two."

She nodded. "I'm sorry I nodded off. I'm usually a little bit better at standing guard."

"Well, you've been working your buns off to open the bakery, not to mention taking care of Sam. You were due a nap."

"Thanks," she said, leaning her head back. "And I see what you did there with your bad pun."

He snickered, which made Sam mumble and burrow his face into Duffy's T-shirt.

"Thank you," she said. "For staying with me. I'm not used to that."

"I didn't mind," he said. "I mean, it's not something I'd want to do once a week, but kids throw up. In my limited experience, that's part of who they are, being gross little monsters, mixed in with moments where they're little angels so you're not overwhelmed with the urge to toss them out of a moving car."

"I've spent hundreds of dollars on parenting books and not one of them managed to define the experience as well as you just did."

"I learned a lot watching Marianne. Lord knows those boys put her through her paces. Did you know that a three-year-old can swallow a boat key?"

"No, I did not."

"Well, Aiden did," Duffy told her. "Twice."

She pulled a face. "I hope it wasn't the same boat key."

"Come to think of it, I didn't ask."

"So, this is my life," she told him. "Behold the glamour."

"Because my life is nothing but red-carpet galas and soirees on my yacht," he told her. "Lucy, I'm not going anywhere just 'cause things get difficult."

"You say that because Mamaw Evie doesn't know about us yet."

"And I'll stick around for that, too. I've lived with or near Donna McCready for decades. Mamaw Evie is an amateur."

"That may be true," she said, reaching for her cell phone, which was on the end table. "Why did Margot send me a text saying that if I find a price tag on your tie from the general store, I am to burn it immediately?"

"It's a long story," he said. "My cousin thinks she is all-knowing and all-seeing."

"She *is* all-knowing. I never gave her my cell number."

"I'm sure someone did," he said. "I'm surprised she doesn't need an extra phone just to keep her contact list. Oh, also, she wanted to know if you would be interested in making her wedding cake."

Lucy gasped. "Really?"

"She said no pressure, but she'd be happy to work with you, if you're interested. I think it was the cake balls that did it."

"I would love to! I've only made a few wedding cakes for friends. But they're an awesome challenge."

"What exactly happens at a cake tasting?" he asked, remembering that his mother had given him and Lana the choice of chocolate or white sheet cake for their quickie wedding, and that was it.

"I make a bunch of cakes and fillings in different flavor combinations and she—and probably Kyle, he seems like an involved guy—taste all of them to see which one they want at their wedding."

"How many combinations?"

"I usually do ten or so. The classics, the standard white cake and white frosting, chocolate with raspberry filling, and so forth. Some brides are really traditional and want to keep things simple. And then I'll throw in some crazy combinations like peanut butter cake with grape jelly filling or banana cake with chocolate."

"How do I get invited?"

Lucy grinned. "Keep being nice to me."

L UCY FINISHED THE last touches on her third coat of Seaside Lavender around the white chalkboard frame, the final decorative touch in the seating area of Gimme Some Sugar. The color scheme and the cabinetry really brightened up the space, made it look bigger and more inviting. She grinned, doing a happy little spin on the recently installed white tile floor. She could just see it, all decorated up with pretty iced cakes filling the maple display cases and people seated at the wrought iron café tables.

She wished her father were there to see it, too. He would have gotten such a kick out of her owning her own business, doing what she loved. But Duffy had promised to bring the entire McCready clan to buy her out on opening day, which was scheduled for the next week. And that would be almost as good.

Sam had recovered fully from his bout of flu, bolstered by FaceTiming the Dawson boys, who were similarly stricken. The

Archer girls managed to remain unscathed, because as Mr. Archer put it, "Margot basically installed an airlock on the house when she heard about the flu going around." The girls were so hopped up on vitamin C they felt superhuman. But the student population was slowly bouncing back from the plague and that was all anybody could ask for.

Duffy's willingness to deal with the nasty parts of life with a kid was weirdly attractive. And he didn't seem to expect praise heaped on him for doing something as simple as getting Sam a glass of water when she was up to her elbows in vomit laundry. Which was a nice change of pace. He'd spent more time in the ugly trenches of parenthood over the weekend than Wayne had in the first two years of Sam's life.

"Stop comparing," she muttered. "It's not healthy. Also, stop talking to yourself. Double unhealthy."

It was difficult not to compare and contrast her experiences with her late husband and Duffy. She didn't feel the pressure to keep Duffy happy, to keep him interested. He was interested in every little thing about her. When she told him about her day, he was engaged. He wasn't just waiting for her to finish talking so he could look at his phone or tell her something about himself. They'd officially rescheduled their date for the coming Wednesday, when Sam would be having a sleepover at the Dawsons'. And Duffy assured her that he had "big plans" and she would be dazzled.

A knock at the bakery's front door caught her attention. Lucy glanced through the door to find a short, squatty man with a shiny bald head and thick mustache standing on the sidewalk. Her mouth pressed into a thin, angry line and she yanked the door open.

Herb Brewster had been balding as long as anybody had known him. Her daddy had said his hairline had started receding in elementary school, but she'd always thought he was kidding. Pete Bowman couldn't stand the man, but mostly because Herb rooted for the St. Louis Cardinals, which Pete had considered a betrayal of the Braves and human decency. Herb was wearing a name badge from the Sackett County Health Department and carrying a clipboard.

"Mr. Brewster, how nice to *finally* see you," Lucy seethed.

"Good morning, Mrs. Garten. I'm Herb Brewster. I'm an inspector for the county health department."

"Mr. Brewster, I've known you since I was a baby. I think you can call me Lucy."

"I've found it's easier if I stick to the proper forms of egress when I'm acting in an official capacity."

"Do you mean 'address,' Mr. Brewster?" she asked, realizing she'd forgotten about Mr. Brewster's little "quirk." Emmaline Brewster had given her son a word-of-the-day calendar for Christmas every year since he was ten. He'd made a bad habit of reading the words on the calendar, but never the definitions.

Mr. Brewster frowned at her. "No. Now, would you like to discuss why I'm here this morning?"

"I assumed it was the appointment for my licensing inspection, which you have rescheduled so many times I've lost track."

"No, I've had some complaints about the cleanliness of your shop and multiple health code violations that could lead to illness and injury for your customers," Mr. Brewster said. "Infraction one, you haven't received certification and approval from the health department."

"I've been calling to schedule an inspection appointment

with your office for weeks. And all I could get from your receptionist was that you would respond 'soon.'"

"That's no excuse, Mrs. Garten."

"Yeah, that makes sense," Lucy said dryly. "But I'm not open yet. How can I be in violation of the health code if I haven't even sold anything to the public? Anything I made for the Sweethearts' Dance was served and sold under Leslie McCready's licensing."

"Yes, and I understand you baked a cake in the shape of a human phallus for Maddie Paxton's bachelorette party?"

Lucy sighed. She was never going to speak to Maddie Paxton again.

"Yes, but I wasn't paid for that cake. It was a favor for a friend, which is really none of your business. Just like if I'd baked a cake in my kitchen for a friend's party, it would be none of your business."

"If you'd baked a cake in your kitchen for a friend's party and someone at that party got sick, it would be my business. And we'd be having this same conversation."

Lucy's jaw dropped. "Did anyone get sick?"

"No."

"Then I really don't get the point of all this," she said, shaking her head.

Mr. Brewster frowned at her, and he looked . . . familiar in a way, like she'd been seeing that expression for years, but not on Mr. Brewster's face. And suddenly, Lucy remembered that Herb was distantly related to Evie's family on their mothers' side.

This was the problem with small towns. Sometimes the people who had authority were related to assholes.

Mr. Brewster squinted at his clipboard and then glanced around the shop. "I understand you've hired Specs Foyle as your assistant."

"Again, what's your point?"

"I'm sure you know that Mr. Foyle has a reputation for having loose moral fiber in this town."

"Loose moral what?"

"He's not exactly the kind of character I would think a mother of an irrepressible child would want to spend time with."

"You mean impressionable? Meaning I wouldn't want my *impressionable* child to be exposed to Mr. Foyle's moral irregularity?"

"I'm just saying, Mrs. Garten, that if you want to run a business that provides a service for the public, don't be surprised if your customers don't want to be served by a person whose character is in question," Mr. Webster said with a sniff.

"Unless hiring someone with a clean criminal record and no other marks against them is some sort of punishable offense, I suggest you move on, Mr. Webster."

Mr. Webster's rheumy blue eyes narrowed at her as he reached into his pockets for a pair of white cotton gloves.

This was going to be a long damn morning.

The inspection was painstakingly thorough. Mr. Brewster literally gave her cabinets, counters, and appliances the white-glove treatment. He measured the temperature of her fridge and docked her points for being one degree *too* cold. He tried to deduct points for not dating/marking her flour and sugar containers. And when she showed that she'd painstakingly marked every container in her pantry with a start date on a removable label system, that he was simply looking at the wrong side of the containers, he insisted on the deduction until she dialed the first six digits of George Pritchett's law office number.

Specs came in at his usual time to find Lucy standing, hands on hips, in the kitchen, looking like she was about to smack Herb Brewster over the head with one of her heaviest cake pans. One of the sixteen-inch wedding cake pans ought to do it.

"Mr. Brewster, my dishwasher is not 'suspiciously clean.' It's just in good working order and we sanitize it regularly. Now, I've tolerated your rudeness and your nitpicking, but this is getting out of hand. I'm FoodSafe Certified, and I worked in kitchens for years in college and I've never seen anybody do half so much in a routine health inspection."

"I believe in being thorough, Mrs. Garten."

"And I believe you're going to keep trying to find something wrong until you have an excuse to shut me down. You've been here two hours and all you've managed to deduct is three points from a hundred."

"Well, what about those jars of supplies?" Mr. Webster said, nodding toward the Jordan almonds and nonpareils in giant apothecary jars, situated on Duffy's shelves in the seating area far above the reach of curious hands. "They're unsealed, undated, and there is no sneeze guard to protect them. And they're a choking hazard for small children."

"They're decorative!" Lucy cried. "I'm not going to use them for product!"

"I think you're getting out of hand here, Herb," Specs said. "Lucy keeps it so clean in here you could eat off the floor."

"Have you, in fact, been eating off of the floor?" Herb asked, frowning.

"It's time for you to go," Lucy told him. She noted that while Mr. Brewster had been openly insulting to Specs and her before Specs showed up, his bravado had now dropped down to nothing.

"You're getting a B-minus rating," Herb said, ripping a carbon copy of her report from his clipboard and handing it to her. "And keep in mind, I have the right to perform a surprise inspection any time I want."

"A B-minus? In what world does a ninety-seven equal a B-minus?"

"You can appeal your score with my superiors." Mr. Brewster sniffed, marching out.

"Oh, I plan on it!" she called after him as he slammed the door behind him.

"He counted hiring me against you, didn't he?"

"You don't know that," she countered.

"He wrote 'person of loose moral fiber on premiere.'" Specs nodded toward her copy of the report.

"What?" she cried. "Okay, first of all, he meant 'premises.' And second, he's not allowed to count off for that, it's just in the notes section. And third, he is such an asshole. Clearly, it's in Evie's genetic code . . . which is a terrible thing to say because my son shares that code, so A-plus parenting from me."

She groaned and flopped her arms down on the counter. According to county regulations, she was going to have to print that B-minus and the accompanying report in bright bold lettering and hang it next to her entrance. Even if she appealed the B-minus, it would take weeks to get a new rating. By then, word would spread that she'd been given a poor report by the health department, and with no apparent reason, people would make up their own reasons. Roaches in the flour. Mouse droppings in the cooler. Drano stored next to the food coloring. She'd be ruined before she opened.

She took a deep breath through her nose and blew it out. She would not accept this. She would not give up. She would not let Evie use her cousin's job to destroy her dream.

"Uh, Miss Lucy, I don't really know what to do here," Specs said.

Sniffing, Lucy straightened up and grabbed a bottle of water from the cooler. "Okay, this is how it's going to go. I'm going to call Marianne and talk to her about securing Mr. Pritchett's services when I appeal the damn B-minus."

"Sounds good."

"And then—"

The bells over the shop door clanged and Specs peered over Lucy's shoulder. His mouth pulled back at the corners into a tragedy mask configuration. Lucy turned to see Lana sauntering in.

She sighed and stared at the ceiling. "Is it International Assholes Stop by a Bakery Day?"

Specs snorted, but covered it with a cough. "I think I'm gonna go in the back, Miss Lucy."

"All right, thanks, Specs."

As Specs made his way to the coolers, out of earshot, Lucy turned to Lana with a level stare. "How can I help you?"

"I heard you were coming back to town." Lana sniffed.

"You know very well I'm back in town. You've seen me in person twice. Now, obviously, the store is not open, so I would like to ask you to leave, please."

Lana pursed her lips into an ugly magenta pout. "Oh, this

won't take very long. I'm telling you, using real small words: keep your pathetic, no-man-having ass away from Duffy."

Lucy burst out laughing. "I know this is going to amaze you, but I really have more important things on my mind right now than whatever the hell is going on under that hardened shell of hair bleach. But just so you know, I don't think you get a vote in who goes near Duffy. You're divorced. Not getting a vote in who your ex-spouse spends time with is right there on the paperwork."

"I'm not talking as his wife. I'm talking as his friend. You're poison to Duffy, do you hear? You fuck with his head and get him all confused. You just use him and get what you want and then when you're done, you tell him he's such a good friend and walk away. You're nothing but a leech."

Lucy whipped her cupcake apron over her head and picked up her purse. "From the woman who cheated on him with two of his best friends? That's rich."

"Duffy and I have a history. He loved me. He loved me enough to marry me. And he's going to love me again. He just doesn't know it."

"He doesn't even like you that much. Now he just feels sorry for you. If you're happy trying to turn a pity-fuck into a relation-ship, well, be my guest."

"He can't really ever feel anything for you," Lana said, smirk-ing. "He just wants to rescue you. That's what he loves to do. Trust me, I know."

Lucy paused, a cold lump of discomfort lodging itself in her throat. Lana had the infernal gift of being able to distill a person's biggest insecurities and turn them into an effective vulgar insult; she always had. And she'd just pinned Lucy's, that Duffy's feelings for her were simply nostalgia and sympathy.

What would happen once that wore off, much like the charm had been sanded away by life with Wayne? But whatever the case, she wasn't about to let Lana get the upper hand on her, in her own bakery, no less.

"You never even knew him," she told Lana. "You still don't. So why don't you march yourself out of that door before I kick your ass up between your shoulder blades?"

"You won't put your hands on me. I'll call the cops on you."

"Do you want to try me? I can afford a better lawyer and everybody who would be chosen for a jury of my peers likes me better than you," Lucy said, backing Lana toward the door. Lana was moving, but sneering at Lucy with hate in her clearly contact-lens-enhanced green eyes.

"Duffy gets confused sometimes, but he is going to come back to me. We're meant to be together."

"Just like you were meant to be together with his best friend?" Lucy asked, giving her a pitying smile while opening the shop door.

"No, that's what I told him just a few weeks ago, when I was climbing out of his bed."

Lucy's eyes narrowed. Duffy had said he hadn't been with Lana in a "while," but Lucy realized now that he hadn't specified a time frame. Hell, Marianne had used the same phrase, but had very deliberately avoided clarifying.

Lana's eyes seemed to flicker with dark glee and she went in for the kill. "What, he didn't tell you? We never stopped sleeping together, not in all these years. Like I said, he always *comes* back to me when it counts."

They'd lied to her. Duffy, Marianne, Frankie. They could have just told her that Duffy had been mixed up with Lana right before she arrived in town, but instead, they'd used vague words and charm to mislead her. Wayne had done the same in the days when he still bothered trying to keep his affairs hidden from her. She'd send him off to "dinner with clients" or "a last-minute meeting" with a smile on her face, only for him to come back smelling of perfume and hotel soap. She'd been trusting and she'd been fooled and she was pretty damn tired of it.

"I'm not doing this," Lucy told her. "We're not in high school anymore and I have no interest in competing with you or trying to prove who Duffy loves more. I came back here so I could raise my son and open my bakery. Your feelings and who you've decided is the love of your life this week are not a priority for me. Now, get out of my shop. Do not bring your mess into my place of business again or the 'ass between the shoulder blades' plan goes right back into effect."

"This isn't over!" Lana called as she walked down the street.

"I have got to keep that door locked," Lucy muttered.

LUCY THREW HER truck into park, her tires crunching to a stop on the gravel of the McCready's parking lot. She scanned the McCready Family Funeral Home and Bait Shop property, spotting the two McCreadys she was searching for sitting on the dock near Sarah's Snack Shack, tearing into one of Leslie's deep-fried creations. Duffy and Marianne looked happy and carefree and Lucy wanted to smack the smiles off of them. Or at least smack their sandwiches out of their hands, because they looked delicious and she'd forgotten to eat lunch.

"Hey, there, Lucy!" Marianne called. "You want a sandwich? Aunt Leslie just figured out how to deep-fry a ham sandwich wrapped in bacon."

"I would love a sandwich, but right now, I'm mad as a wet cat," Lucy said, pointing her fingers at her sibling targets. "You two owe me some answers."

"Is this about me putting your bakery on Yelp already?" Marianne asked. "I got overexcited. I'm sorry."

"What? No! Well, I guess, we'll get to that. Duffy, I'm mad at you because I just found out *from Lana* that you two didn't stop sleeping together 'a long while ago.' She said it was more like weeks ago, meaning right before I showed up in town. Which means you and your sister lied to me about how recent things were with Lana and Duffy and I feel like an idiot."

Duffy cringed. "Now, technically, I didn't lie."

"You really think this is the time to argue semantics?" Lucy asked, pursing her lips.

"No, no, it is not," he admitted. "Look, I'm sorry. I was just embarrassed. It's not exactly a flattering picture of me, sleeping with somebody I've been divorced from for years, somebody I don't have feelings for and I'm definitely not in a relationship with. And I didn't want you to know because I was afraid you would think I was some sleaze, not somebody you'd want to be friends with, much less date."

"Well, I'm not thrilled about that. I'm not gonna say otherwise," she told him. "It shows a pretty serious lack of judgment on your part. But I'm way more upset by the idea that you just . . . omitted a pretty big piece of information. You left me to find out from Lana, so she could see my reaction to that."

"I'm sorry," Duffy said.

"And you?" Lucy asked Marianne.

"I didn't want to say anything to mess up Duffy's chances," Marianne said, her cheeks flushing. "I'm sorry, Lucy, it was wrong. I just wanted to see Duffy happy."

"Well, you both made me real unhappy. I don't like being tricked. And I don't like being lied to," Lucy told them as Marianne stared into her lap. "I had enough of that with Wayne. I don't want to smile while I'm being fed a load of bullshit."

"I'm sorry, Lucy," Duffy said again.

"Maybe it's better that we found this out before our date, before we did anything that could permanently mess up our friendship." Lucy turned to leave, only to have to Duffy jog around her and take her arms in his hands.

"I don't want to lose that, either," Duffy protested. "I'm sorry. But I don't think we should not see each other over this. I'm sorry, I won't do anything like this again."

"I just can't," Lucy said, attempting to pull away and step around him. In a movement one could accomplish only when they were used to walking around unstable boat decks, Duffy turned her on her toes and pulled her mouth to his. He delivered a kiss so hot and demanding that Lucy's traitorous knees gave up the fight entirely and melted like butter on a hot sidewalk. Her fingers clutched at his shirt as she sagged and he caught her around the waist as he ravaged her lips.

She whimpered. God help her. She whimpered into his mouth as he claimed every bit of hers with teeth and tongue. He pulled her closer, aligning their hips, and he splayed his huge hands across the small of her back. The little flutters of *want* she'd felt before were shoved aside for full tremors of desire, seizing her belly and making it that much harder to remember why she was angry with Duffy.

"Please don't give up on us before we even get started," he whispered against her lips.

"Did you just shut me up with a kiss?" she asked him.

"I wouldn't put it that way," he said, his voice still husky. "I like to think of it as imploring you to reconsider in a highly physical manner."

Lucy snorted. "I'm still irritated. I don't want us to fail before we get started, but I won't stand for you being dishonest with me. Is there anything else you want to tell me? Some other wife I don't know about? Charming illegitimate children stashed somewhere in the next county?"

"No," he promised. "That's it. I showed crap judgment with my ex-wife. But I've barely spoken to her since you came back into town, and when I have talked to her, I've made it clear I'm not going to take up with her again."

"Well, she's got a lot of confidence that won't last," Lucy told him.

"I'll make it clearer," he said. "I won't mess this up, Lucy, I swear to you."

"All right," she said, kissing him lightly. "I don't want to lose you, either, you know."

He pulled her tight against him, peppering kisses along her cheeks. Lucy groaned and wrapped her arms around his neck.

"Um, guys, I'm still sitting right here," Marianne said.

"Deal with it!" Lucy said. "I'm still a little pissed at you for breaking the girl code."

Marianne sighed. "Fair enough."

12

THE LAST TUESDAY in March marked the annual McCready family business meeting, to review how the previous year had run and plan for the next fiscal year. Tootie and Aunt Leslie made a fancy lunch of tiny curried chicken salad croissants, minted fruit salad, and individual chess pies. Tootie had been served that menu at a Ladies Auxiliary luncheon in 1982 and considered it the height of businesslike elegance. Each family member presented a report for their individual area of the business, including notable disasters and ideas for improvement. The addition of Margot to the office staff meant a lot more pie charts, but Duffy had to admit, it was a lot easier to understand their profit margins when they were outlined in lime green.

Honestly, it was nice to see the profit margins at all. While McCready's hadn't exactly suffered in the aftermath of the water dump, they'd never seen the kind of gains highlighted on Margot's graphs. It was a relief to watch E.J.J.'s and Stan's shoulders relax just a little bit, as if letting go of the weight they'd been carrying for the last five years.

Frankie proposed that the business's *official* motto be changed to "Because everybody dies." Which she did every year. And as usual, E.J.J. voted her down, "for the sake of the family dignity," which *he* did every year.

And Donna didn't come, because everybody agreed that was safer.

"Anyone have new business?" E.J.J. asked.

Bob cleared his throat and raised his hand. "I do!"

Every set of brows at the table rose—except for Margot's, because she didn't know how rare it was for Bob to bring up new business. Normally he reported on the funeral home's licensing and order rates and that was it.

"So, some interesting news from the county commission. A land developer out of Chicago called and wants to set up a meeting with us. They're thinking about buying the Wheaton place on the west side of the lake, building some condos, maybe even a resort."

Duffy frowned. The Wheaton place was a two-hundred-acre hog farm well outside of town, with prime shoreline. The Wheatons had once been a sprawling family with lots of branches, big enough to run the farm without hiring on help. But over the years, fewer and fewer of the youngsters chose farming, moving out of town to take up professions like law, medicine, and HVAC repair. The last of the cousins to be listed on the deed had retired to Florida years before. And now, apparently, the land was valuable enough that some big developing outfit wanted to buy it.

"I guess it's good news," E.J.J. muttered. "If somebody wants to develop the land, it has to be worth something. They must think people will want to spend their vacations here, which means the rebound from the water dump is just about finished."

"Yeah, but around here, that means little group cabins or some dinky motel. Hell, sometimes it's just a campground," Margot said. "Condos or a full-service resort would take permanent 'summer people' and maybe even retirees moving into town. That could mean a lot of economic growth."

"It could also mean an influx of strangers with their traffic and hissy fits over Wi-Fi access," Stan grumbled.

"I never had a hissy fit." Margot sniffed. "I merely made sternly worded inquiries."

Stan snickered.

"It could mean chain restaurants and Starbucks and things that Lake Sackett never had before. Stuff that brings more people in, yeah, but it would also mean more competition for the locals," Frankie said. "I'm not saying it's the end of the world. I just don't want us to turn into some overcrowded, homogenized tourist trap where you can't even get down Main Street in the middle of a weekday."

"We may be borrowing trouble," E.J.J. said. "This might not even come to pass."

"What's the name of the company? I can reach out to some of my friends in Chicago, ask about their reputation," Margot offered.

Bob looked relieved and slid a slick-looking prospectus across the table. "Yes, please."

"Maybe I can fly back to Chicago for a weekend to investigate the company and do a little baby shopping," Margot added casually. "Maybe a little wedding dress shopping."

"What was wrong with the dress shop in Atlanta?" Tootie asked. "They had some beautiful dresses there, from those fancy designers I can't pronounce."

"Yeah, but those designers don't have maternity lines," Margot muttered. "And I know a couple of seamstresses in Chicago who would make me a custom gown without making the 'aw, that's okay, honey' face at me when I say I need an elastic panel over the belly."

Leslie clucked her tongue and patted Margot's shoulder. "We'd be happy to come with you to Chicago to shop for a dress."

Margot's smile was strained. "Okay, that would be good."

Frankie snorted. "Hey, Lucille Bodine offered to let you borrow her wedding dress."

Margot shuddered and held up her hand. "We're not going to talk about that."

"What's wrong with Lucille Bodine's wedding dress?" Duffy asked.

Margot lowered her head to the conference table. And appeared to be praying.

"A lot of bows," Tootie whispered. "Including one great big one over the stomach area. Miss Lucille was about eight months gone with Mike when she got married."

"As interesting as all this wedding talk is," E.J.J. said, coughing slightly.

Bob shrugged. "I like wedding talk. There's usually cake."

"Speaking of cake, Lucy said she'd be thrilled to make your wedding cake," Duffy told Margot. "Just go by the shop to set up a tasting. She'll even do up a couple of off-the-wall flavors like peanut butter and jelly and banana and chocolate."

"A chocolate and banana wedding cake sounds amazing," Frankie said.

"I think I'd like to try that peanut butter and jelly one," Stan said.

"Now I really want a piece of cake." Margot sighed. "And a guacamole burger with bacon. And cheese grits."

"Well, now I want guacamole," Duffy muttered.

"Children!" E.J.J. barked.

Bob cleared his throat again. "The commission is going to meet with them in a month to consider their offer, with any additional input Margot happens to find."

Margot offered him a salute, but she was very clearly still thinking about cake. "But they're going to ask Marianne to find some fancy lawyer in Atlanta to go over any offers so we don't accidentally sell them the lake or something."

"Probably a good idea," Frankie noted, as Duffy nodded, leaning back in his chair until only two legs rested on the floor.

"Any other business?" Tootie asked.

E.J.J. raised his hand. "Yes, I have here a proposal from Donna. She would like to step down as director of the marina, letting Duffy take over, and implement a plan that allows her to retire in five years."

"What?" Duffy sat up suddenly, his shifting weight throwing the chair off balance. He tumbled backward and whacked his head against the floor. "Ow."

Frankie jerked her thumb toward her cousin's prone body. "Our future marina manager, ladies and gentlemen."

"What do you mean my mom wants to retire?" Duffy demanded, hauling himself up and righting his chair.

"She's been talking about it for years," Leslie said.

"Not to me, she hasn't!" he exclaimed.

Leslie reached over the table and squeezed his hand. "She's getting older, honey, it's getting to be more of a chore, physically, hauling tourists around the lake. And she's getting to the point where she's afraid she'll be too old to enjoy fishing in her retirement. Junior didn't quit working until he absolutely had to, and she doesn't want to get to the end of her life and realize that she never took time to enjoy herself."

Duffy swallowed heavily. Why hadn't his mother even mentioned this subject to him? It wasn't like it wasn't his business. He was replacing her, for goodness' sake. Why hadn't she told him that she was feeling her age? He would have stepped in and taken on more of her charters if he'd known she was getting tired. Why didn't she ever express anything to her own son besides irritation?

"Well, it's not as if you're not ready to take over the marina, Duff. You know how everything runs and what to order, the paperwork and such," E.J.J. said. "You and Donna have been doing the same job for years. She just has the title is all."

"I know, it's just, I'd be running it on my own. It's a big change for me," Duffy said. "We might have to actually hire somebody else to do charters, or work in the store."

"Aw, Duffy's gonna have to take his last big-boy step into adulthood," Frankie teased.

"I'm not taking shit from somebody wearing a cartoon kitty robot T-shirt," Duffy countered.

"Swear jar!" Tootie crowed. "And Frankie, stop teasing your cousin. I happen to remember you passing out the first time you had to fill out the death certificate paperwork on your own."

"I skipped my morning snack that day," Frankie grumbled.

"You'll do just fine," Margot told him. "If you can survive working for your mother, you can survive anything."

Duffy pursed his lips and nodded. "True enough."

"I move we accept Donna's proposal and promote Duffy to interim director of the marina for a six-month probationary period, as is McCready's policy," E.J.J. said.

"Seconded," Margot said, raising her hand.

"All in favor?" E.J.J. asked.

Everyone in the room said "aye."

"Accepted," Tootie said. "Congratulations, honey."

Duffy slumped back in his chair as his family cheered. He'd gotten a promotion, sort of. It was no small thing to gain authority in a business structure that consisted of less than ten of his relatives. The next generation of McCreadys was taking over the business.

"So, that's old business, financial review, Frankie tries to change the motto, E.J.J. says no, and the new business. Any other new business?" E.J.J. asked, checking items off the agenda. "If not, Tootie and I have an announcement." Every person at the table blanched because that was highly unusual. Tootie was smiling broadly, Duffy noted.

E.J.J.'s mouth was just slightly tremulous. "We're going on her cruise to Aruba. She's worked real hard for it and I'm proud of her," he said, though his voice was hoarse, as if he'd just announced he had end-stage something awful. "I'm just pleased as punch that we finally get to follow her dream all the way down to another country."

Frankie gasped. "Really?"

"I'm sure the business will be in good hands while we're gone," he told Bob. "And when we get back, you and I probably need to talk about a new schedule, where I spend a little more time at home. Y'all are ready to take the reins and I'm ready to . . . uh . . ."

"Retire," Tootie called down the table. "The word you're looking for is 'retire.' And you're going to be just fine, honey. I promise."

"It's about time," Duffy said, slapping the table.

Margot smiled warmly and hugged E.J.J. "Congratulations, both of you. I'm so happy for you."

"Oh, just imagine, a cruise to all those exotic places." Leslie sighed. "Let me know if you like it. Maybe Bob and I can go on a cruise."

But poor Uncle Bob didn't hear Leslie's broad hint for what was probably a much-needed vacation. He seemed to be considering his future without E.J.J. running the office, because he looked ready to fall over.

The business was changing and Duffy wondered if he and Frankie and Margot were up to the task of carrying the weight into the future. It would be challenging. It would involve a lot of hard work. But it certainly wouldn't be boring.

PARKING HER TRUCK in front of Duffy's cabin, Lucy felt a strange anxiety ripple through her belly. It certainly wasn't guilt over leaving Sam for the night. Her son had practically shoved her out the door so he could get straight to playing with the Dawson boys. And she knew she wasn't doing anything wrong. She wasn't moving on too fast. It had been months since Wayne passed. And she had closed that door in the hallway of her life.

She just really, really wanted this to go well. She wanted to feel that "zing" of being close to someone she was attracted to, of flirting and knowing it was going to lead somewhere. But she'd been married to her high school sweetheart for her entire adult life. She knew Duffy was a great kisser, but she had a feeling this date might end in a much more . . . well, naked fashion. And she wasn't sure she knew how to be with anyone else. What if dating and sex had gotten much more complicated while she was being a wife and mom and she didn't know what to do anymore? What if there were spin moves involved? She didn't know any spin moves.

But this was Duffy. And things rarely went bad when Duffy was around.

She took a deep breath and slid out of the truck. She was wearing an older cotton floral dress she was pretty sure she'd had before Sam was born. She'd kept her makeup minimal and her hair in a ponytail. Duffy had been a little mysterious about their plans for the night and told her to dress "comfortable and any damn way you please." So this was her compromise instead of jeans and boots.

The man himself came out of his cabin, looking downright polished in a blue dress shirt. He'd left the jacket and tie at home, which was probably for the best, given the fate of the last set.

"I meant to pick you up!" he exclaimed as he jogged down his porch steps.

"Well, I had to drop Sam off at Marianne's house, which means driving past your place, and I thought it might be a little silly to drive all the way back to my house just so you can pick me up at my door."

"There's a principle to the thing," he grumbled under his breath, then kissed her cheek.

"Well, this is postmodern feminism at work, buddy, so get used to it," she told him. "I pump my own gas and clean my own gutters and everything."

"Of course you do," he said, glancing down at her dress. "You look so pretty in that dress. I think I like it even better than the red or the blue. This may be my favorite so far."

"Thank you. You look nice, too," she said, straightening the collar of his shirt.

"So Sam and Nate are up to shenanigans tonight, huh?"

"Dinosaur-shaped chicken nuggets are being consumed as we speak."

"Eventually you're going to have to tell that kid that they don't come out of the chicken that shape."

"No, I will not," she said, reaching into the passenger seat for a small purple soft-sided cooler with GIMME SOME SUGAR stamped on the side. "I do feel kind of weird asking Marianne to babysit so often."

"Don't. Sam's so well-behaved that he sets a good example for Nate. And Nate finally gets to feel like a big brother instead of the baby of the family, which is probably going to be a rare opportunity for him, because as Marianne put it, her baby factory has closed."

He tucked her arm into his elbow and led her toward the dock. A pontoon boat with a navy blue shade, named *Ain't Misbehavin'*, was tethered on the far end. "So I thought that we might take a little sunset cruise."

"On a pontoon boat?"

"Yeah, it will be pretty comfortable. It's basically a couch that floats," he said, helping her step onto the boat.

"Did you bring wine and cheese?" she asked with a laugh.

"I brought beer and my aunt Leslie's deep-fried macaroni-and-cheese balls," he said, stepping onto the pontoon boat and lifting the lid on a bright red Coleman cooler.

"Oh, thank God," she said. "I hate wine. I know it's lowbrow to admit it, but it always tastes awful to me, like salad dressing gone bad. Give me a Bud Light any day. I will accept cheese in pretty much any form, though."

"That's why you're one of my favorite people," he said, holding her hand as she picked a seat across from the pilot station. "I panicked for just a second there."

"I think we both need to relax a little bit," she told him.

"Probably," he said, hauling the cooler onto the boat. "All right. Just sit back and enjoy the ride."

"When have you ever known me to do that?" she asked, holding her hand out imperiously for the keys. When he balked, she chuckled. "You're not going to let me drive?"

"It's not a sexist thing, I just like driving boats."

"Duffy, of the two of us, which one has run a bass boat into Marv Burnside's dock?" she asked.

"I was seventeen! And the tiller was stuck!"

"You threw poor Carl thirty feet into the air!"

"His collarbone healed up just fine," Duffy insisted.

She peered over the rims of her rounded black sunglasses. He sighed and dropped the keys into her hand. "Fine."

She chuckled, sitting behind the wheel as he cast the lines off. "Where are we going?"

"Head toward Deer Tick Bay and then turn left," he said, flopping back into a nearby seat.

Lucy's nerves thrilled at the sound of the engine starting. It had been far too long since she'd been out on the water. The last time she'd been on a boat, it had been a luxury cruise ship bound for Belize. It had been absolutely lovely, and was one of her fonder memories of Wayne, but it was a far cry from puttering around the lake on her father's old Alumacraft. She loved gliding across the surface of the water—at a slow, responsible speed, since Duffy seemed to have outfitted the boat for a pretty leisurely pace.

It was a chance to see Lake Sackett from a different angle, to realize how small and insignificant you were compared to the complicated workings of nature. Dying sunlight danced in splashes of orange and gold on the water. Birds took flight at the sound of the engine.

Speaking of which, Lucy thought maybe the engine sounded off, too thin. As if it was struggling to keep up with even the low demands Lucy was making of it. By the time they'd traveled a few miles, reaching the perimeter of Make-Out Island, it was sputtering like an old man's cough. She cut the engine and let them coast in under their own momentum. Duffy was already standing, moving toward the engine to lift the cover.

"I thought it sounded thin, but it's been a long time since I've been out on a boat," Lucy told him.

"Yeah, but the engine looks okay to me," he said. "I just tuned it this week."

Lucy glanced at the instrument panel. And saw the gas gauge. "Duffy?"

He crossed the boat and saw the red indicator flopping toward E.

"Really? We ran out of gas?" Lucy scoffed, smirking at him. "What is this, high school? In 1957?"

"What?"

"What's next, are you going to have Frankie run out of the woods dressed like the hook man and scare my clothes right off?"

"I checked the tank right after lunch today and it was full, I swear," Duffy said, his voice rising. "I wouldn't put you in a stalled boat, Lucy."

In any other man, she would suspect deceit, but Duffy's upset seemed so genuine.

"Well, I could have checked the gas gauge before I started the boat," she said, shrugging. In the distance, the sun was sinking into the horizon, casting a golden-orange glow over everything it touched. A cool, pleasant breeze drifted off the water, smelling of woods and the honeysuckle that grew on the island in abundance. The lake lapped against the boat in a quiet, endless cycle of white noise. In terms of being stranded, it could have been worse.

"Who was it that suggested you take me out on the boat tonight?" she asked as Duffy tossed the anchor, lodging them just off the island.

"Frankie. She said it would be romantic to take you out to-ward Crooked Ankle Inlet because you can see the sunset really well from here this time of year . . . aw, sonofabitch." He sighed. "Frankie."

Lucy nodded. "Yep."

"So do you think that she was trying to get us close to Make-Out Island as a misplaced swing at nostalgia?" he asked. "I mean, she must have measured out the gas with an eyedropper."

"Probably. I love your cousin, but she's about as subtle as a sack of hammers."

He sighed, picking up the shortwave radio attached to the dashboard. She opened the cooler, because at this point they were stuck and might as well enjoy themselves. Lucy unloaded the foil-wrapped fried goodness onto the little table near the front of the boat. The beers were kept cold in a separate compartment. She grinned, impressed. Duffy had really planned this out.

"Dammit, Frankie, come in," Duffy barked into the receiver as the sun slipped behind the hills and the light became purple and soft.

Frankie responded far too quickly, as if she was hovering over the radio, waiting to pounce . . . and gloat. "I will only respond to the code names we established when we were kids."

Duffy sighed and tapped the receiver against his forehead. "'Dammit, Frankie' *was* the code name I gave you when we were kids."

"Negative, Ginger Terror. I will only respond to the code name we *agreed* on as kids. Otherwise, how will I know it's you? Someone could be pretending to be you." Frankie's voice echoed over the surface of the lake, startling a pair of herons that were wading in the shallows.

Duffy gritted his teeth, which made it sound really strained when he grumbled, "*Divine Glitter Unicorn Empress of the Universe*, please come in."

Lucy snorted into her mac 'n' cheese ball.

Frankie hit the button quickly enough for Duffy to hear Eric say, "I thought code names were meant to save time. That name doesn't sound like it saves time."

"I hear you, Ginger Terror, what can I do for you?" Frankie asked, her smugness radiating from the speaker.

"You can explain what the hell you were thinking stranding me out in the middle of the lake at dusk with Lucy on board."

"But you're not in the middle of the lake, are you?" Frankie asked. "If I was going to guess, I would say you're safely anchored somewhere near Make-Out Island, cracking open the beers."

"You don't know me," he scoffed, just as Lucy opened a beer and handed it to him.

"And instead of hurrying back because you're worried about Sam or She Who Shall Not Be Named or any of the dozen other things y'all two take onto your shoulders, you're going to have a time-out. By yourselves. In private. Just enjoy yourselves. We'll be by to pick you up in an hour or two. You'll thank me later. Divine Glitter Unicorn Empress of the Universe—out."

"She's in therapy. I thought that was supposed to make you *less crazy*," Duffy said incredulously, staring at the receiver.

"Eh, therapy is more about dealing with the crazy you've already got," Lucy said as he sat next to her and accepted a paper plate filled with snacks.

"So you tried it?" he asked.

"Yeah, after Wayne died, and a little before, to be honest. It helped."

"You don't seem all that upset about this," he said, gesturing to their increasingly dark surroundings.

"Well, I can't say this has been the best date I've ever been on, but I'm with you," she said, shrugging. "I'm safe when I'm with you."

A pleased, proud warmth crossed his face. "Thank you."

"I can't remember the last time I just sat and had a beer in the quiet," she said, sighing. "I feel like I've been running for years now. Errands and meetings and appointments and getting Sam up every morning and getting him to bed at night. I can't remember the last time I just . . . sat, even just to read a book that wasn't written by a pediatrician or didn't have a cartoon fish on the cover."

"Marianne feels that way too sometimes. I actually found her faking going to a book club meeting so she could eat a burger all by herself."

"That sounds amazing," she said. "I mean, I love my son more than anything in the world, but there are times when I dream about being able to take a bath without someone's little fingers poking under the bathroom door while he asks what I'm doing."

"Well, you know, set small goals."

They ate their snacks and drank their beer in companionable silence, her head tilted against his shoulder, enjoying the sights and sounds of night falling on the lake. Duffy put his arm around her and all the nerves she felt melted away. There was a certain freedom in knowing that you *couldn't* hurry up and get back to work or dishes or whatever else you had hanging over your head because you could only sit and enjoy yourself.

"So, I think it's good that we got our first kiss out of the way already," she told Duffy as she finished her beer. "Takes the pressure off."

"I agree, but I think we're pretty good at it. No pressure."

"I agree with your agreement," she said. "And I think we should see what else we're good at."

Duffy reared his head back. "Right now? Here?"

"We've got time and privacy, something that's pretty rare for both of us," she said. "And I don't think anybody else is going to be coming out to Make-Out Island at this time of year."

"Are you sure it's not rushing anything? I mean, don't get me wrong. There are no words for how much I want to do this, but I don't want you to do anything you don't want to do yet. I'll wait for you . . . Dammit, woman, I'll wait for you forever."

She kissed him lightly and he moaned into her mouth. She pulled away and rested her forehead against Duffy's. "We've waited long enough, McDuff McCready."

He nodded, kissing her and pulling gently at the ties holding her dress at her shoulders. She slid her fingers through his thick gingery hair and climbed into his lap, straddling his hips. Something very firm and solid was waiting there for her and she laughed against his mouth.

"I told you," he exclaimed. "I've been waiting a long time for this. Like, since before I understood how *this* worked."

"No," she assured him. "It's good. It's a big confidence booster to know that I'm wanted. It's been a long time since I've done this."

"How long?"

"More than a year. Closer to two," she said as his eyes went wide.

"Well, that's what I'm here for," he told her as she giggled into his shoulder. "Food, drink, travel, self-esteem building. I'm a full-service man-friend."

"Man-friend?"

"I feel a little old to be someone's boyfriend," he told her.

"We're parked on Make-Out Island with no gas," she noted.

"You're going to have to let that go," he told her as he pulled her mouth to his, even as she shook her head, because no, she would never let that go. She plucked at the buttons of his shirt, revealing skin that was tanner and firmer than she seemed to remember it being. Duffy's hands were busy at her neck, stroking the skin, touching her pulse points, lifting her hair so he could

reach the sensitive spot behind her ear he had no business finding intuitively. She traced the curve of his jaw with her teeth
and then bit down gently on his earlobe, making him jump and
roll his hips. She gasped and ground down against him, because
damn. The way he looked up at her, like she was the center of the
universe, was enough to make a girl drunk with power.

And just when they seemed to be getting comfortable with
each other, Duffy pulled away. "Oh, wait, wait, wait. I don't have
any condoms. I mean, I went to the doctor to get checked out.
I'm all clean. I just didn't want to assume anything, but now it
seems like I shot myself in the foot by trying to be polite."

She sighed, tipping her forehead against his. "Well, I appreciate that you didn't want to assume anything, but yeah, condoms
would be a good thing to have right now. I'm on the pill, but
honestly, I don't think I'm ready to take any chances." Lucy
chewed her lip for a moment. "Why don't you look in the glove
compartment by the steering wheel?"

"Why?"

She laughed. "I just have a feeling about it."

Duffy pulled the compartment door open and brightly colored foil packets of condoms rained onto the carpeted boat floor
by the dozen.

"I mean . . ."

"Frankie had a lot of faith in us," Lucy said, nodding.

"Still, even with the condoms, we don't have to do anything
you don't want to do," he promised.

"Hey, Duffy."

"Hmm?"

She jumped at him, knocking him back on the carpet and
climbing onto his lap again. Though traffic on the lake at this

time of night in the low season was pretty limited, anybody could pass by and see what they were doing. And she found that she just didn't care. She wanted Duffy. And she was going to have him.

He rolled over her, sliding his hands up her thighs, leaving warm trails on her skin as they relaxed open. Her skirt rode up to her hips and he slipped her panties down. Just to feel that pressure on her skin, the closeness, sent tremors down her spine. The only sounds she could hear were the chirping of crickets and their heavy breathing, making her feel like they were the only people on earth. Duffy ghosted his fingers over her flesh, finding her wet and ready, and did she mention it had been a while? Because she clenched around the steady curving rhythm he started with surprising and near-embarrassing speed. He barely had to circle the place that . . . previous partners couldn't find with multiple hints and blatant direction and she was crying out, throwing her head back against the floor and arching into his hand. When the delicious little tremors stopped, she was clinging to Duffy's shoulders with her face buried in his neck and he was smiling like she'd given him a gift.

Duffy rose to his knees and scooted her dress down her body, until she lifted her hips and let him toss it aside on the seat. He cradled her hips in his hands and thrust forward. Bless him, he was going so slowly with her, filling her so sweetly and slowly, while kissing her with the same gentle thoroughness that made her love him in the first place. And as nice as it felt, there would be time for that later. She dug her nails into the curve of his ass as she planted her feet and rose up to meet him.

"I'm not made of glass, you know," she whispered against his ear. He grinned and bit down on her shoulder, dropping reverence and gentleness in favor of doing what felt even better. And when they were finished, the sweat cooling pleasantly on their skin, listening to the insects chirp and the water move, she sighed into his neck. "That was a very nice way to take advantage of an empty gas tank."

"I just want to point out one more time that I had no idea what she was doing and I'm not responsible for the actions of my family members," he said, kissing her hair.

"It would serve her right if she rolled up here to see your bare ass, but I think we should put our clothes on."

"I hate it when you're right," he said with a sigh.

She shrugged into her clothes with a quickness understood only by mothers whose toddlers considered showers to be a stunning betrayal of maternal loyalty, then slipped into her dress. While Duffy yanked his clothes on, she opened her little purple cooler and offered him an eight-by-eight square foil package.

"What's this?"

"Your favorite," she said, peeling the foil back to reveal a golden lattice of crust over cinnamon-dusted peaches. "I remember, my mama made one for you when we were eleven and you missed my birthday party because it was an all-girls sleepover. Mama was so afraid your feelings would be hurt that she made you a cobbler."

"I ate the whole thing myself in one sitting, because my dad was a notorious cobbler thief," he said, taking a plastic picnic fork out of the cooler and breaking the crust. "I have never been so belly-sick in all my life."

"So, clearly, this is your favorite."

"It's delicious," he said around a mouthful of peaches and

pastry. He scooped a forkful toward her mouth. She accepted it, and had to admit that even for one of her cobblers, it was damn tasty. The secret was poaching the peaches in just a little bit of bourbon before baking.

"But it's not my favorite," he said.

"What!" she exclaimed, nearly choking on her own cobbler. She chewed her bite carefully and asked, "But you said it was delicious!"

"It is. And I love it, but it's not my favorite."

"You are a tough nut to crack, McDuff McCready, but I will figure this out."

"Or, I play the long game, never tell you if and when you find my favorite, and I get amazing desserts for life."

"It's a good thing you're freaking adorable, you know that?" she grumbled.

"Yep."

"And you're not bad in bed."

"Thank you, but I would like to point out, this is not in fact a bed. This is a boat. In a bed, I am much better."

Lucy snickered and they shared the rest of the cobbler. They drank their beers and talked about everything and nothing, about old classmates and new additions in town, about Margot and her efforts to rebuild Lake Sackett one Yelp review at a time, about Stan's sobriety and the Junior League meetings in Texas.

It was very pleasant to just sit there and talk. And not think about the next place she needed to be, the chores she needed to get done. Frankie might have gone a little psycho in her agenda, but removing the option of leaving had given Lucy the excuse she needed to relax. Her son was in good hands. She'd just enjoyed some pretty spectacular sex. And now she was drinking a cold beer. That was a pretty banner day as far as she was concerned.

But she was going to carry an extra gas can wherever she went just in case.

Almost exactly two hours after their distress call, a boat engine sounded in the distance. Frankie's Day-Glo orange emergency windbreaker was clearly visible even in the dark. One of the McCreadys' bass boats was outfitted with a revolving red-and-blue police light, a searchlight, and a magnetic vinyl sign slapped on the side of the hull that said SACKETT COUNTY SHERIFF'S DEPARTMENT, WATERFRONT DIVISION.

"For the record, I did not know she was doing this until you were already out on the water," Eric called after he shut the engine off.

"Did you special-order a bubble light off of the Internet just for this moment?" Duffy asked Frankie.

"Yes, on the day I heard Lucy was coming back to town," she said, handing him a gas can.

"Yeah, that makes me super uncomfortable," Lucy told her. "You ever heard the word 'premeditated'?"

"Trust me, I've discussed that word with her," Eric promised.

"I am going to get you back for this," Duffy said.

"You can't threaten me with violence in front of my cop boyfriend," Frankie told him. "His citation-writing fingers get all itchy."

"No, I made an agreement with your dad and E.J.J. that I wouldn't let you talk me into charging people just because they annoy you. Bob actually made it a term of my employment, after the fact," Eric said.

Frankie pouted. "Well, that blows! What's the point of dating the sheriff if I can't abuse his power?"

"I'm a good man and I love you . . . ?" he suggested as Duffy fitted the gas can spout into the pontoon's gas tank.

"Fine. Bring logic and reason into it." She sighed and kissed him. "And you do have those washboard abs, which you definitely should have added to your boyfriend résumé."

"You both suck," Duffy informed them.

"I was just trying to help!" Frankie exclaimed. "And I wanted to make up for that whole Lana misunderstanding."

"This was your version of helping?" Lucy asked.

"Oh, please. You're smiling so bright we barely needed a flashlight to find you. Besides, I gave you just enough gas to get to Make-Out Island safely, and, Duffy, I knew that's where you would go if I told you about it, because you're real suggestible when you're nervous. And if you'd bothered to look in the emergency kit, you would have found a note informing you that there was a backup gas can in the bench, under the life vests, with just enough gas to get you back to the marina."

Lucy's jaw dropped. "That's super dangerous."

Frankie shrugged. "Eh. Worth it."

13

THE NEXT DAY, Carl and Duffy were "rebuilding the truck" like they normally did on Thursday nights. Of course, the part for Carl's truck still hadn't come in, so they were actually working in the McCready woodshop. They were up to their ears in sawdust and Carl came dangerously close to losing a pinkie, but they were happy as pigs in slop.

The McCready woodshop had been added to the compound sometime in the 1960s, when making caskets on-site became less of a demand and the uncles wanted a place they could practice their hobby closer to home. It was basically a glorified shed, with gray cinder-block walls and a corrugated metal roof. But Duffy's father, Junior, had been meticulous about keeping the open space clean and organized. The tools were always sharp and the large worktables were oiled and clean. The air smelled of warm pine and sharp, clean chemicals, a scent Duffy closely associated with his dad. Carl was using a jigsaw to cut wood into patterns to match the frame Duffy had built for Lucy's chalkboard menu.

Duffy was employing woodworking skills he hadn't used since high school to carve Lucy's name into the boards. The power tools were so loud, the men barely heard Lucy pounding on the door to the shop.

Carl was startled when she burst through the door, resulting in him damn near losing the other pinkie.

Duffy whipped off his safety goggles and shut off the saw before Carl hurt himself. Lucy's big brown eyes were shimmering with unshed tears and her face was ashen.

"Hey, sweetheart, what's wrong?" he asked. "Is Sam okay?"

"Sam's fine. Um, but I have a situation, in my truck," she said, her voice quavering.

Duffy and Carl practically chased her out of the shop. Sam was a few yards down the "compound" on Tootie's porch, playing with the dogs under Tootie's careful supervision. She and E.J.J. waved, and Tootie called, "I've got him, honey. You just take care of Lucy!"

Lucy's big red truck was parked with the bed facing away from Tootie's place, so she got a full view of Carl and Duffy's reaction when Lucy yanked the tarp off of the strangely lumpy shape she'd hidden from her son.

It appeared to be a collection of yellow plastic parts, held together with bolts, jutting out at a dozen different angles as if someone had been playing Jenga drunk and tried to make their creation permanent.

Duffy recoiled. "What in the hell?"

"Is it one of them ironic postmodern sculpture things?" Carl asked, his head tilted to the side.

"It's Sam's birthday present," Lucy said, reaching into her truck's passenger seat and yanking out a plastic bag full of plastic bits and bolts and an instruction booklet labeled BIG YELLOW PEDAL TRACTOR. While the little boy pictured in the black-and-white illustration looked very happy to be playing with the tractor, the booklet was about as thick as a copy of *Field & Stream*.

"Did Sam do something to make you mad?" Carl asked. Duffy took off his cap and slapped Carl on the back of the head with it.

A tear slipped down the curve of Lucy's cheek and Duffy's heart damn near broke. He put his arm around her and pulled her close as he rubbed her arm. "Okay, uh, Carl, help me carry this into the shop without Sam seeing."

"Sure thing," Carl said, picking up the reshrouded pile of parts and hoisting it through the door with Duffy's help.

"I tried to assemble it myself while Sam was busy watching cartoons, but the instructions are just . . . nonsense. I do not get why it's this hard!" she exclaimed. "I'm the one who installed our Wi-Fi. I rewired my stand mixer when the extension cord fell off. I built his crib, his baby bed, and his race car bed. I know how to use tools! But these instructions are just ridiculous! And I don't understand why I'm so upset and this is so embarrassing for so many reasons."

"Don't feel bad," Carl told her. "Marianne had to put together one of those plastic pirate island play sets after Aiden's birthday a couple years back? I was working late and she said don't worry, she could handle it. I came home to all these little plastic pirate bodies dismembered all over the carpet and the pirate fort in pieces. I said, 'Wow, Aiden, must have had a big ol' pirate battle.' And Marianne burst into tears because Aiden hadn't even played with it yet."

Lucy sniffed. "That does make me feel better, thank you."

"You knew it was important for this to be built right because Sammy needs to be safe when he rides it. You knew when to ask for help. That counts, hon," Carl told her, laying a hand on her shoulder.

"Thanks, Carl," Lucy said, smiling at him.

"No problem," Carl said. "I'll call Marianne over here to bring some sandwiches. And some moral support. And some beer."

"He's the redneck Prince Charming," Lucy said as Carl stepped out of the workshop.

"Sure is, but you haven't seen anything yet. Wait until Marianne has a birthday. It's disgustingly cute."

"I think it's sweet. I'm glad they're so happy together."

"We've got this," Duffy promised her, kissing her lightly. "Don't worry."

"Well, I'm going to help. Despite showing up in tears because the mean tools beat me, I'm not that big of a damsel in distress."

"Absolutely," Duffy said. "The first step is taking apart whatever the hell it is you did here and saving all the parts."

"Okay," she said, setting her toolbox on the closest worktable. The lumber Duffy had been working with caught her eye. Duffy supposed that was normal, considering it was her name he was carving into it.

"What are you doing there?" Lucy asked.

"Oh, uh, this was supposed to be a surprise," he said. "It's one of those proprietor signs for the front of the bakery. It's got your name on it and the year you're opening. And the scrollwork matches the frame for—*oof.*"

Lucy threw her arms around Duffy's neck and cut off his air supply.

"Thank you," she said, sighing into his neck. "You don't know how much it means to me that you're helping me with the bakery. Hell, that you think it's a good idea, that just—"

She was crying again. And Duffy didn't know what to do other than pat her on the back and let her do it. "It's been a real long day for you, huh, sweetheart?"

She nodded without lifting her face from his shirt.

"It's not just the tractor, is it?"

She shook her head back and forth.

"Come on, honey, let it all out at once. You'll feel better for it."

"It's just . . . everything all together, I guess. Being outsmarted by the mean tools. Sammy's birthday—it's the first one without his daddy and I know that's going to be weird for him. And I didn't want to bring it up on our date, but I got a ninety-seven from the health inspector the other day," she said, sniffing and wiping her nose.

"But that's great."

"Well, Herb Brewster—you know, Evie's cousin—said that the ninety-seven is a B-minus."

"On what planet?"

"That's what I said!" she exclaimed. "So I appealed the score with the health department and the director said that they would send someone out for a follow-up inspection but it won't be for another three weeks, which means if I want to open as planned, I'm going to do it with a big, bold red B-minus on the front of the shop, which doesn't exactly put a lot of confidence in me, customer-wise. And it's just so frustrating, dealing with small-town politics and extended families and I'm just—I kind of got pushed to my limit today."

"Well, that's understandable. But why wouldn't you want to bring that up on our date?"

"I don't know. It felt like such a downer. I didn't want to splash my worries all over you when we were trying to have a nice time. I wanted to put on a happy face and enjoy myself."

"I don't want you putting on a happy face when you're hurting. I want you to tell me what's hurting you. I'm not him, Lucy. I won't content myself with the easy parts of your life."

Lucy nodded and wrapped her arms around him. "Thank you."

"And we'll figure out some way to work around this health department thing. You're gonna open on time. I promise."

"I hate leaning on you this way," she said as Carl quietly rejoined them in the workshop. "I hate asking you for favors."

"It's not leaning on me. It's applying skills that I happen to have to a problem that you happen to have. If I had a cake emergency in the middle of the night, would you help me with it?"

"A cake emergency?"

"You haven't seen what happens when I turn on an oven," he said.

"It's true," Carl said. "He made a pan of brownies once and we used it for a boat anchor."

LUCY SAT ON her porch, sipping iced tea, watching Sam pedal his tractor around on the grass, making engine noises with his mouth. She'd mowed the grass herself just that morning to make sure it was a manageable height for the adorable little wheels. Before her toy-related meltdown, that is. Fortunately, Tootie had kept Sam entertained for the hour it took Duffy and Carl to take apart her Rorschach toy installation and reassemble it into a tractor shape.

Evie had called again that morning and asked if she could come to Sam's birthday party. The problem was that Lucy wasn't planning a party for Sam. All of his friends were in his preschool class, and from what Marianne told her, Lake Sackett parents were notoriously bad at RSVPing for children's birthday parties, and even worse at showing up for them. So the previous day, she had brought dozens of brightly decorated dinosaur-themed cupcakes to Sam's preschool for him to enjoy with his class. Maybe she would throw something more involved with his kindergarten classmates the next year, but for now, this seemed like the best way to guarantee a celebration with his friends. Today was a quiet Saturday at home with his mom and the giant plastic tractor he was using to mentally dig up the lawn.

She checked her phone and right on time, Duffy's truck came rolling up the driveway, with passengers up front. She grinned as Sam stopped his one-man tractor pull and waved to Duffy. "Sam, sweetheart, come here."

Sam immediately hopped off his tractor and came running to her. "Is Mr. Duff here for my birthday? Are we having another party? Did you make me another cake?"

"Yes, Mr. Duffy is here to see you on your birthday. No, we're not having another party. But I wanted to talk to you for a minute, okay?"

Sam's back was turned to the truck and Tootie and Duffy climbed out. Prince was cradled in Duffy's arms, frantically licking his bearded face.

"Now, five is a big birthday. You're not a baby anymore. You're a big boy and I think you're ready for some big-boy responsibilities. So, I was thinking that Prince could come and live with us, and you could help me take care of him."

"Oh, yes, PLEASE, Mom!" Sam squealed.

"Now, look, we're adopting him, which means he's a member of the family. He's not a birthday present. He just happened to show up today."

Behind Sam, Tootie grinned and flashed a thumbs-up while Duffy silently removed a big red bow he'd obviously tied to Prince's collar.

"I promise I'll take care of him. I'll feed him and give him baths and clean up after him," Sam swore.

"Okay then, turn around."

By then, Duffy had set Prince on the ground and the puppy gamboled straight for Sam, almost knocking him over.

"Thank you, Miss Tootie," Lucy said as Sam and Prince rolled on the grass together. "I know you don't take these adoptions lightly."

"Oh, honey, I've never been so sure about letting one of my babies go. You three will be just fine together."

"And the McCreadys send gifts," Duffy said, bringing out several gift bags printed with brightly colored paw prints. "Dog bowls, dog bed, leashes, puppy shampoo, everything to get you guys started. The whole family chipped in."

"Aw, that's so sweet," Lucy said. "I was gonna make a run to the pet store later, but this is great. Thank you."

"Thank you!" Sam cried as Prince chewed on his shorts.

"We hadn't quite started obedience training yet," Tootie said, watching the spectacle.

"We'll work on it," Lucy promised. "He was going to outgrow those shorts anyway."

Lucy went inside to fetch some iced tea for Tootie and Duffy, and when she came back out, she found that Evie had arrived with a comically large gift box wrapped in Superman paper. Sam had never cared for Superman, who had been Wayne's favorite growing up. Sam preferred Batman.

While Tootie and Duffy wore strikingly similar expressions of distrust, Lucy tried to appear neutral. Though for a split second, she was worried that Evie had purchased another tractor for Sam. This was Sam's grandmother, and it was a normal thing for a grandmother to want to see her grandson on his birthday. Of course, it would have been preferable for Evie to call and *ask* Lucy if it was okay to come over, but . . . yeah, Lucy had no excuse for her. It might be selfish of her, but she was thoroughly annoyed that Evie hadn't called ahead.

As Sam was tearing the paper off the box, Lucy was struck with a sense of foreboding. She had no idea what was in that box, but she was well aware of what Wayne's family considered appropriate gifts for kids. A Christmas involving lottery scratch-offs and promotional beer koozies came to mind immediately.

"Look what Mamaw Evie brought me!" Sam thundered as he pulled the box up and revealed a weathered bicycle with a body that had once shone red and a banana seat that had been reupholstered with new vinyl. This bike looked vaguely familiar.

"Oh . . ." Lucy said, nodding. "Okay."

Lucy looked to Duffy. The grim expressions on both his and Tootie's faces assured her that the helpless sense of rage she felt was not just a product of her feeling annoyed by her mother-in-law.

Sam was not ready for a two-wheeler yet, definitely not a two-wheeler that had been built for a much bigger boy, with no training wheels. Frankly, she thought she was pushing it with getting him a dog. Lucy should have been asked. It was shitty of Evie to just show up with this giant parenting decision in a box and leave Lucy no recourse but to take something away from her son.

"Sam, why don't you and Miss Tootie take Prince inside? He probably needs some water."

"Sure thing." Tootie took Sam's hand and followed him into the house. Duffy, probably sensing a storm brewing, stayed on the porch, waiting.

"What were you thinking, giving him Wayne's old bike?"

"It was his daddy's!" Evie cried. "I got it for Wayne's birthday when he was a little boy!"

"Yeah, I remember him riding it to school in third grade. Wayne got it for his *eighth* birthday! It's way too big for Sam. He could get hurt trying to ride it around. And he doesn't have pads or a helmet."

"He'll be fine, he just has to get used to it," Evie insisted. "It's only right for him to have something that belonged to his daddy. It's like keeping a part of Wayne alive."

"A part of Wayne is alive! In Sam!" Lucy cried. "But that won't last if he has an accident on a bike that's way too big for him, with no helmet. Look, I'll hold on to it for him for a couple of years and when he grows into it, we can try it then."

"He doesn't need to wait! I came all the way over here and I want to see him ride it now!"

"You would be surprised how little I care about what you want," Lucy told her. "You should have talked to me about this before you brought it over."

"Well, I didn't talk to you about it because you don't want to talk to me about anything having to do with my grandson. You didn't talk to me before you decided to open that *bakery* or when you decided to take up with some man. My Wayne would be ashamed of you, carrying on the way you do. After all your years together, I just expected a little more loyalty. He wouldn't have moved on this quick if you died," Evie snapped.

"We don't know that, Evie. And I'd like to think that Wayne would want me to be happy."

"Well, I don't like the idea of you bringing some man around Sam who's not half the man my Wayne was. It's not as if he's ever going to replace Sam's father."

"Uh, I'm standing right here, Miss Evie," Duffy said.

"What do you mean, *some man*? That's Duffy McCready. You've known him since he was a baby. You went to high school with his parents. And I don't talk to you the way you want me to about Sam because you seem to think that means you get to tell me whether I'm raising him right. I don't talk to you about financial decisions because it's none of your business. And Wayne can't be embarrassed, because he's dead. He can't be replaced because Sam only has one father. Who I date is none of your business, as long as it doesn't affect Sam, which it hasn't."

"I *thought* I knew him until he married that Lana Newton, but clearly, he's got a screw loose if that's his idea of a good decision."

"Still standing right here," Duffy muttered.

Lucy continued as if she hadn't heard him. "I'm trying to include you in our lives, but you never just take what I offer, it always has to be more than what I want to give, the way you want it. You're making this way harder than it has to be!"

Evie sniffed. "Well, you're just making my job easier. The

more people see you out acting this way, the easier it will be to take you to court."

Lucy's belly went cold and it was all she could do not to stumble back onto the porch. She'd been waiting for this tactic since Wayne had died, the threat of enforced visitation and dragging Sam into court to talk to strangers about who he loved best. She'd hoped Evie would never play that particular card, that Evie would respect Wayne's memory more than that. Obviously, Lucy was naive to the point of being sort of a dumbass.

Lucy worked to keep her voice calm, even as her brain screamed at her to take her son and run. "If you want to go that route, and stomp all over what little love I have left for you, go right ahead. But you need to know that Wayne's money you're so worried about? Would pay for a pretty amazing big city lawyer."

"This is bullshit!" Evie yelled. "I can't believe you would hurt me like this!"

"Well, you reap what you sow," Lucy snipped.

Evie's eyes narrowed; she was clearly aware that Lucy was throwing her own words back at her. But oddly enough, Lucy didn't feel a bit of triumph in it. This whole situation sucked and she was incredibly weary of it all.

"Look, I don't want to keep Sam away from you, even though my life would be a lot easier and a lot less stressful if I didn't let you into it. But you have to prove to me that you can put him first, to keep him safe and happy. You don't get to just make demands and expect me to fall in line."

Evie sniffed. "We'll see."

As she stomped toward her car, Duffy put his arm around Lucy's waist. "You okay?"

"No, I am not."

Lucy sank until her butt hit the porch steps.

"Hey, it's still a good day," Duffy told her. "Your son is safe and happy and has a puppy he's in love with already."

"I don't want to put Sam through some awful court battle. That's part of the reason I didn't divorce Wayne in the first place."

"I honestly don't think it's going to come to that. The only lawyer in town likes you much better than her," Duffy said, kissing her cheek.

"I hate feeling this way, but it's like I can't trust her at all with any little thing. I mean, you saw what she did with a birthday present. It just turns into this awful mess every time."

"It's not an easy road, honey. It never was going to be. But you're handling it really well. And you look super-hot when you've got blood in your eyes."

Lucy laughed. "That's wrong."

"I find you hot in all forms. I regret nothing."

"Weirdo."

"I'm your weirdo."

"Yeah." She sighed, leaning her head against his shoulder. "You are."

14

THE MOMENT THE doors of Gimme Some Sugar officially opened on a beautiful early April morning, the bakery was packed. Lucy suspected it had as much to do with curiosity from her neighbors as with people wanting cupcakes. But she would take any business she could get. Her plan was to lure them in with gossip and keep them coming back with quality baked goods.

All the painting and tiling and cabinetry had combined to create a colorful, inviting space that kept the focus on the display case full of cupcakes, luscious-looking fruit tarts, and cookies in a dozen flavors. A section of wall painted in chalkboard paint and framed by Duffy's work listed the *Daily Specials* in curli-cued yellow chalk letters. The tables were already crowded with locals sipping their coffees and devouring their sweets. A line at the counter had formed swiftly and was getting dangerously close to the door. Specs, bless him, had taken to counter service like a champ, cheerfully filling the little purple Gimme Some Sugar boxes and sending people away with a nod.

So, despite Evie's dire predictions, it seemed people did want baked goods in Lake Sackett. Even when there was a B-minus on the door. Marianne had helped Lucy pore over the county's health and safety regulations to find that while the letter grade must be displayed prominently at the entrance, there was no law against blowing up the health inspector's notes to an equally large size and displaying to the public that the chief complaints were "Fridge is one degree too cold" and "Dishwasher is suspiciously clean." Lucy's shop came across as "suspiciously clean" and Herb Brewster came across as an asshole.

A clang of bells at the door made Lucy look up. Donna waved and offered her a rare smile as she quietly joined the others in line. Lucy felt her heart lighten as a happy rumble of voices filled her shop. She lost herself in the soothing rhythm of filling orders and counting change. She was so busy, she barely noticed when Melody slipped into the shop, but the lone glowering face in the crowd finally caught her attention. Wayne's sister glared at every single customer for daring to look happy while standing in Lucy's "den of sin." Of course, that could have been related to one of the daily specials carefully written on the chalkboard: *Devil Woman's Food Cupcakes with "Sinful by Nature" Dark Chocolate Filling.*

Lucy thought it was funny, but clearly, Melody did not. Her sister-in-law stewed in her righteous juices right up until she reached the counter. "Just a plain sugar cookie, please. Everything else looks like it's too rich for me."

Lucy handed it to her with a smile. "No charge. Now please leave."

Melody glared at her while unwrapping the cookie and took a big bite. She immediately shrieked as if in pain and dropped the cookie to the floor. She clutched her mouth and cried out, "Oh, my tooth! I think I broke my tooth on that cookie. You must have baked the eggshells in it, Lucy! Or a big chunk of metal! I knew you didn't know how to run a bakery! You're gonna kill somebody!"

Around the shop, people stopped eating the pastries in their hands and subtly inspected them for foreign objects. Lucy's heart jumped into her throat. This was the sort of scene that could ruin a new business. She should have known that Melody would pull something like this. She should have known she wouldn't just skate through this opening unscathed without Wayne's family making some trouble for her. Lucy watched the door and noted that while people were edging away from the counter, they weren't backing out the door. They were staying to watch the spectacle.

Lucy cleared her throat and rounded the counter, picking up the dropped cookie from the floor. She inspected it, with her hands clearly visible to everybody standing in the shop. It was crumbly and buttery and smelled like vanilla—and lacked any sort of foreign object or poison. Lucy said very loudly and firmly, "Melody, I don't see a single thing wrong with this cookie, other than it's been dropped on the floor."

"But my tooth!" Melody cried, crumpling to the floor in a blond heap, clutching her face.

"If you honestly think there's something wrong with your tooth, you need to go to the dentist," Lucy said. "I'll pay the bill myself if you can prove I did something to damage it."

"No, I just need everybody in the shop to pray for me," Melody insisted. "Please, all you good people, lay down your sinful sweets and pray to deliver me from my pain caused by *this woman!*"

Lucy's mouth dropped open and her cheeks heated, but it was obvious that no one was stepping forward to lay hands on her sister-in-law. They seemed frozen, unsure of what to do. And then Donna parted the crowd, putting her hands on her hips. "Melody Garten, you get your ass up off that floor and stop acting a fool. You should be ashamed of yourself."

"But my tooth!" Melody cried.

Donna turned and scanned the faces of the customers. "Caroline!"

Caroline Dodge, the tall, willowy daughter of Fred Dodge, stood up on her toes, her dark cameo of a face rising above the other customers. "Yes, Miss Donna?"

"Could you come on over here, honey?" Donna said, in the same sweet tone she used with Lucy. "Now, you've been studying real hard at dental school, yes?"

"Yes, ma'am, I wouldn't waste my daddy's hard-earned tuition money," Caroline said, her brown doe eyes wide with alarm. "I'm home on spring break."

"Would you recognize a broken tooth if you saw one?"

"Sure. I mean, I'm not licensed or anything. I wouldn't be able to do anything about it. But I would know what I was looking at," Caroline said.

Donna helped Melody to her feet. "Could you take a look at Melody's mouth?"

Melody shook her head. "Now, look here, I don't want some person I barely know looking in my mouth! I don't need a dentist! I need prayer!"

"You're gonna need a lot more than that if you don't act right," Donna warned her. "Now, open up."

Caroline's own mouth pulled back at the corners. "Are you

sure about this, Miss Donna? I could get in trouble for examining somebody who doesn't want it."

"If Melody is gonna claim that Lucy broke her tooth, she needs to be willing to let someone who knows what they're doing take a look," Donna said in a very loud, deliberate, *I am making a point!* voice.

Suddenly, Melody shouted, "I'm healed! It was divine intervention! I don't need anybody looking at my teeth!"

"Because there was nothing wrong with them in the first place." Donna snorted. "Now, get on out of here."

Melody wrenched her arm out of Donna's grip and stomped toward the door. "I wouldn't eat anything from this bakery if it was delivered like manna from heaven!"

"Did she just invite me to throw pies at her house?" Lucy asked Donna. "Because that sounds like a plan."

The heavy silence that hung in the air with Melody's departure practically clogged Lucy's throat. The customers were still frozen in an awful tableau that could be titled *People Who Just Don't Know Where to Look*. Now that the crisis had passed, Lucy's cheeks flushed and her eyes grew hot and wet. She was already strung so tight, and dealing with her sister-in-law's bullshit right now was just beyond anything she could handle. And oh, Lord, she was gonna cry in the middle of her shop on her opening day—

Donna put her warm, firm hand on Lucy's arm and murmured softly, "Honey, you need to get yourself together. Don't let them see you cry, because then they'll know they got to you."

Lucy pressed her lips tightly, remembering her own words to Donna in the grocery store so many years before. She took a deep breath through her nose. "Yes, ma'am."

"If any of y'all are dumb enough to believe anything that crazy-ass Melody Garten says, you might as well clear out. But if you leave, don't come back and expect Lucy to wait on you again. So you're gonna have to choose between that sweet goodie in your hand, or supporting somebody who's looked down her nose at damn near everybody in this room," Donna said, her eyes sweeping across the café area. No one moved. No one even twitched toward the door. "Good. Now when you go home, talk about how good Lucy's cupcakes are, not Melody acting like a jackass."

Donna turned to Lucy, who was already planning an enormous boat-themed cinnamon spice cake for Donna's next birthday. "Go serve your customers. But save a cinnamon roll for me."

"You got it," Lucy said, squeezing her hand. "Caroline, you get a free coffee for putting up with a weird public scene on your first visit."

"Thank you," Caroline said, her shoulders sagging as she blew out a breath. "That was indeed weird. And extreme."

"I'm sorry I used you as cannon fodder, honey, but I knew she wouldn't want to get looked at by anybody who would be able to call her on her bullshit," Donna said as people milled forward and reformed the order lines. "Whatever you want is on me."

"This is turning out to be a pretty good day for me," Caroline said with a grin, pointing at a bear claw so Specs could retrieve it for her.

The day continued on and sales were steady. Despite Lucy's heart's thundering against her ribs, she kept on her most pleasant smile and did small internal dances of joy while the display case emptied. And then Ike Grandy walked through her door, his blue eyes scanning the room. She swallowed thickly. Ike had pretty much cornered the breakfast business in town since the Dunbar bakery had closed. She couldn't imagine that he was happy to have competition again. She liked Ike. She didn't want a confrontation with him, especially if it meant losing access to his cheeseburgers. She loved Ike's cheeseburgers.

Lucy watched out of the corner of her eye as Specs served the customers in the other line. Ike moved forward slowly, choosing a half dozen pastries from the case. He took them and a cup of black coffee to one of the café tables and methodically worked through the pastries, taking one bite of each. Every time, he nodded, as if in approval, took a long drink of coffee, and then moved on. The very last item was her cinnamon roll. He took an even larger bite and chewed thoughtfully, in a way that made Lucy's belly drop into her shoes. He rose and stood beside the line until there was a lull, waiting patiently as she emptied her display cabinet into the pantries of her neighbors.

"Can I talk to you for a minute?" he asked. Lucy glanced at the ladies in line.

"Oh, you go on, Lucy," Mrs. Bodine told her. "I need some time to make up my mind."

Lucy motioned for Ike to follow her into the kitchen.

"I don't really know how to say this, so I'm just going to come out and say it." Ike sighed, as if he was about to confess to multiple murders and inventing telemarketing. Lucy's eyes went wide. "The cinnamon rolls at the Rise and Shine? They're not homemade."

Lucy's mouth dropped open. "What?"

"I buy them at the bulk store and sneak them into the diner in an empty lard box when nobody's looking. I have for years."

Lucy reached out to take his hand. "Oh, Ike, I had no idea."

"It's the one thing I don't know how to make. It's the damn yeast dough. I never can get it to proof right. Give me a drop biscuit or a pie crust any day."

"But Mr. Dunbar was running a bakery here for years before I opened up," Lucy whispered.

"Yeah, well, I never did get on with Bud Dunbar. He called my French fries soggy in 1979 and after that I refused to buy so much as a doughnut off of him."

Lucy pursed her lips. "Sounds like a reasonable response."

"So do you think you could make me a few dozen of those cinnamon rolls every morning? And some of the bear claws? I'd put a little sign out telling people the pastries are from your shop and telling them they should try your place for dessert. I'd pay full retail price, just so I wouldn't have to keep that damn lard box around."

She mentally calculated the amount such an order would add to her coffers as a dependable income. And grinned. She extended her hand. "I think I can make that happen."

Ike grinned. "Thank you."

AT THE END of the day, she and Specs were sitting at one of the café tables splitting a bottle of sparkling nonalcoholic apple cider, toasting the nearly empty display case. Lucy took a picture of it to post to the shop's Instagram account with #VICTORY.

"My feet are aching and I feel like my face might fall off from smiling so much, but we really accomplished something today."

"And we gotta do it all over again tomorrow," he reminded her.

"Just let me have my moment, Specs."

He laughed. "All right, boss. Have your moment."

"I bless the day you walked through that door, Specs. I couldn't have done it without you."

"Aw, sure you would have." His wrinkly face went pink. She sipped her cider. "But it would have been a disaster."

She choked on her cider, spitting it back into her cup as he laughed at her.

"I bless the day you hired me, too, Lucy," he said. "It's been good for this old man to get out of bed and have some purpose. Your daddy would have been real proud of you."

"Thank you," she said, blinking hard as she finished her drink.

"So," she said, pulling her point-of-sales system's analytics for the day, "the blueberry muffins sold out, as did the raspberry-lemon muffins. The bran-walnut crashed and burned. They are the only ones left in the case, just as you predicted, so I owe you five bucks. No bran-walnut tomorrow. The bear claws and the cheese Danish were the big winners for breakfast pastries, defeating all other breakfast pastries in combat. The chocolate chip cookies outsold all other cookies two to one. Snickerdoodle and peanut butter ran second and a close third. And all cupcakes sold out. All of them. Even the chocolate-espresso-almond, which you said were too pretentious for this market, so you owe *me* five bucks, which makes us even. I'm going to keep Devil Woman's Food on the menu forever just for the bullshit that Melody pulled today. Also, we will be adding Black Forest and caramel cinnamon apple to the lineup for tomorrow and rotating out the carrot cake and the mocha. I'll leave those recipes on the counter for you, but honestly, it's nothing you can't handle."

"Sure thing, boss lady."

A loud knock sounded at the front door.

"We're closed!" she called without turning around. "Completely sold out!"

The knock repeated, sounding even more determined. Lucy turned to see Herb Brewster standing at her door, waving a clipboard at her.

Lucy sighed. "Aw, sonofabitch."

DUFFY FOUND LUCY on her front porch swing, drinking a beer. He had more beer in a cooler for her, and some of Leslie's famous fried chicken. And when she could barely muster a smile for him, he winced.

"Damn, that bad?" he said, flopping down on the swing next to her. "Tootie said the opening went great! You had a huge line most of the day. I drove by a couple of times—not that I was being creepy about it. Just, you know, supportive, from a distance. Where is Sam?"

"He's inside, sleeping. And the opening went fine. Big sales numbers. Happy customers," she said, draining her beer. "It was after closing that was the problem. Herb Brewster did not appreciate me appealing his rating or blowing up his notes so everybody could see he was being an unfair jackass. His follow-up inspection was even more brutal than the first, because he'd received an 'anonymous report' that a customer had been injured while eating one of my cookies."

"What?"

"It's a long story. I got an eighty-four. He dinged me for having garbage in the garbage cans. At the end of a busy day. Apparently, in his opinion, garbage cans are merely decorative."

"Wow, that's rough. What was your rating?"

"I got a C." She sighed. "And I'm not allowed to appeal it again for six months."

"C is still passing," he said.

"I know," she said. "It just feels like an enormous failure. And did it have to happen on my opening day? Couldn't I have just one day? I know this is going to sound paranoid, but I can't help but think Evie had something to do with this."

"I would say that's an overreaction, but she did have Herb shut down the only Italian restaurant we've ever had because the owner made a comment about Evie eating too many of the breadsticks," he said, taking another beer out of the cooler and handing it to her.

"Part of me feels sorry for her, because I know she's grieving. She lost a son, whom she loved. But at the same time, she's just so freaking frustrating to deal with, and she is trying to shut down my business, which is a really messed-up thing to do. And at the end of the day, I don't want her to try to use Sam as some sort of replacement for Wayne. And I just don't trust her enough to leave him alone with her."

"Okay."

"Well, what do you think of that?"

"I'm not going to tell you how to parent, Lucy. I am the definition of underqualified there."

"Duffy, tell me what you think or you'll never see another one of my cupcakes."

"Wow, you're cutting deep."

"I'm a desperate woman."

"You have the right to make all of the decisions about your son. That's what it means to be his mama. But even with that aside, the bakery thing is really messed up and Evie and Melody had no right to do that. So go after them hard, there."

"Oh, I intend to."

He cracked open his own beer. "How?"

"I don't know yet," she admitted.

"I'm going to tell you the same thing I tell my mom. I can only pay so much bail money, so watch yourself."

"Aw." She gave an exaggerated puppy-dog face. "You would bail me out of jail?"

"You are on the very short list of people I would bail out of jail."

"Oh, honey, I'm touched," she said, splaying her hand over her heart.

"In the head."

"Shush."

15

THOUGH THE SHOP was closed on Monday, Lucy had arranged to meet Margot there for her special tasting. She figured it was a lot more professional to meet in her workspace than to haul a bunch of cupcakes over to Margot's, where there was a possibility they would be devoured by the Archer girls. Or the Archer dogs.

She had stayed up into the wee hours of the morning to make cupcakes in a dozen flavors, finding the perfect specimen for each batch to offer as the tasting sample. Lucy was certain she'd never prepared so much for one meeting in all her life, not even that time she got saddled with gathering items for the Junior League's Spring Spectacular "Lap of Luxury" Charity Auction. No one appreciated how difficult it was to separate rich people from their money.

Honestly, it wasn't the prospect of baking Margot's wedding cake that made her nervous. She'd baked tiered cakes before, so the involved construction—cardboard circles, wooden dowel rods, plastic support tubes—didn't scare her. It was the idea that this was one of the most important cakes of someone's life, and she could seriously screw it up and there would be no way to fix it. That Margot could look back at her wedding day with joy and nostalgia, and then scrunch up her face and say, "But the cake."

It didn't seem so important when she was just making a cake as a favor for a friend. It seemed like an opportunity for a funny story. "I let my college friend make the cake and it ended up melting right off the stand and into my table full of uncles in the middle of the reception."

Now, making a wedding cake for a former fancy event planner? Seemed like an opportunity for professional suicide.

After dropping Sam off at preschool, where he promised he would draw at least two pictures of Prince, Lucy stopped by the McCready compound. She'd left one of her Wilton wedding cake idea books at Duffy's place, and the McCreadys never bothered locking their doors. Duffy was supposed to have that morning off, but took a last-minute charter. She'd sent him a text letting him know she would be dropping by, just in case he had something lying out he wanted to warn her about. He texted back, **Sure thing, baby doll. See you at my place tonight for pizza and Pixar!**

A few minutes later he texted again, **Um, there's no sequel to UP, right? Asking for a friend.**

She laughed. Poor Duffy had not been prepared for the emotional upheaval that was Carl and Ellie's love story. She texted back, **Nope, but there are two more Cars movies.**

Duffy's response was a string of gifs of Luke Skywalker, Michael Scott, and Marty McFly yelling, "NOOOOOOO!" which had her giggling the whole drive to the McCready compound.

The laughter died the moment she spotted Lana's El Camino parked near the gravel entrance to the compound. Her mouth turned down at the corners and she parked in front of Duffy's cabin with a resigned weight on her chest.

Whatever was waiting for her on the other side of the door, she did not think she had the mental fortitude for this bullshit without several more hours of sleep and a metric ass-ton of coffee.

Crossing the porch, Lucy pulled the door open to find Lana shimmying through the living room in one of Duffy's old John Deere T-shirts. Her blond hair was mussed and her long, tan legs were bared, the hem of Duffy's shirt barely covering a pair of cheap-looking magenta lace panties. She giggled and preened midturn. "Hi, sweetie! Welcome ho—"

Lana stopped mid-"ho," but a sly smirk spread across her features. "Oh, sorry, I was expecting Duffy."

"I'm sure you were," Lucy deadpanned.

Lana didn't bother to try to cover up. "He just ran out to grab us something for breakfast."

Lucy took a deep breath and dropped her purse by the door. She crossed her arms over her chest, the cuffs of her old jean jacket snagging at the neckline of her floral dress. "Sure."

"I know, it's probably hard for you to find out this way, Lucy, but it's for the best. I mean, it's not like he's cheating on *you*. I'm his *wife*. And really, I think I should be thanking you. 'Dating' you, or whatever you call it, has made him see the light. It was just like I told you. After getting a taste of that boring apple pie, he realized how much he loved me, that he can't live without me. So you can just run along. I'll take care of Duffy from here."

"Lana, I'm going to stop you there. I am not dumb enough

to believe that Duffy slept with you recently or was planning on sleeping with you today. He's too decent a person, and he's not dumb enough to tell me to come on over to his cabin if he thought you were going to be here. So why don't you pick up your clothes and what's left of your dignity and go on home? I'll leave Duff a note about fumigating the place."

Lana's face went purple with confused rage when she realized her lure wasn't working. And given that she wasn't the type of gal to have a backup plan, she opted to just go on the attack. "You think you're so special because you managed to snag some guy who never got over you in high school?" she snapped. "It's pathetic. You know you're too old and saggy to get someone new, so you settled for Duffy. You've never loved him. You're just using him. You're a selfish bitch and one of these days, Duffy's going to figure it out and drop you on that flat ass of yours."

"And then he'll go right back to you, huh?"

Lana nodded. "Where he belongs. It's just a matter of time. He slept with me right before you got back to town. I don't see any reason that'll stop."

Lucy's face set in rigid, glacial lines. "Well, I guess we're just going to have to see." She yanked the door open and held it there without looking at the frame. "Now, get your shit and get out."

Lana scooped her clothes up from the floor and snarled at her as she stomped out the door, her jeans in her hand. "This isn't over!"

"I'm sure it isn't," Lucy said with a sigh, pinching the bridge of her nose as she heard Lana storming up the gravel drive.

"Oh, this is stupid," she told herself, sniffing slightly. "Don't let her get to you. Don't let her dumbass skanky supervillain plan work."

Lucy snatched the Wilton book off the coffee table and shut the door firmly behind her. "I'm never having sex with Duffy in that cabin. Ever."

An hour later, Lucy sat at the slightly larger "consultation table" she'd arranged in the café area with an array of cupcakes staged on a tiered tea tray. Even with the different colors and frostings, it looked very pretty. Her swirls were even and comparable. Her little toppings were centered. It was perfect, but not obnoxiously so.

Margot stepped through the front door of the shop, looking like an ad for maternity business wear, her expensive designer sunglasses slid back like a headband in her thick blond hair. She glanced at Lucy and her dark gold brows knit together. "You okay, sweetie? You're looking a little 'down in the mouth,' as Tootie might say. *I* wouldn't say it, but the term definitely applies to you this morning."

"No, I'm fine, just fine," Lucy assured her. "And I hope you're ready to eat sweets for breakfast."

"I can't tell you how much we're looking forward to this," Margot said as her eyes lit on the cupcake display.

"We?" Lucy tilted her head. "Is Kyle coming?"

Margot patted her swell of belly. "No, just me and the peanut. Kyle is stuck at school. It's Pet Show-and-Tell Day, which has a history of going horribly awry. We've been craving cake for days, just thinking about it."

"You may be having a boy. I swear, when I was pregnant with Sam, I wanted nothing but Ho Hos and rocky road ice cream. My friends who were having girls wanted fruit salad and grilled chicken."

"A boy wouldn't be so bad, to balance out the estrogen in the household. All Kyle has is Arlo and Charlie. They hardly count."

"You haven't found out the gender?"

Margot sank into the chair beside her with an "Oof." Lucy handed her a glass of water, which she sipped from gratefully. "Nope, we're going to be surprised. It keeps things exciting."

Lucy grinned. "I think that's sweet. So we have a selection of cakes here, both lightly flavored and intense, fruity and chocolate. And a spice cake, even though it's not a good fit for a summer wedding. But it's a good 'get it out of the way quick' rejection option."

"A summer wedding," Margot said, frowning. "Right."

"You don't think you'll be ready by summer?" she asked. "Duffy said you haven't set a date yet."

"I'm sure it will be fine," Margot said, though Lucy noted that Margot didn't give her a date. "So, I'll start with the white cake and white icing, the boring end of the spectrum."

Lucy snorted. Margot took a bite of the cake and shrugged. "It's moist and delicious."

"But about as exciting as unflavored Jell-O?" Lucy guessed. Margot nodded. Lucy spun the stand to show her a lemon cake with Swiss meringue frosting. "Slightly more exotic."

"There we go." Margot sighed, chewing thoughtfully. "This is a front-runner."

Lucy handed her the glass of water. "Can you stand the smell of coffee? It's a good palate cleanser between flavors."

"I have no problem with coffee. I would make out with you right now if you'd recently had coffee," Margot told her. "The whole family has me on caffeine lockdown. Even the sweet tea they give me is decaf."

"Sorry, all I can offer you is this," Lucy said, holding up a sugar shaker she'd filled with whole coffee beans for just such an occasion.

"I'll take it," Margot said, snatching it from Lucy's hand and pressing it to her nose, inhaling deeply.

"Okay, and chocolate is a good complement to the coffee beans you're trying to lodge in your nasal cavity."

"I regret nothing," Margot declared and took a big bite of a devil's food cupcake with double chocolate frosting. She moaned, sitting back in her chair. She closed her eyes and held up one finger. "I'm going to need a minute."

Margot consumed the entire cupcake without further comment. "I really want a chocolate wedding cake. The baby thinks I should have a chocolate wedding cake."

"I agree with the baby," Lucy said. "It could be great. Nontraditional, fun. We can do full chocolate frosting with brightly colored flowers or fondant decorations. I have some wedding cake books you can look over to give you some idea of what's possible. Or you can just give me some details about the decorations or even the invitations, and I can work something up myself."

"Right," Margot said, nodding. "More details."

"Honey, I know we're not close friends, but I tend to worry about people when they make this face when they talk about their wedding." Lucy made an expression that looked like nausea mixed with the pain of getting punched in the boob.

"There's just so many choices," Margot said, sipping the water. "I mean, I used to make these decisions all the time when I was planning events. But now that it's for me? I only plan on doing this once. I know everybody says that, but I mean it, I will *never* do this again. And what if I pick the wrong thing? What if I look back and wish I'd done something different?"

"That's not really helping the amount of pressure on me as one of your vendors, Margot."

"But it's not just the cake, I'm like this with everything," Margot insisted. "The napkin colors and the type on the invitations and the way we phrase every single damn thing—because of my weird parent situation and at the same time, I don't want it to seem like I'm gloating over Maggie. She died and I have her husband and children now."

"What does Kyle think?"

"He and Maggie had a big white wedding the first time around, and he had a lot of input. He feels it's kind of unfair not to give me everything I want this time. So even if he has a preference, he just tells me to do what I want," she said, shrugging. "I just, I thought it would be easy, you know? Because I have so much experience with this sort of thing, and I know what I like. But this . . ."

"You know, if you don't want to be married, you don't have to do anything you don't want to do. The baby complicates things, but lots of people have babies without being married. I know this is small-town Georgia, which adds to the pressure, but it's not like they're going to sew a big red A on your clothes."

"It's not that I don't want to be married. I love Kyle. I want to be with him, and only him, forever and ever. I don't see my life working with anyone else, or without the girls, even if things have moved a lot faster than I thought they would. It's taken a lot of work for me to recognize that it was my mother's marriages I was afraid of, not the institution itself. It's the idea of the wedding and all those people and . . . I know what some of them still think of me, even though they smile and call me 'Stan's girl.'"

"You don't have to do a big white wedding."

"I know." Margot sighed. "But if I don't, that would hurt Stan's feelings, Tootie's feelings, Aunt Leslie's feelings—everybody's feelings, basically."

"And your feelings in all this are . . . where?"

Margot's eyes narrowed. "Please don't be wise and insightful with me right now."

"Seriously, this is the limit of my folksy wisdom. If you weren't knocked up, I would be plying you with booze," she said, hugging Margot. "Talk to Kyle and see how he feels about paring things down a bit. I'll still make the cake, no matter how small. Hell, I'll make you a wedding cupcake if you want."

"I hate wedding cupcakes, they're a cop-out."

"See, that's one decision made, right there, though thousands of brides disagree with you," Lucy said. "And you didn't like the white cake, so that's another. You favored the lemon and the chocolate. And if you decide you like any of the other flavors, we can do a bit of everything. Lots of people do multiple flavors in tiers or cupcakes. It's more interesting and you cater to your guests' tastes. The mark of a considerate bride."

"You're right." Margot sniffed. "I'm overreacting. It's just these stupid hormones and feelings and I'm not used to having either. I don't get paralyzed over decisions. I don't cry over things like this. I *make* people cry."

"You sound oddly proud of that."

"I am, a little," Margot confessed.

"It happens to everybody," Lucy assured her. "When I was eight months pregnant with Sam, my dad gave me this awful Raggedy Andy doll that my mama had kept in storage for me, from when I was little. I mean, this doll was the stuff of nightmares. And I cried happy tears so hard I scared my dad."

"That sounds oddly familiar," Margot said.

"You want some more cake?" Lucy asked.

Margot nodded. "Desperately."

Lucy spun the tiered tray again and offered her another cupcake, topped with toasted coconut. "Now, I like to call this my Almond Joy cupcake."

Margot practically recoiled.

"Is that coconut?" she asked, turning slightly green.

"Yeah, chocolate cake with a coconut cream frosting."

"Lucy, I'm really sorry about this." Margot leaned over the wastebasket and threw up more than Lucy considered humanly possible.

"Oh, hell, is that one of your morning sickness triggers?" Lucy gasped and tossed the cupcake over the counter. Where it landed, she had no idea, but it was out of Margot's nose range.

Margot groaned as Lucy pressed the water into her hand. "Coconut, and raw meat, and fucking peanuts of all things."

"Yeah, motherhood is a disgusting miracle." Lucy patted her back as Margot leaned back over the trash can. "You know, there was a lot more vomit involved in this bridal appointment than I expected."

"Me, too," Margot grumbled.

ONCE MARGOT WAS feeling better, Lucy gave her a bottled water and a pecan pie to go, and sent her home. Then she boxed up a few dozen cookies she was going to take to Sam's class later that afternoon. They were having a play day at Sackett Memorial Park and Miss Lilah had asked her to bring a snack just before pickup.

But for now, she closed the shop. She figured making a customer throw up was probably an omen. She drove to Sackett

Memorial Park, cookies in hand. But when she pulled into the parking lot for the large playground area, recently finished with funds from the Lake Sackett Optimists Club, she didn't spot Sam running around with the other kids on the brightly colored plastic equipment. A small flare of panic building in her gut, she scanned the playground, searching for his familiar shock of blond hair.

Her eye caught on a little boy on the sidewalk behind the playground, beyond Miss Lilah's line of sight. He was standing with a familiar figure, Evie, who was coaxing him onto a faded red bicycle.

"Shit!" Lucy yelled, tearing off her seat belt. She hopped out of the truck and ran across the park. Sam wasn't even wearing a helmet and Evie was "helping" him balance on a bike so tall he couldn't even reach the pedals without standing on them. Lucy saw the determined look on his face and her heart dropped. Lilah noticed Lucy running and froze at the expression of frightened rage on her face.

"Evie!" Lucy yelled. "Get him off that thing right now!"

All of the kids stopped playing as Lucy ran past the playground. *Faster, faster,* she had to move faster to get to her baby. Over the blood pounding in her ears, she could barely hear Evie chattering encouragements to Sam about what a big boy he was and how proud his daddy would be to see Sam ride his bike in the park just like Wayne had.

"Evie, stop!"

Evie turned to see Lucy running at them and let go of the bike. Sam pumped his legs, but with his body weight shifting wildly, he only coasted a few feet before gravity caught up with him, the bike wobbled, and he flopped onto his right side, his head barely missing the far edge of the concrete and thumping against the soft dirt. Sam shrieked in pain, and Lucy saw that one of the joints of the bike was pinning his right arm to the sidewalk.

"Now, he'll be just fine. No reason to panic," Evie said, her voice maddeningly calm as Lucy lifted the bike gently off of Sam. "Every boy takes a tumble off his bike now and then. It's not a big deal. He just has to get right back on and try again. It's what his daddy would have wanted."

"You shut your mouth right now," Lucy growled as Sam whimpered in pain. His wrist was bent at an odd angle and was swelling like proofed yeast dough.

"Oh my Lord, Lucy, I'm so sorry!" Lilah cried, kneeling by Sam's side. "There are so many kids running around and I didn't even see Evie sneak up here."

"I didn't sneak anywhere!" Evie yelled. "This is public property! I just thought it would be nice for him to have a bike to play with while his class was in the park!"

"So, what, you went to my house and took it out of my garage?" Lucy exclaimed. "That's crazy! And I told you he's not big enough for this bike. He didn't even have a helmet on. Did you see how close his head came to hitting the sidewalk?"

"Oh, no one ever wore helmets when Wayne was growing up. He never got hurt," Evie said. "You're making too big a deal out of this. You're the one who's scaring him. Sam, honey, you're fine. Aren't you? Tell her you're fine and you want to take another ride on the bike Mamaw gave you."

"No, I want to go home. Mama, please. My arm hurts." Sam rubbed his tearstained face against Lucy's shoulder. She kissed his sweaty hair and rubbed his back.

"You need to be a big boy, Sam," Evie said, her voice sterner. "Now, stop that crying."

"Shut. Your. Mouth," Lucy told her, gingerly holding up Sam's wrist so Evie could see the swelling. "You did this. This is your fault. No one else's. You just had to have your way. Well, you got it. Congratulations."

Evie's face went white, then green. "I didn't mean for him to get hurt. I only wanted to have some time with him. I taught his daddy to ride a bike in this park and—"

"I don't want to hear it," Lucy seethed, standing with Sam's weight in her arms. "Lilah, I'm gonna take Sam to the doctor to get his wrist checked out. I'm pretty sure he's going to need an X-ray. I'll sign whatever paperwork needs to be signed later, okay?"

Lilah nodded. "Sam, you feel better, okay? You come back to class as soon as you can."

"It's okay, Miss Lilah. I love you and I'll see you later."

Lilah looked like she might burst into tears. "I love you, too, Sam."

"It's gonna be okay, Lilah," Lucy said. "I'll call you as soon as I know anything about the wrist."

Lilah nodded again.

"I'll come with you," Evie said, picking up the bicycle. "I can keep Sam company in the waiting room."

"You must be out of your damn mind," Lucy told her. "I don't want you in the waiting room. I don't want you at the hospital. I don't even want you in the same county!"

"Lucy, please! Don't be unreasonable!" Evie cried as Lucy power-walked Sam's limp body across the park.

"My arm hurts," Sam moaned. "And I want ice cream."

Lucy's lips quirked despite the extreme shittiness of the situation. "I'll give you all the ice cream you want after we see the doctor."

"What's an X-ray?"

"It's a picture of your bones," Lucy said, buckling him into his car seat.

"That sounds cool. Can I keep it?" he asked, cradling his wrist to his chest.

"I'll see if I can get you a copy," Lucy said, running her fingers over his hair.

"With my ice cream?"

"With your ice cream."

FOUR HOURS AT the urgent care clinic, two scoops of mint chocolate chip, and a soft cast later, Evie settled Sam down in his bed with some Tylenol and his favorite stuffed dog. It was only seven when they returned home, but Sam was already nodding off. Prince seemed aware that something was wrong with his boy and had immediately cuddled up at Sam's side over the covers. Lucy didn't have the heart to tell him to get off the bed.

"Can my friends sign my cast, Mama?" Sam asked with a yawn.

"Well, it's not that kind of cast, baby, but I wouldn't be surprised if Miss Lilah had the kids make a get-well card for you."

"That'll be nice," he said, running his fingers over Prince's floppy ears. His eyes closed and he added, "I'm sorry I rode the bike."

Lucy swallowed thickly. "It's not your fault, honey. Mama should have been there to keep that from happening."

"Okay." Sam sighed, turning his face into his pillow.

Lucy sat there on his bed, listening to her son's breath evening out. She scratched Prince's head and said, "I'm going to make an exception tonight, but I'm trusting you not to pee on anything important."

Lucy clicked on Sam's race car nightlight and walked down the hall. She put on her comfiest sweatpants and a track and field T-shirt so old it was soft as butter. She sank onto the couch and found she was tired, the kind of tired that seeped into your bones and weighed you down like lead. She hadn't been this tired since the day after Wayne's funeral, when she realized she would have to start her life over entirely. She wasn't just weary in body but in spirit. Her baby had been hurt, because she was distracted, busy. She'd been just a minute too late and her son had literally suffered for it.

Everywhere she turned, there seemed to be some reminder of something she wasn't doing right. Sam's toys on the floor. (*Oh, the son that you seem to be dropping off with one of the McCreadys every other day when you and Duffy have plans? The son that Evie has threatened to take you to court over, because she doesn't think you're raising him right? The son who got hurt today because you weren't there?*) Brochures for the shop, spread out on the coffee table. (*Right, the business that is sort of, kind of getting off the ground, but could topple at any moment because your mother-in-law could turn the tide of public opinion against you? The business that could close if the local health inspector gets his way?*) A Braves cap Duffy had left on the end of the couch. (*Duffy? The man you're not quite brave enough to make a com-*

mitment to, even though you love him, because you both have too much baggage? The guy whose half-naked ex-wife snuck into his house and tried to convince you that she'd just slept with him that morning, because that's something people outside of soap operas do? The guy who could be an amazing husband and father figure to your son, but bringing someone into Sam's life that permanently could cause so many problems with Evie and Lana and unknown relationship forces you probably haven't even figured out yet?)

The voices of doubt in her head melded together to form a gospel choir proclaiming her multilevel failure. Everywhere she looked, she saw some battlefront she had to attend to, work that had to be done, and she was just so damn tired of fighting. She was worn thinner than a flour-sack dress, and she was feeling it down to her soul. She pulled the afghan off the back of her couch, wrapped herself in a blanket burrito, and drifted off to sleep with a heavy heart.

She gasped when she realized someone was standing over her, and came up swinging. Fortunately, Duffy was quick on his feet and ducked out of the way before her fist could connect.

"Duffy!" she cried, still half-asleep. "What the hell?"

"Sorry! Sorry! I heard what happened with Sam at the park and I wanted to check on you. Margot said you weren't quite yourself this morning. She actually used the phrase 'down in the mouth,' which I find alarming because Margot has resisted most Southernisms. I didn't know if you'd still be up for our plans tonight—"

"So you just show up to my house?" Lucy asked, sitting up and squinting at him.

"I tried calling and you didn't answer. You also didn't lock the front door."

"I'm sorry." Lucy pressed her fingertips into her cheekbones. "I've just had a really long day. Why don't we go outside? Sam's sleeping down the hall and I don't want to wake him."

"How's his arm?" he asked as he followed her out the door. "Aunt Leslie said Lilah was just beside herself over him getting hurt."

"It's fractured. The doctor said it's pretty common in a fall at his age and he'll be fine. But honestly, it's just the topper of a shit day. I had a little bit of a run-in with Lana this morning, who was prancing around your cabin half-dressed and tried to convince me that she was waiting on postcoital doughnuts. And then Margot vomited her way through our cake tasting this morning. And my son got hurt and I just realized that I forgot to stop at the grocery store to get the ingredients for pizza. I just sort of collapsed."

"So you forgot. It happens. We can just order pizza. It's okay."

And something about the cheerful, blithe forgiveness Duffy was offering made rage, hot and ugly, boil up from her gut. "No, it's not okay and you shouldn't be willing to accept it. I'm half-assing everything. Parenting Sam, dating you, running the business. There is not a whole-ass attempt in that whole list."

Duffy scoffed and rubbed his hand over hers, and she flinched away. "What are you talking about? You're amazing."

Her voice broke as she insisted, "I'm not amazing. I'm no-where near it. I'm clinging to this earth by my fingernails just to keep from getting thrown off. I can't just keep rolling with the punches. I can't keep the fight up on every front. I've tried it before and it's too much to ask of one person. I can't keep fight-ing for my bakery and my relationship with you and be a decent mother to Sam, and maybe if I just let something go I'll be able to feel like I can breathe again. Maybe I'm not ready for a relationship. Maybe in a couple of years I will be, but right now . . . I don't think I can do this anymore. Between those three things, I've gotta choose Sam and providing for Sam."

"What does that mean?"

"It means exactly what it sounds like, 'I don't think we can do this anymore.' "

Duffy's face flushed an unpleasant color, his hands dropping to his sides. "So you're willing to drop me just like that? Walk away like I'm nothing? Again?"

"What are you talking about?"

"This is high school all over again! You walked away and you never looked back. You chose Wayne, you left with him. And I didn't get any say, any warning," he said, his voice rising. "It's happening all over again."

She sighed, letting her head drop. So they were finally having this conversation. They couldn't just pretend it hadn't happened, that everything was okay and they'd moved on from whatever wounds had been inflicted when they were teenagers. But instead of looking at the situation rationally and trying to respond with some amount of emotional maturity, Lucy shot back, "I don't know if anyone has told you this, but fixating on something that happened ten years ago is not real attractive. And it's not like I owed you something because we were friends. You don't get dibs, Duffy."

"I'm not angry because I think that you owed me love because I loved you. I'm angry because you wasted your time on an idiot who treated you like a damn lifestyle accessory. And it disappoints the hell out of me, Lucy."

"That's none of your business."

"Why did you stay with him? You could have left him years ago, when you figured out you weren't happy. We could have figured this out *years ago*, before you got bogged down in guilt and grief and whatever the hell is going on with you right now that is making you come across a lot like my mother."

"That's none of your business! And I'm sorry, but I don't think I'm going to take crap from someone who lets his ex-wife back into his life whenever the wind hits her wrong, because you don't want to make her feel bad for being a terrible fucking person."

"Well, maybe some people don't just cut folks out of their lives as easily as you do," he said.

"So that's what you really think I'm doing with Evie?"

"Not necessarily, but it's a real pattern with you. You cut me out. You cut out all your friends here. Hell, you cut out the entire town and ran off to Texas."

"I'd much rather live that way than coddling her, which is what you do with Lana. If you stood your ground with her, maybe she wouldn't feel comfortable sneaking into your damn house half-dressed."

"So this is about Lana?"

"No! It's not about Lana or Evie or even Sam. It's about me. I'm not ready to be what you need me to be. And God, I appreciate that you've been there for me over the last few months, but I let this go too far too fast and I just can't keep up anymore."

"So I'll help you," Duffy said. "That's what people do for someone they love. They step in and they help."

"Me becoming more dependent on you is not the answer here," she said. "I need some time to myself, where I can focus on what's most important and get my shit together."

"So no matter what I do, I don't get a vote in this," he said. "You've already made up your mind."

She nodded, even though every nerve and muscle in her neck wanted to clench up and prevent her from doing something so very stupid. How had this happened so fast? How had they gone from funny gifs this morning to her spewing an angry torrent of insults at him this evening? And why was he so angry with her in return?

"Well, I guess there's nothing left to say," Duffy growled, turning on his heel toward the door.

"I'm always gonna love you, Duffy," she said quietly. "And I hope someday we can be friends again."

His face grew red, and for the first time in their lives, Duffy looked like he was truly angry with her. "No, Lucy, it's not going to work like that. I can't go back to being your friend. Not anymore."

"Then I hope someday you'll forgive me. I'm sorry."

"Yeah, you are." He crossed to the door and slammed it behind him. Lucy buried her face in her hands and wept.

16

DUFFY DID THE only thing he could think of when he was hurting, which was to go to the dock at McCready's and drink. On this particular evening, the sun was setting over the lake and most everybody was gone for the day. Even Frankie, seeing the way he'd screeched his truck to a halt in the parking lot and the rigid set of his shoulders as he stomped down the dock with his six-pack of beer, knew enough to leave her cousin alone. Aunt Leslie left a wax-paper-wrapped sandwich on the bench near the Snack Shack and disappeared silently.

He watched the light dance across the water and wondered again how the hell things had gone so wrong so fast. One minute, he and Lucy were planning dinner, and the next, they were yelling. He'd said horrible things to Lucy, like all of the ugliest resentments written on the back side of his heart came bubbling up from his lips. And she'd had some whoppers in return. The problem was that neither of them was wrong. They'd both messed up. They'd both had old hurts they hadn't confessed to, and the sad thing was he wasn't surprised by the words coming from either of them.

Her doubts about herself had taken him off guard, though. He knew that she worried about mothering Sam, about being enough for him on her own. But he never would have guessed she felt like she was failing at *everything*. He never would have described her as half-assing anything. It wasn't like he wasn't accustomed to fighting in a relationship—he'd had more screaming matches with Lana than he could count. But this felt different . . . and potentially permanent.

"Son, I know I say I'm disappointed in your choices pretty frequently, but this is a new low."

He looked back to see his mother standing on the dock, her long, thin arms crossed over her chest.

It was at times like this that he missed his father desperately. Junior McCready hadn't been a great scholar, but he'd always been able to cut to the heart of the matter and find the most gentle way to advise Duffy. His father never looked at him like he'd shit in his own hat.

"I called Lucy to check on Sammy after Leslie told me all about the accident at the park. I've never heard her sound so upset, Duffy. Not even when her daddy died. What did you do?"

Duffy sniffed. "I'm pretty disappointed in myself, too, so welcome to the club."

"You finally man up and tell the girl you love her. You find out she loves you, too. You were making it work. And then . . . what? You have a little fight so you sulk here, waiting for some sort of mystery sign, drinking yourself stupid?"

"Well, what do you expect me to do?" Duffy asked. "She told me she didn't want to keep seeing me. It wasn't just a 'let's be friends' speech. She wanted to end things because she wants to be a good mother to her son. That just proves what a good person she is, that I was right to love her in the first place. That's not the kind of thing you argue with."

"And you believed her?" She rolled her eyes, sitting down near him. "Oh, son, I didn't teach you anything about women?"

"Well, you taught me that they're seventy-five percent crazy mixed with twenty percent surly, and the remaining five percent is up to chance. So thanks for that."

"She's scared, Duffy. That's normal, considering her situation. And it's normal to lash out, too. Lord knows I did."

"Yup," he muttered.

"But you don't just give up on her. You go back, try to talk to her."

"Well, that would make a lot of sense if I hadn't said a lot of bad shit, too."

Donna wrinkled her thin features. "Like what?"

"That I was pissed at her for choosing Wayne and leaving with him, for staying with him when she was miserable, and that she was a coward for running again."

"I swear, idiocy runs in the McCready male line." She sighed.

"So what do you suggest I do?"

"Apologizing would be a good start," she said. "Hoping that she apologizes, too, but not expecting it for a while. Not giving up, or looking for an excuse for giving up because you're scared, too. I like that girl, and you know I don't like a lot of people. She brings out the better parts in you. Love like that, the kind of love that I had with your daddy? That doesn't come along every day. And if you're dumb enough to let that go, you're no son of mine."

"Does all of your motherly advice have to come wrapped up in insults?"

She thought about it. "Yep."

"Fine," he grumbled. "Is this a flowers-level apology or am I looking at jewelry and maybe a kidney?"

Donna shrugged. "You've got two kidneys. You'll be fine."

Just then Duffy heard tires crunching on the gravel behind them. He turned to see Lana's El Camino parking next to his truck. "Oh, shit."

"Did she have something to do with your problems with Lucy?" Donna asked.

"Not exactly, but she didn't help," Duffy said, standing.

"All right, that's it." Donna pushed to her feet and took off running down the dock.

"Shit." Duffy sighed again, chasing after her. By the time he caught up to Donna, she and Lana were screaming insults at each other, circling, like they were trying to figure out who was going to throw the first punch. Donna impugned Lana's parentage, moral fiber, character, and intelligence. Lana cast aspersions on Donna's ability to be anything but a bitch. That was pretty much all she had. Frankie and Eric came running out of the morgue entrance. Eric's face was in full cop mode and he rested one hand on his can of Mace.

"Would you two just *stop!*" Duffy thundered, somehow reaching a volume that could be heard over them.

They stepped apart, both breathing heavily. Lana tried to paste on a sweet smile. "Sorry, honey bear, you know your mama and I just don't get along. Of course, your mama doesn't get along with anybody."

"Bite me," Donna muttered.

"Lana, it's over. I'm seeing Lucy and I don't want to mess it up."

"I've heard this song before," she said, grinning at him. "Change the station."

"No, I mean it."

"You've meant it before," she told him, pulling at his T-shirt. "Is this about the thing at your cabin this morning? Lucy just overreacted. You know how she is. It's just all a big mix-up. No big deal. Besides, I don't know if I like you spending so much time with Lucy. You got so tore up over her last time. All she does is confuse you and screw with your head."

"I think you mean you don't like it because I started saying no to you," Duffy said.

Donna snorted, and Duffy glared at his mother. She put her hands up and stepped back. Duffy turned back to Lana. "I am done. I apologize if I was unclear by continuing to sleep with you after our marriage was over. We are over. I don't want to continue this sick, crappy thing between us anymore. It's not good for anybody. And I'm done with it. I don't want to see you anymore. I don't want you to come by my house or the business."

"So what, you're gonna go play daddy to some boy who isn't even yours? Now that Lucy's back you're going to drop me and go running after her again?" Lana sneered.

"One has nothing to do with the other."

"You'll be back. There's something between us, Duffy. There always will be. You made vows to me. You don't just walk away from that."

"*You* walked away from that," he noted.

"And I always come back," Lana whined. "Lucy's going to walk away and leave you in her dust, just like she did before. And you'll be right back where you belong, with me."

"No, it's not going to happen," he told her. "I'm done, even without Lucy. I can't come back to you. It's not good for either one of us. Just stay away from me, stay away from my house, and definitely stay away from Lucy and her shop."

"We'll see." Lana sniffed, turning away and walking back to her car. "You'll be sorry, and this time, I won't take you back. See how you like that."

She climbed into the El Camino and peeled out, flinging gravel in her wake. Donna laid her hands on Duffy's shoulder.

"And you." He turned on his mother. "You're gonna tone it down. We've let you get away with behaving like a pissed-off wet hen for years because we knew that you were mourning Dad. But enough is enough. You've already chased Marianne off. She barely talks to you. I would really like to have a conversation with you that doesn't involve you insulting or threatening me. Hell, you didn't even tell me that you were thinking of *retiring*! You're going to leave me in charge and you're not even going to talk to me about it? You couldn't tell me that you were getting tired and sore? That you had things you want to do or that you're afraid of working until you're dying? Mom, I would really like to have the kind of relationship where we actually tell each other what we're thinking, instead of expressing everything through hurtful sarcasm. If you don't think you can scrape up that much 'gentleness' or 'softness' for your son or your family, you really need to look inside yourself and figure out what sort of person you want to be."

Donna pursed her lips and looked ready to shoot back an angry insult, but instead nodded and said, "Okay."

"And you!" He walked up to Frankie. "You will never do anything like that bullshit boat stunt again, do you hear me?

Your wacky antics are going to get somebody hurt one of these days."

Frankie raised her hands in a defensive posture. "Okay."

"Great!" Duffy yelled, and stomped over to his truck. "Now all I have to do is get Marianne to agree to some boundaries, and I'll have the trifecta."

IN THE WEEK that followed, Lucy tried to tell herself that this was better, that her life was less complicated now that Duffy wasn't in it. She told herself it was better that the relationship stopped before it became clear to Sam that they were a couple. Right now, Sam thought they were just friends, just as they'd been since they were kids, and he wouldn't think much of it if one of his mom's friends stopped coming around. He wouldn't blame himself or regret the loss of Duffy in his life. She didn't have to worry about sending Sam to be watched by someone else while she went out, which seemed so selfish now. She didn't have to worry about time with Duffy leaving her too tired to keep up with her bakery schedule.

And sure, Marianne and Margot both said that they would not lecture her on the subject, since they were obviously biased, but Lucy also noted that the texts from the McCready women, while polite, were a bit more reserved and certainly less frequent. But even that was better, because she didn't have the distraction of keeping up friendships that took her away from her work and home life.

Life was simpler, if emptier, now. She got up. She got Sam ready for school. She went to the shop. She sold her pastries and cakes. She made dinner and spent time with her son. And at the end of the day, when the house was quiet and she sat on her couch alone, staring into space, all she felt was exhausted. It was a good sort of exhaustion, knowing that she'd worked hard all day to provide for her family and make sure her son felt loved, but she couldn't help but feel there wasn't much left at the end for her.

Maybe that was the problem with Lucy: she was selfish. Lots of women went to bed alone and exhausted but content, knowing they'd done their best and their children were thriving, and that was enough for them. What gave Lucy the right to want more?

Duffy needed someone with fewer issues and fewer demands on her. This was for the best. And if she grew a little quieter every day, her smile a little more brittle, well, that was something she was just going to have to handle. Even if she did have daily nightmares about Duffy coming into the shop with a faceless bride, asking Lucy to bake their wedding cake. The worst ones were when that faceless bride turned out to be Lana and Lucy woke up yelling.

It was after one of these nightmares that Specs walked into the bakery bright and early to find Lucy standing at the counter, her face buried in one of those ridiculously oversize travel mugs of coffee that you could only find in truck stops.

Specs frowned at her pale face and the dark rings under her eyes. Even her apron seemed melancholy, with its repeating pattern of sad pandas.

"Miss Lucy, go sit down. We need to talk," he told her.

Lucy peered up at him over the rim of her comically large mug. "I'm still the boss around here, I think. My name's on the door and everything."

"Sit," he said again, pointing imperiously to the closest café table.

Lucy pouted a bit but took her mug and flopped into a chair. Specs took two blueberry muffins out of the case and put them on plates, which he set on the table.

"Talk," he said. "That McCready boy hasn't stopped by lately. And you've obviously got something eating at you, so talk."

"We don't have time for this, Specs. The shop opens in twenty minutes."

"The cases are full. There's obviously coffee made. You cleaned everything in a fit. What else do we have to do?" Specs asked. "So spill it."

And it all came bubbling forth: her growing feelings of exhaustion, her doubts, the scene with Lana, the fight with Duffy. Her problems with her mother-in-law—with which he was already unfortunately and intimately familiar. Her coffee was halfway gone and her eyes were hot and glassy, but her cheeks were dry. "I thought I was doing the right thing, trying to keep my priorities straight, but now, I feel . . . just fucking awful. Pardon my French."

He snorted into his coffee and sipped it contemplatively. "You want to know what your daddy would have said?"

"Desperately." She sighed, trying not to let her eyes well up at the thought of her father.

"Running and hiding never solved anything. You tried that once, running from this place to make a life with that idjit boy."

Lucy frowned at him.

"I know, it's not nice to speak ill of the dead, but the Garten boy was an idjit. Your daddy worried over it just about every day when you were gone, that the boy didn't appreciate you, that you didn't seem happy when your daddy talked to you on the phone," Specs said. "Duffy McCready? He's loved you your whole life. He never stopped loving you. And that doesn't mean you owe him nothing. It doesn't mean he has dibs. But it does mean he has staying power. Course he's also an idjit, but not in a way that would hurt you."

"I don't want to hurt him," she protested.

"Then you won't. At least not on purpose."

"I just don't want to get hurt again."

"Then go live in a plastic bubble," Specs said. "That's the only way to keep that from happening. There are no guarantees in this life, girl. You know that better than anybody. There's gonna be hurt. There's gonna be tears. And it's a hell of a lot harder to deal with that alone."

"Even harder to deal with it with the wrong person," Lucy said.

"You would know," he said, clapping his hand on her back. "And no, maybe this doesn't come at the most convenient time in your life. The good things don't always fit right into a neat little box. Things are hard now, but they'll get better. And even if they don't, it's a hell of a lot easier dealing with them with someone behind you than doing it alone. I get running, and I get hiding. I spent a good bit of my life doing both. You know what I got out of it?"

"I'm almost afraid to ask."

"I got drunk. That's pretty much it. Lost a lot of jobs. Got kicked out of a lot of places. Never had a family. So now, I spend a lot of time at AA meetings and volunteering at the VA. And I have a nice job with this crazy gal who spends too much on aprons. And it's not the saddest story ever told, but it could have been a lot better if I'd pulled my head out of my ass when I was your age."

"I thought you said there were no guarantees."

"No, but given that you're not an idjit, I'd say you got a better shot than most."

"Thanks, Specs."

"Nothing to it," he said. "Now you sit here and finish your trough of coffee while I flip the 'Open' sign."

"Check to make sure my name is still on it," she called after him.

17

*I*T TOOK DUFFY several days just to work up the nerve to show up at the bakery. He waited until she would be just about closed, because he didn't want to make her uncomfortable in front of customers.

He'd decided against flowers or kidneys, because she would see through either. He determined that he would throw himself at her feet, apologize, and hope for the best. He parked his truck outside the shop, wiping his sweaty palms on his jeans for ten minutes before getting out. Not because he was nervous, or even hesitant to apologize, but because he was afraid she would reject him. What would he do if she did?

He'd sat down with Margot, whom he considered his only sane female relative at the moment, even with the hormones and the crying, and he'd written out what she called a very nice apology with multiple bullet points. And he'd read it, over and over, until he was sure he could give it to Lucy without forgetting one bit.

And now he was parked outside her shop and he couldn't

remember a damn thing. He knew he should have brought it with him. Inhaling deeply, he stepped out of the truck and went to face the firing squad . . . a firing squad armed with cupcakes.

Thankfully, the shop was empty, and from what he could see, so were the display cases. It seemed like the bakery was making a real go of it. Lucy was in the back of the kitchen, sweeping. Specs froze in place as he saw Duffy walking through the door. He called, "I'm gonna go . . . somewhere." And then immediately bolted for the front door.

Lucy was wearing an apron with little cactuses on it and he hoped that wasn't some sort of sign. Her face remained maddeningly neutral as she spotted him. She stopped sweeping, one corner of her mouth lifting as Specs fled.

Coming around the counter, she motioned toward one of the café tables. He sat and she took two Cokes out of the fridge to set between them. They stared at each other, her eyes bright and her lips trembling the slightest bit.

"I don't even know what to say to you," she told him. "I should be angry with you, but you weren't wrong about some of the things you said. Just like I wasn't wrong about some of the things I said. But I was wrong when I said I needed to live without you, that I couldn't make you a priority in my life. I keep thinking about you in terms of my marriage, in terms of 'one more thing I have to take care of.' And that's not fair to you. I should know you better than that. I felt overwhelmed and instead of coming to you for help, I shut you out, and I'm s—"

"No, you shouldn't say you're sorry first," he said, interrupting her. "*I'm* sorry. I don't know why I got so angry, but I shouldn't have taken what you were trying to tell me and made it about me and my feelings."

"You got angry because you were angry with me. You've probably been angry with me for a very long time. And that's okay. I mean, I didn't hurt you intentionally, but that doesn't make your hurt feelings any less real. I don't know why I stayed with Wayne. It was a cowardly thing to do. I told myself I wasn't giving up on my marriage. And then I told myself that I was doing the right thing by staying and making sure that Sam had a father. And then, I just didn't know how to get out.

"He didn't hit me. He never kept money out of my hands. He never threatened to take my child away. He just didn't seem to love me, or feel anything for me, really. He liked how I looked. He liked how I made him look, but that's a pretty creaky base for a marriage. And I was afraid to leave because I didn't want to come back to Georgia and admit that I'd married the wrong man and messed up my life. If I had known, back then, the way you felt, it would have been different. But we were kids. And we don't know how things would have turned out if we'd gotten together back then. We could have gotten sick of each other in two weeks and broken up before prom. Probably earlier, if you had the sort of judgment that told you dating Lana was a good idea. So, yeah, it's probably better that we get together as adults. What I'm saying is that I'm sorry I hurt you. I didn't mean to. I hope that we can move past it."

Duffy's eyebrows rose. "That was a lot."

She nodded. "Yep."

"I don't know if I have as much to say. You're right about the Lana stuff and I've already talked to her and made it clear that I'm not putting up with any more bullshit, that we're over. And I had no business making those cracks about you shoving Evie out of your life. I know you were scared, and instead of sticking around and trying to figure out why you felt like you were failing, how I could make it better, I just let loose on you. I did love you, and yeah, sometimes the resentments and the regret get to me. But it's not right to lay that at your feet.

"Frankie helped me find one of those app things for a therapist?" Duffy said. "I'm gonna talk with a guy in Atlanta once a week over video chat. He thinks I have some issues to work out, from my dad dying and the whole traumatic-first-marriage thing. I want to be sure that if we get back together, it's right. I don't want to mess this up."

"I saw someone after Wayne died. It helped," she said, squeezing his hand. "And if you forgive me—"

"I do."

"Great. I forgive you, too. So I think it's fairly certain we're going to be together."

Duffy leaned over the table and kissed her, thoroughly, with his hands buried in her hair. "I'm so sorry."

She laughed, wrapping her arms around him. "We hit a bump. It happens to most couples, but most couples don't have decades of history between them, waiting to spring up and hit them in the face."

"Probably true."

"I love you, Duffy McCready. I always have."

"I love you, too," he murmured against her mouth. "I know that you're not going to get married right away. Sam still has to get comfortable with me and we both have some stuff to work through. It could be years from now, and I understand that. I'm willing to wait."

She laughed. "So this is not a proposal?"

"No, this is a promise. I love you, Lucy Bowman. I've loved you for a long time and I'm not going to stop anytime soon. When you're ready and I'm ready, we're going to do this right. And I'm going to make a life with you."

"Deal," she said.

"Good," he said, pulling her into his lap. "Now, I didn't bring flowers or cake tools this time, but I did bring something better."

She leaned her forehead against his. "And yet, you appear to be empty-handed."

"Herb Brewster and his supervisor, Daryl Platt, will be arriving at your shop bright and early at ten a.m. Friday for a reinspection. So be ready."

"I thought I wasn't allowed to file another appeal for six months?" she cried.

"Well, you know how Herb is related to Evie and she used her influence against you?"

"Yes, I am vaguely familiar with those circumstances," she said, nodding.

"Well, Daryl Platt is distantly related to Grandma Tootie on her mother's side. And when she called in to complain to Daryl about one of his inspectors misusing his power and bending health and safety regulations to the point of breaking to harm a girl she considered family, which Tootie found to be very distressing on a personal level, Daryl felt the need to review your case and schedule a meeting to make it right. Herb should be coming by tomorrow to deliver the notice."

Lucy gaped at him. "So you used small-town nepotism for good instead of evil?"

"Grandma Tootie doesn't play that card very often, but when she does, it's a beautiful thing. Daryl was not impressed when he heard what Herb considered a B-minus. Herb is going to have to go through multiple retrainings."

"This is better than flowers," she agreed, kissing his cheeks. "Much, much better."

IT HAD BEEN a long time since Lucy had voluntarily visited the Gartens' double-wide. As usual, the outside was immaculately kept, with carefully cultivated forsythia bushes blooming on either side of the door. Lucy suspected that the lush grass was due to Dewie's obsession with lawn mowers . . . and probably his desire to get away from Evie as often as possible.

"Nope, that's not the right attitude to approach this with," she chided herself. "Nope nope nope."

She kept repeating "nope" until she reached the door and pressed the doorbell . . . which happened to chime the opening bars of "How Great Thou Art," the Elvis version.

She's making this difficult already, Lucy thought.

Evie blanched when she opened the screen door. "Lucy? Is Sam all right? How's his arm? I just haven't slept a wink since the accident. I just feel so bad."

"Evie, stop. I came here to talk, and you need to listen," Lucy said as calmly as she could.

Evie lifted a brow and admitted her into the house. The furniture was still kept in plastic, just the way Lucy remembered it. And Evie still seemed to think that a portrait of Jesus cradling a bald eagle in his arms made for good art.

"You want something to drink?" Evie asked, still obviously uncomfortable.

"Just some sweet tea, if you have it made up."

"Always," Evie said, fetching the Tupperware pitcher from the fridge. She nodded to the tiny oak dinette set. "Have a seat."

"Sam's arm is in a cast. His wrist was fractured, because he fell off of a bike that was way too big for him. A bike you went to my house and picked up, then took to the park specifically to make him ride it, when I'd said that it was too big for him and he wasn't ready. But it was more important to you to relive some moment in Wayne's life, using my son, than to make sure that child was safe. You put what you wanted ahead of my son's well-being and that cannot happen again if you hope to have a relationship with him. For the sake of being honest with you, you need to know that I've already called George Pritchett's office and given him a copy of the ER report with the doctor's notes and the X-rays, and a statement from Miss Lilah saying that the injury happened while Sam was being supervised by you. If you still plan on filing for visitation of Sam, I will have George include those reports with my legal response."

"I won't. I won't file for it. I'm so sorry," Evie whispered, her eyes brimming with tears. "I've just felt so lost since Wayne died, and having Sammy there, it's like a little version of Wayne all over again. I just wanted to see him alive again, that little boy I loved so much. And when you said no to the bike, I got so mad, I just wasn't thinking straight. I shouldn't have done what I did, and if you let me see Sam again, I won't do anything like it."

"I think we both need some cooling off before we even think about a relationship between you and Sam," Lucy said. "When we're ready, I'll call you and set up a time when you can visit while I'm there to supervise. But we're not going to make set plans for holidays or camping trips or anything for a long time."

Evie opened her mouth to protest, "But—"

"Do you really think you have room to argue with me?"

"No," Evie said, slightly sulky. While Evie normally would have fought tooth and nail against anything resembling limits, Lucy realized this Evie had been humbled. Her actions had resulted in Sam getting hurt and that was the sort of thing people didn't forget.

Lucy sat a little straighter in her chair. "And any visits with you and Sam will not involve Melody. She can't behave the way she did at the shop and expect me to sit by while she plays auntie to my son."

"But—"

Lucy cocked her head. "Again, do you think you have room to argue?"

"I'll tell her myself," Evie grumbled.

Lucy sipped her tea and traced patterns in the condensation gathering on the glass. "I think I need to make myself clear. I loved your son when we got married. I went into our marriage with the best of intentions. I think we both did. But we'd stopped loving each other the way a married couple is supposed to love each other a long time before he died."

She took a deep breath and added, "And I know you're not going to want to hear this, Evie, but he'd made a habit of sleeping with other women. He made it clear he wasn't going to stop because he didn't see anything wrong with it. And when he died, we'd been talking to a counselor twice a week for almost six months."

Lucy pressed her hand over her mouth, the weight of this burden slipping from her shoulders. And to her surprise, Evie didn't look incensed at Lucy besmirching her son's memory by implying he was anything less than a perfect husband. Evie didn't even look that surprised.

"You think I don't know you two were unhappy?" Evie scoffed, sipping her tea. "Of course I knew. I knew my boy. I knew when he was faking. And as for cheating, well, he came by that honestly. They say when you grow up seeing that, that you think it's okay to do it yourself."

Lucy's brows rose. "You mean . . . Dewie?"

"Naw, Dewie would never dream of it. It's part of the reason I've stayed with him for so long. But Wayne's daddy thought that as long as he came home at the end of the week with a paycheck, and didn't drink too much or slap me around, that anything else he did was his business. He wasn't exactly sneaky about it. And Wayne was always the smart one. He knew what was going on. And he just put his daddy on that pedestal so high . . . I imagine telling him that he was wrong to do something his daddy did went over like a lead balloon."

"And I suppose you're going to tell me that I should have just sucked it up and been happy with the life your boy provided for me?"

"Well, it wouldn't have hurt," Evie said with a shrug. "But I know what it's like to be that unhappy in your marriage, and I guess you modern girls don't have to worry as much about being happy where you are. You have more options."

"But you always talked about Wayne's dad like he was a saint. I mean, you've been with Dewie forever, but you've never married him."

Evie lit a Virginia Slim and inhaled deeply. "Oh, hell, I loved the man, don't get me wrong, but he could be a prize asshole when he wanted to be. But the kids were so young when he passed, and I just couldn't bear for them to know that. I thought it would be better if they thought their daddy was some perfect man, taken from them too soon. A damn sight better than telling them there was a good chance their daddy would have run off with a carnival if he'd lived any longer."

"You're probably right." Lucy sighed, sinking back in the seat. "So you knew we weren't doing that great, and you didn't say anything? I'm shocked."

"I thought that if I moved to Texas and took some of the pressure off of you, that you two would have more time together and it would help."

"And the fact that you would have twenty-four-hour access to your son and grandson would just be a side benefit, right?"

"It wouldn't have hurt," Evie said again.

"Okay, so item two is that the store is open and I'm not closing it. It's a going concern now and it's going to support me and Sam. And your means of interfering through Herb is about to come to a halt, so please, just leave me be."

"I only sent Herb after you the once," Evie insisted. "'Cause I thought I could catch you off guard before the opening and delay it while I worked on you to close up. But after you were open, I figured what was the point? Damage done."

"So why did Herb come back?"

"He did not appreciate you questioning his authority."

Lucy snickered. "Well, he's about to get in trouble for misusing his authority, so I am comfortable with that."

Evie flicked a long column of ash into her Kissimmee, Florida, ashtray. "And what about Wayne's money?"

"I will not be paying your bills, or Melody's bills or Davey's bills. That money is to take care of Sam and pay for his college tuition."

Evie flopped back against her seat, her expression sour for a moment. "I guess I get it. I just don't want to see you waste it. I don't want Sam to have to go without the way Wayne did. And yeah, we got used to having Wayne give us a little extra, to ease the way. And I got a little panicked at the idea of not having that anymore. I can't say I handled my son's death in a way that was entirely graceful."

"No, I'm not sure any of us did," Lucy said. "I think it might help you to see a grief counselor to help you deal with Wayne's death. Not just because I think that it would be healthy for you, but because it might get you to the point where I feel comfortable letting you see Sam again without an armed police escort."

Evie opened her mouth to protest, but then pinched her lips together. "I'll think about it."

*L*UCY TIGHTENED THE straps of Sam's life vest around his little frame.

"Are you sure Prince can't come on the boat, Mama?" he asked. He'd grumbled about being forced into puffy lifesaving equipment, but he was very excited about the prospect of fishing.

Lucy ruffled her fingers through his hair. Though Duffy had offered to take Prince on their first boat outing, and even bought him a little dog life jacket, Lucy thought taking a small child *and* a dog on a watercraft, without knowing how either would react, would be a little much for their first try.

"Prince is going to be just fine at home," she promised, clipping the little life vest Duffy had bought for Sam, which matched Prince's. "He's got his toys and his blankie and his water. He'll get to come with us next time."

"Okay."

Lucy checked the fasteners on Sam's soft cast, grateful that they didn't have to worry about him damaging the waterproof cast on the boat. While Evie had been respectful of Lucy's request for silence and space, Melody had called Lucy's cell phone and the bakery repeatedly to tell her what an awful godless bitch she was for holding Evie accountable for Sam's injury, that obviously all Sam needed was his grandmother's precious love and prayer to heal him. Lucy was ignoring but logging the calls for now, just in case she needed to get Eric involved.

"Are you excited about fishing?"

"Do I have to put the worm on the hook?" he asked, frowning.

"Not on the first try. We'll help you work up to it."

"It's nice that Mr. Duffy is taking us out on the boat."

"I think so, too."

"Do you *love* Mr. Duffy?"

"I think I do. I loved him as a good friend for a long time. But now, I think I love him like . . ."

"Like Miss Marianne loves Mr. Carl?"

"I don't think anyone will ever love anyone the way Miss Marianne loves Mr. Carl," she said, "because that relationship is just against all laws of probability, but yeah, I love him how married people love each other."

"Are you going to get married, like Miss Margot and Mr. Archer?"

Lucy certainly hoped that any future marriage of hers didn't involve an unplanned pregnancy and cake-related vomiting, but she figured that would be a lot to explain to a five-year-old. "Someday, maybe, way off in the future, when we've spent a lot more time together and talked about it much more, we might get married. But I promise to talk to you about it first, okay?"

Sam scrunched up his lips, like he was thinking about it. "Would I have to call him Daddy?"

"No, you don't have to do that ever if you don't want to. Duffy is not going to take your dad's place in our family, he's just joining it. Like Margot is joining Mr. Archer's family. We didn't have a Duffy before, and now we do. It's one more person to love."

Lucy thought about making a comparison to adopting Prince, but that seemed like a step too far.

"It would be okay," he said. "As long as he doesn't try to take my room."

Lucy pursed her lips. "I can guarantee he would not try to take your room."

"Okay, it's fine, then."

Lucy laughed as Duffy carried the fishing poles and gear down the dock. "What's so funny?"

"Oh, just talking about Sam's room," Lucy said. "He's very attached to it."

"As he should be. That Batman vinyl thing you put on the wall is amazing," Duffy said.

"Your aunt Leslie left this with us," Lucy said, nodding toward the cooler. "There are drinks and sandwiches, none of which are deep-fried, some of which contain actual vegetables."

"Wow," Duffy marveled. "You've worked some sort of evil mind-control voodoo on my aunt."

"No, I just refused to take anything that was soaked in canola oil," Lucy told him as he carried the gear onto the boat.

"And I made this face," Sam said, poking out his bottom lip.

"Has Prince been giving you lessons?" Duffy asked, holding his hands out to Sam.

"Nope." Sam leaped toward Duffy, who caught him around the waist. Sam giggled as Duffy set him on his feet.

"Okay, first rules of the boat," Duffy told him. "That's your seat, by my seat. We always stay in our seats while the boat's moving, because otherwise you fall off the boat, you get hurt or sick, and your mom gets really mad at both of us."

"That makes sense," Sam conceded.

"No swearing where other adults can hear you. No beer for people who haven't started elementary school. No acts of piracy." Duffy ticked the "rules" off on his fingers. "No Viking funerals. And no accurate measurements of the fish we catch. We always exaggerate by at least fifty percent."

"I don't know what that means," Sam said, laughing and rolling onto his seat.

"We'll figure it out," Duffy told him, reaching out to Lucy.

"I'm not going to jump at you," she told him.

"I can handle it," he said. "You ready for this?"

Lucy's mouth pulled at the corner as she watched her son settle on a seat that seemed way too big and way too high and way too close to the water. "As much as anyone can be."

"I'm not going to put a hook in the worms!" Sam announced as Duffy cast off.

"Understood," Duffy replied.

"How long are we going out on the boat?" Sam asked. "Are we going to sleep on the boat? Like on a cruise?"

"Well, I have to come back in time to meet Margot for another cake consultation. Hopefully she will make it through this appointment without yarking."

"Is that when you throw up a lot?" Sam asked. "Ew."

"Yeah . . . I meant to tell you, Kyle and Margot have decided to elope," Duffy said, grimacing.

"Oh, thank God." She sighed, dropping her face into her hands.

"What? I was worried about telling you! I thought you were excited about doing Margot's wedding cake!" Duffy exclaimed.

"Yeah, and then I realized how badly it could go if I screwed up her cake, considering I now think of her a friend and may end up related to her someday."

His face brightened at the mention of someday being related to Margot.

"I'm related to half the county somehow," she told him. "Don't get all riled up."

He chuckled.

"I'm just saying. Can you imagine having to face someone at holidays, knowing that you'd screwed up their wedding cake? Every Thanksgiving, 'Happy Thanksgiving. I haven't been thankful since you screwed up my wedding cake.' Every Christmas, 'Merry Christmas. I haven't been merry since you screwed up my wedding cake.' Every Labor Day, 'Happy Labor Day, I wish you'd labored to give me a better cake.'"

"Yeah, okay, that would be bad," Duffy agreed. "And maybe it's better if Kyle and Margot get everybody used to the idea of eloping. You know, in case we decide that my family is too crazy to trust with anything fancier."

"It can't be that bad."

"You say that because you weren't here for Carl and Marianne's wedding."

"Well, on the subject of cake, I have something for you."

"Aw, you didn't have to bring anything!" he exclaimed as she reached into Leslie's cooler and handed him a small purple box.

"I saved it for you. I figured out your favorite," she told him. He opened the box to reveal a half dozen beautiful red velvet cupcakes with cream cheese frosting.

He grinned. "Yes, you did. How did you figure it out?"

"This was the first thing I ever made for you," she said as he took a big bite. "It was for the class Christmas party, back when we were still allowed to bring homemade treats to school."

He leaned forward and kissed her, leaving a bit of frosting on her lip. "You gotta remember, I was used to my mom's cooking, which was basically an unspoken threat. Your cupcake was magical."

"And that's when you fell in love with me?" she asked.

He kissed her. "Well, no, but it certainly didn't hurt."

"Gross," Sam said, shuddering.

"All right, all right, no more kissing your mama," Duffy promised Sam as he fired up the boat engine.

"Good!" Sam yelled over the noise, though he was grinning to beat the band.

Lucy settled against his back, leaning her cheek against Duffy's shoulder while he steered. She watched Sam's hair go vertical in the wind, smiling as he batted his hands at the water that spattered over the hull, though Duffy was driving as carefully as possible.

For the moment, this was as happy as she could expect to be. She wasn't looking for perfect. But this was pretty damn close. She suddenly raised her head from Duffy's shoulder.

"Hey, Duffy, you've checked the gas tank this time, right?"

Duffy glanced down at the instrument panel. "Yep. It's full."

She blew out a relieved breath. "You brought a backup can, too, right?"

"Uh." Duffy chewed on his lip, turning to Lucy. "Maybe we should head back to the dock real quick."

Lucy nodded. "Yep."

"What happens if we run out of gas?" Sam asked, his eyes wide.

Lucy and Duffy shared a look over his head and blushed simultaneously. "Uh, we'd have to call Frankie and Mr. Eric for help," Lucy told him.

"Well, that wouldn't be so bad," Sam said.

"Yeah, let's not put that theory to the test," Lucy said.

"Can I steer the boat?" Sam asked.

"Is this about steering the boat, or about yelling 'yar' like a pirate?" Lucy asked. "Because you tend to throw up both hands when you yell 'yar' and we need one hand on the wheel, at least."

"I want to yell 'yar,'" he admitted.

"You can *help* me steer," Duffy said. "And yell 'yar' all you want."

"Good!" Sam hopped up and Lucy held his life jacket loosely while he crossed to the steering seat. Duffy let Sam stand in front of him, and held the wheel steady while Sam tried to pull it back and forth. Cartoons were not good training examples for how steering works on boats.

"YAR!" Sam howled, making Duffy cackle. Lucy sat back on the seat, watching her son laugh into the wind, and knew that no matter what the future brought, they were going to be just fine.

Acknowledgments

As ALWAYS, THANK you so much to my agent, Natanya Wheeler, and my editor, Abby Zidle, for getting me through this book, which was written during a cross-country move. I wrote parts of it in my old house in Kentucky, my parents' house, a moving truck, a coffee shop, and our new house in Michigan with no furniture. (It is shocking how hard it is to write in a house where there is nowhere to sit.) Abby and Natanya, I would not have finished this manuscript without your patience and encouragement. The same goes for my fellow Setonians— Kathleen, Anna, Jenn, and Therese. I am thankful every day for your support and your ears. And Jeanette, you are the best writing partner and friend a girl could ask for. Thank you to David, Judy, Darcy, and Carter, who unpacked and organized the house so I could work. I'm very grateful to have all of you in my life.